"PRIORITIES?"

"The recovery of the enriched uranium," Brognola said. "That's the top threat. Next, we need to know just how far the connection between the WWUP and these domestic and international terror organizations goes."

"On it," Lyons said.

"Coordinate through Barb to have the Farm deliver anything additional you'll need," Brognola said. "I'll arrange for a liaison with local law enforcement both in Chicago and wherever the trail ultimately takes you."

"You sound like you have someplace in mind."

"I might. Reginald Butler has long been a political activist. He's one of the richest men in America, and if he's mixed up in any of this, or even if he's simply letting his company sell the Seever units to foreign nationals with ties to terror, I want him taken down."

"Could get sticky," Blancanales said dubiously. "Government operatives pressuring an American entrepreneur who's already complaining about governmental harassment."

"We don't exist," Brognola said. "We do, therefore, what we have to do."

DON PENDLETON'S

STONY

AMERICA'S ULTRA-COVERT INTELLIGENCE AGENCY

MAN®

DRAWPOINT

A GOLD EAGLE BOOK FROM

WORLDWIDE®

TORONTO • NEW YORK • LONDON
AMSTERDAM • PARIS • SYDNEY • HAMBURG
STOCKHOLM • ATHENS • TOKYO • MILAN
MADRID • WARSAW • BUDAPEST • AUCKLAND

Recycling programs
for this product may
not exist in your area.

First edition June 2009

ISBN-13: 978-0-373-61985-6

DRAWPOINT

Special thanks and acknowledgment to
Phil Elmore for his contribution to this work.

Printed in U.S.A.

DRAWPOINT

PROLOGUE

UVC Limited Milling and Processing Facility,
Meghalaya, India

Patrick Farrah paused to light a cigarette, groping for the pack and lighter that weren't there, cursing as the realization hit him for the fifth time in as many hours. He swore under his breath as he overrode the impulses so deeply ingrained in his mind and muscle memory. He fished out a pack of gum and stuck one of the pieces in his mouth, muttering under his breath as he chewed the hard stick into pliancy. Quitting smoking was something he'd promised his girlfriend he'd do. He'd live longer, Jody had told him. Well, maybe he would. But that didn't make it easier.

Twilight had brought little relief from the subtropical humidity. Meghalaya, as the wettest state in India, received an average rainfall that ranked it among the wettest places on Earth, not just in the nation. The idea still staggered Farrah, but the country, for all its moisture, was relatively moderate in terms of day-to-day climate. It was also lush and beautiful, exotic in a way the States would never be. He had easily fallen in love with the place.

The work was relatively easy, too. Sugar Rapids Security, the company for which he contracted, was among those backfilling private security details in Afghanistan and Iraq. Farrah's girlfriend, safe back in Upstate New York, had been none too happy about his accepting the assignment in India, even if it was just for a year. But Farrah knew she'd have been a lot more unhappy if he'd agreed to the even riskier jobs available for triple pay in those war zones. No, the pay for the India posting was high enough to make it attractive, and safe enough that he didn't have to keep Jody up nights worrying if he was going to make it back.

He really couldn't complain about the work. A year spent in the beautiful West Khasi Hills area was almost like a vacation, as far as he was concerned. And how hard was it to guard a bunch of mining equipment overnight, make sure it wasn't stolen or meddled with? The owner of the equipment, Uranium-Vanadium Consortium, Limited, gave the SRS subcontractors little grief and plenty of cash. Except for occasional checks by his Sugar Rapids supervisor, Farrah was on his own most of the time. It was peaceful and, if a little boring, steady and honest work.

He did worry, with a sort of superstitious dread, about being stationed near the milling plant. He supposed it was better than pulling duty closer to the laser enrichment facility, where things really glowed in the dark. He'd heard the whole thing was experimental, too, the latest in UVC technology subsidized by the Indian government. But apart from the technology itself, the idea of uranium dust just kind of scared the crap out of him. There were plenty of safety protocols in place, he'd been assured up and down. But all of the SRS contractors with whom he worked were a little nervous around stuff that could poison you and make you sterile if it didn't kill you. He'd worked nuclear plant security in the States and was no stranger to the vague sense of unease radioactive material produced. He'd learned to live with it.

He understood just enough of the process to steer clear of the dangerous areas. The uranium ore was mined from the shafts recently sunk here in the Meghalaya hills. The discovery had been a shock to everyone involved except UVC, apparently, who had been counting on their new proprietary technology to open up new markets.

On a typical evening, Farrah made a long, slow circuit around the facility, giving the milling plant a wide berth. The enrichment plant was down the dirt road, beyond his specified territory; Ranjhit Bhatt patrolled that part of the complex. Bhatt was a good guy, a local who spoke fluent English and played a mean game of cards. The two sometimes met on their breaks to sneak in a few quick games.

Farrah tried to vary his routine slightly, but there were only so many ways to walk the perimeter and check on the various outbuildings in this part of the fenced compound. This night was no different. He shrugged mentally and started for the metal storage shed that was his mental landmark for the start of his circuit.

The shed exploded.

One moment it was there, the next it was a flaming cloud of debris. A wall of heat hit him, scorching his face and drying his eyes as the shock wave bowled him over. Farrah hit the ground hard, feeling the breath rush out of him in one great, wracking cough. He had the presence of mind to shield his head and roll over, painfully, as scraps of burning metal rained down. He had a moment to wonder what was happening before he heard it—a whistling noise increasing in pitch. When the heavy chunk of concrete struck him in the head, he didn't have time to wonder what it was before his world went dark.

When he opened his eyes again to a throbbing pain in his skull, the night was aglow with flickering orange fire. He could hear the crackling flames and smell the smoke as he watched, his vision blurred from the blow to the head. Afraid to move from where he lay sprawled on the ground, he watched as trucks roared past. He coughed as their diesel exhaust plumes rolled over him, but tried otherwise to remain still. The trucks—he didn't recognize them—were moving away from the enrichment plant. Men clung to the running boards on either side of the truck, men armed with what Farrah recognized as AK-47 rifles.

His brain fogged with pain and confusion, Farrah struggled first to one knee. Lurching to his feet, stumbling and getting up again, he fumbled at his belt for his pistol as the last of trucks roared past. There was only one man clinging to the side of the vehicle, a battered Toyota Land Cruiser. Farrah forced his blurred vision to cooperate just long enough to get his .45-caliber Springfield XD out of its holster. He fired once, then twice, then a third time, into the night.

He tripped and fell. The stumble saved his life, most likely, as return fire from a gunner in the rear of the Land Cruiser scored the air above him. Then the truck was gone, leaving only the burning wreckage of the UVC facility in its wake.

He groped for his radio but couldn't find it. He wasn't sure if he'd dropped it or if maybe it had been taken while he lay unconscious on the ground. With nowhere else to go, he staggered for the front entrance to the camp, where the chain-link gates had been knocked down. The trucks had probably driven through them.

He heard footsteps scraping through the dirt and brought up his gun, closing one eye in an attempt to fight back the double vision creeping into his sight. The bloody figure that emerged, backlighted by the flames, was Bhatt.

"Bhatt!" Farrah said in relief. "You're alive!"

Bhatt tried to speak but fell to his knees, choking and coughing. Farrah reached for him but Bhatt waved him off, trying to catch his breath. Farrah turned and almost tripped over the body.

A dead man was sprawled on the dirt road.

The corpse wore olive-drab fatigues and a balaclava. An AK-47 had been dropped not far from the dead man. Also near the body was a square box the size of a large phone or personal data device. Farrah picked it up gingerly, fearing it might be a detonator of some kind. He turned it over in his hands, but couldn't figure out what it might be. It looked like a complicated phone. Why would a guerrilla be carrying such a thing? And who were these people?

Bhatt coughed loudly and said something. Farrah turned to him and helped prop him up. Bhatt was flushed and choking, but he looked determined to choke out what he had to say.

"What is it?" Farrah asked him. "Bhatt, what it is?"

"Uranium!" Bhatt finally managed. "Enriched uranium!"

"What about it?" Farrah asked, his stomach sinking.

"They took it!" Bhatt said. "The trucks...full of drums of enriched uranium!"

"Full?" Farrah went pale. "Are you sure?"

Bhatt nodded.

Farrah looked down at the dead man, the man he'd

killed, the first life he had ever taken. Then he looked back to Bhatt.

A single death was nothing compared to the potential mass murder that had just left through the main gate.

CHAPTER ONE

Aurora, Illinois

Carl "Ironman" Lyons sipped black coffee from a foam cup, surprised at how good it was. The former L.A. police officer had done more than his fair share of stakeouts, subsisting on gut-wrenching, greasy takeout leavened with bad coffee. He'd had coffee so bad, in fact, that it could make a person wince. But this was good coffee. The proliferation of designer coffees and trendy joints to drink it in had pushed the fast-food empires to keep pace. Lyons counted himself among those benefiting from this free market.

"I've never seen a man so thoughtful over a cup of Joe," Hermann "Gadgets" Schwarz commented. The electronics expert and veteran commando—whose nerdy demeanor concealed a hard core forged on many a battlefield—frowned and brushed a lock of brown hair out of his eyes. He shifted in the passenger seat of the black Suburban, glancing over at the bull-necked blond man who hulked behind the steering wheel sniffing at a coffee cup.

Lyons grunted at his teammate and turned back to watch the street. Encouraging Gadgets would only get him started, and it was too early in the morning to deal with his ribbing just yet.

The two members of the covert counterterrorist unit known as Able Team were parked down and across the street from the Illinois headquarters of the World Workers United Party. Even now, the third and final member of Able Team, Rosario "The Politician" Blancanales, was inside that building, patiently waiting to speak with the local director of the primary chapter of the WWUP. The gray-haired, dark-eyed, soft-spoken Hispanic was an expert in both the psychology of violence and in-role camouflage. He had needed no special disguise or even a particularly complicated cover story to get an appointment with the WWUP's director. He had simply posed as an interested potential donor and made an appointment through the chapter's secretary.

What had brought Able Team to the streets of this Chicago suburb was far more complicated. The brief had first been transmitted to him through the computer experts at Stony Man Farm, the covert organization under whose umbrella Able Team operated. A lot of it had caused Lyons's eyes to glaze over in boredom, but he had of course been able to get the gist. The WWUP had a lot of money for a fringe political party, and the transfers of funds to and from the party had finally tripped whatever monitoring algorithms the supercomputers the Farm were using to monitor worldwide data transfers. More significantly, transfers of funds to the WWUP were being routed to the group from outside the country. The Byzantine web of laws governing political contributions was not something Lyons pretended to understand, but that didn't matter. The key was that when the money tree was shaken hard enough, Stony Man had been able to link monies sent to the WWUP all the way back to offshore holding companies that were themselves linked to the Earth Action Front.

As Lyons had been so recently informed, the EAF was a notorious ecoterror group whose members were more than happy to use violence to achieve their aims. They had gone from total unknowns five years earlier, to the preeminent "green" terror group worldwide. While they'd started small-time—spray-painting EAF on "gas-guzzling" SUVs parked at American sales lots, or staging denial of service attacks on the networks of corporations overseas they deemed to be polluters—they'd long since graduated to acts of violence that bordered on mass murder. In the past month, in fact, the EAF had claimed responsibility for a housing development fire in California that had killed three—in the name of stopping "suburban sprawl"—and for the ill-planned bombing of a nuclear power plant in France that had killed a security guard. While international in scope, the EAF was known to have a significant presence domestically. And that presence was thought by many, including Stony Man Farm's computer wizards, to include the WWUP.

Compare the World Workers United Party membership rolls to the EAF's in the United States, Lyons imagined, and you'd most likely get more than a little overlap. That, by itself, was a matter for the FBI or other federal organizations, or so Lyons had thought. He had placed the call to the Farm to express this opinion, only to be gently persuaded otherwise by Hal Brognola, director of the Sensitive Operations Group's and Lyons's boss. Lyons had, of course, used the diplomacy for which he was well-known when discussing the issue with Brognola.

"This, Hal," he'd said over the secure satellite phone, "is a steaming pile of horseshit."

"Usually it's David who gives me grief," Brognola had said, referring to David McCarter, the leader of Stony Man Farm's international counterterrorist unit, Phoenix Force. "What's the problem?"

"Don't we have bigger fish to shoot in a barrel?" Lyons had thrown back, deliberately mangling the metaphor. "Able Team is better used on just about anything other than rousting some play-acting Commies."

"WWUP is a remarkably powerful organization," Brognola'd said, "whose professed ideology is admittedly socialist or Communist, depending on whom you ask. They are far from pretenders. There is serious talk of WWUP fielding a viable third-party candidate in the next presidential election."

Lyons had hit back. "Since when does a third party have a chance? You expect me to take these people seriously?"

"You don't have a choice," Brognola had told him. "*We* don't have a choice. The WWUP didn't exist before a few years ago. It's rushed in to fill a perceived void in domestic politics, becoming a very real Communist movement."

"And the WWUP is getting its funding from a global gang of environmentalist whackos. That's still a job for the FBI."

"This isn't just about 'environmentalist whackos,'" Brognola had insisted. "Ecoterror is on the rise, globally and domestically. Now, don't get me wrong. We're not talking about conservationists or legitimate environmental defense groups. We're talking about extremists, those willing to commit violence to achieve their aims. And we've long gone past some animal rights activists releasing minks from cages, or vandals throwing bricks through the windows of fast-food restaurants. Our friends at the FBI, in fact, have a couple of thousand cases of arson, bombings, theft and vandalism on the books in recent years, all of them attributable to 'green' terrorist groups. My sources within the Bureau say they're ranking it a greater emerging threat than the hot-button domestic terrorists of a decade or two ago—neo-Nazis, paramilitary groups, Klan splinter factions, and so on. And while the crimes are rising here in frequency and in violent intensity, they are rising simultaneously in developed nations across the globe."

"So what's the link?" Lyons had asked him.

"For whatever reason," Brognola had said, sounding tired, "the radical, violent fringe of the environmentalist or 'green' movement has become the new home for collectivist politics domestically. The radical greens often tout a socialist agenda as part and parcel of the economic and environmental reforms they advocate. The more violent Communist and socialist groups are happy to embrace them. There's a lot of cross-pollination between and among the various terrorist and fringe groups involved."

"I'm not a politician, Hal. And I'm not a cop anymore."

"I'm not asking you to be one," Brognola had said, "and if this was about politics or could be taken care of by the local authorities, it would have nothing to do with the SOG. But Aaron's team has identified an exponential trend in fund transfers to WWUP from accounts that can be linked, ultimately, to ecoterror groups, most notably the Earth Action Front. Most of the transactions are being routed through a single person at the top of the chain, the director of WWUP's Chicago chapter." Aaron was Aaron Kurtzman, head of Stony Man Farm's cyber team.

"Why Chicago?"

"It's the domestic headquarters for WWUP, the hub of their network of chapters throughout the country. Any decisions implemented by WWUP, including their potential presidential campaign, are ultimately made in Illinois."

"So you want Able to…what?"

"There's a timetable at work here," Brognola'd confided. "The people behind WWUP, and especially their donors, have to know that their monetary transactions will look suspicious eventually. The Farm caught it a lot earlier than the usual domestic institutions would, but they'd have noticed it eventually, too. Campaign finance laws, IRS regulations, standard federal banking policies…any of these could have raised a few flags in a few hundred computers. For the WWUP and their backers to be acting so brazenly tells me that something is going to happen. Something big, considering the risks, and considering the scope of the WWUP in the United States."

"What are you telling me, Hal?" Lyons had said, finally losing his hostile tone.

"I've got Aaron and his people looking into the wider implications, tracking both financial data and terrorist incidents at home and abroad," Brognola had explained. "But our working theory is that a force or forces outside the United States is or are working very hard to exert political influence inside the country. Specifically, we theorize that one or more of these terror groups are funding a seemingly legitimate incursion into U.S. politics using, among other means, violence. Whatever they're planning is coming to a head, or they wouldn't be risking financial exposure. The top of the pyramid is in Chicago. I want you to take Able Team and poke your head in the dragon's lair."

"To see if we get roasted alive?"

"Something like that. If we're wrong, we lose a little time and a little effort. If we're not, we get in on whatever the WWUP is plotting, maybe make them nervous enough to expose themselves, tip their hand. The clock is ticking, Carl. Something big is ramping up, and my instincts tell me we have to move now, stop it before it can get out of control."

The big Fed had been right about this kind of thing more than once, Lyons knew. "All right, Hal. We'll take a look. We'll see what we can shake loose. But I'm not promising anything resembling diplomacy."

"Do what you do, Ironman," Brognola had said. "That's what I'm counting on."

Now Able Team was on site, parked on Ogden Avenue in Aurora, Illinois. At least, two-thirds of the team was sitting in the SUV. The last member of the team, the man they called "the politician," was on the inside, his every word monitored by the microtransceivers each member of the team wore in his ear.

The little earbud devices, nearly invisible when worn, had an effective range of half a city block. The one Blancanales wore would, if anyone noticed it, appear to be nothing more than a small hearing aid. Gadgets Schwarz had helped develop the minuscule units for the Farm's use.

Schwarz's banter notwithstanding, the two men kept their idle chatter to a minimum as they watched the front of the WWUP building, a converted storefront nestled between a pack-and-ship mailbox store and a sheet music shop. Blancanales could hear every word they said, so there was no point in annoying or distracting him with unnecessary chatter. As the two men waited and listened, they could hear the ringing of office telephones in the background. Now and again they could hear the WWUP receptionist's voice, though her words were indistinct at Blancanale's presumed distance from her. The wingnuts inside, Lyons reflected, had kept his teammate waiting for at least half an hour past his appointment time. Whether this was simply business on their part, or a calculated tactic, he couldn't be sure. It didn't seem likely that they'd antagonize a potential donor by making him cool his heels unnecessarily.

Even as he considered it, Lyons sat up. There was rustling on the other end of the connection as Blancanale put down whatever newspaper or magazine he'd most likely been pretending to read. A voice that Lyons recognized as the receptionist's, closer now, told the man that the director would see him.

Schwarz, next to Lyons, press-checked his silenced Beretta 93-R, ready to go operational at Lyons's command. As Schwarz holstered the weapon, Lyons ran through his mental checklist, idly patting himself down with one hand to verify that all of his gear was in place. His .357 Magnum Colt Python was secure in his shoulder holster. While the SUV held a concealed locker in which the team's heavy weapons were locked, they'd opted to travel more lightly for this initial probe. Concealed under the gray business suit Blancanales wore, Lyons knew, was a Beretta 92-F in a shoulder holster, which should prove sufficient if he got into any trouble inside. Still, there was an element of risk in all such operations, especially since the man was placing himself at the mercy of potential enemies, cut off from the team by distance and a few doorways.

The Able Team leader listened as Blancanales and the

director, who introduced himself as Timothy Albert, exchanged pleasantries. Lyons allowed himself a tight smile as Blancanales ran through a spiel on the injustices of "world capitalism" and "corporate rule," intended to put Albert at ease, persuade him—momentarily, at least—that he was speaking to a fellow traveler ideologically. The two traded what, to Lyons, sounded like pompous slogans that would be lame coming from college radio jocks. Eventually, though, Blancanales moved in for the kill. Lyons tensed as he heard it coming, nodding to Schwarz. If he managed to shake anything loose, it would come now.

"Much as I would like to continue this conversation, my friend," Blancanales was saying quietly, "there is the matter of the World Workers United and its status as a political party in the United States."

"How do you mean?" Albert asked, sounding polite but puzzled.

"Illegal distributions of cash to your party," Blancanales said, his tone equally polite. "Funds from overseas. Funds that violate campaign finance laws, just for starters, and that perhaps violate certain other laws intended to prevent the exchange of monies to and from terrorist groups."

Albert was silent. Lyons pictured him gaping like a fish.

"You do not deny that your party receives significant funding from the Earth Action Front, do you?" Blancanales asked. Now his voice took on an edge.

"I... Well, I'm sure I don't know what you're talking about..." Albert stammered.

"Justice Department," Lyons heard Blancanales say. He pictured the soft-spoken Hispanic flashing the Justice shield Brognola had issued to each of the member of Able for occasions such as this. "And you, sir, are under arrest.

We have a warrant and we'll be searching the premises. This search extends to seizures of your computer equipment. If you'll step away from the desk, sir…"

Albert muttered something Lyons could not hear.

Schwarz and Lyons both winced involuntarily as the earpieces they wore cut out in bursts of white noise.

"Gunshot!" Lyons was already jumping out of the SUV, his Colt Python in his fist. Schwarz was close behind him with the 93-R. They ran full-tilt for the WWUP building, dodging cars as they dashed across the street. Lyons ignored the honking and the shouts from irate drivers—though one particularly loud commuter shut up fast when he noticed the mammoth revolver in Lyons's big hand.

The twin glass doors at the front of the WWUP building slapped open, banging in their frames. Two men leveled pistols from the doorway. One of them was dressed in a blue security guard's uniform, while the other wore a button-down shirt and tie. Lyons shoved Schwarz away from him bodily as the electronics expert came abreast. Gunshots burned through the air between them.

"Pol!" Lyons shouted. "Pol, come in!" He triggered a single round. The 170-grain jacketed hollowpoint round dropped the security guard in his tracks, booming like thunder in the crisp morning air. Simultaneously, Schwarz triggered a 3-round burst from his 93-R. The suppressed weapon chattered, stitching the other shooter across the chest. He fell in a crumpled heap with his necktie flapping across his face.

"Go, go, go!" Lyons ordered. "Blancanales! Come in, damn it!"

ROSARIO BLANCANALES flashed the Justice shield. "Justice Department," he said. As he informed Albert that the man was under arrest, threatening search and seizure of the computers in the office, he watched the man carefully for his reaction. This was the moment of truth. If he was innocent of any wrongdoing, or perhaps simply a white-collar criminal looking to finance his party with extralegal funds, he would plead ignorance or try to cut a deal. If the World Workers United Party was dirty, however—

Faster than Blancanales would have thought possible, the slim, well-dressed, middle-aged Albert wrenched open a desk drawer and yanked out a Smith & Wesson .38 snubnose revolver. Blancanales threw himself backward behind a chair without thinking. The first shot punched a hole in the wall of the office, directly behind the spot where he'd been standing.

As he fell, Blancanales ripped his Beretta 92-F from its leather shoulder holster. Without aiming, he hosed the front of the desk and the air above it with withering gunfire. He didn't expect to hit Albert; he only needed to drive the man back to foul any follow-up shots that might be coming.

A door slammed. Blancanales surged to his feet, the Beretta in a two-handed grip. Albert had fled through a second door in the rear of his office. Before the Able Team commando could give chase, however, he heard gunshots from the outer office, where he'd been kept waiting. These were answered by the boom of what could only be Lyons's Python, something he'd heard countless times before. Too experienced to freeze up with indecision, Blancanales rushed forward, trusting his teammates to take care of their part of the operation. He pushed through the rear door, going low and fast, waiting for more gunshots. They did not come. His earbud was producing noises, but he ignored it for a moment, focusing on the immediate threat that Albert presented.

A fire door slammed. Blancanales hustled down the narrow corridor in which he found himself, the Beretta leading the way. He hit the crash bar on the fire door and plunged through.

"Pol!" Lyons voice came in his ear again. "Come in, damn it!"

"Albert has gone out the back," he responded. "I'm in pursuit."

"Two down in at the front door," Lyons barked. "The secretary's screaming her head off, but she's not hit and she's not a hostile."

"Understood," Blancanales said. He rounded the corner at the rear of the building, taking it wide, "cutting the pie" to give him an angle for a return shot if Albert was waiting. A car door slammed and an engine churned to life. Blancanales stuck his head out of the alleyway and saw Albert starting a late-model Taurus.

"Ironman!" he said. "He's coming your way, out the front! Maroon Taurus!"

"On it!" Lyons responded.

Blancanales took aim and pumped the remainder of his Beretta's clip into the rear of the Taurus. The car was already putting distance between them; his 9 mm rounds having no noticeable effect. Then the black Suburban bearing Lyons and Schwarz was roaring up to him, barely stopping. Blancanales threw himself into the back of the vehicle, narrowly avoiding catching his leg in the door as momentum slammed it shut.

Schwarz was already on his wireless phone, calling the Farm to arrange for a clean-up team to run interference with local authorities—and see to the bodies. Lyons drove with a white-knuckled grip, pursuing the Taurus through heavy traffic. The reinforced truck howled on its extra-heavy-duty tires. Blancanales imagined he could hear the overpowered engine sucking in gasoline as the armored SUV roared in response to Lyons's foot on the accelerator. Schwarz was forced to hang on to the overhead handle to keep from sliding back and forth in his seat as the Suburban weaved and dodged. Blancanales smiled grimly and held on to the back seat.

"What happened in there?" Lyons asked, his eyes never leaving the traffic in front of them.

"You heard him," Blancanales said. "I played the Justice card and he froze. When I talked about seizing and searching his computers, he went for the hardware. Who were the other two?"

"Security, I guess," Lyons grunted. "Moved on us the second your boy opened fire. Must have made our stakeout. They were too quick to come at us, otherwise."

"So they were already waiting for trouble," Schwarz mused.

"But why would they just open fire? What's to be gained?" Lyons asked. "The second we show up they start popping caps. Why?"

"Whatever the reason, this means Hal's suspicions were well-grounded," Blancanales replied.

"And a big, black Suburban parked on the street isn't as subtle as we thought it was," Schwarz said wryly.

"Gadgets, the clean-up team," Lyons said, whipping the steering wheel hard left, then right. "They know to secure the computers?"

"Yes," Schwarz said. "They'll search the network and

pull the drives for us. That's if nobody activated some sort of sweep-and-clear doomsday program. We might come back to find their drives have eaten themselves."

"Let's hope not," Lyons said. He came to a clear stretch of road and tromped the pedal to the floor. The Suburban growled and shot forward with renewed speed. "Got him now," Lyons said.

Blancanales craned his neck, looking forward out the windshield from where he sat. The Suburban slowed for a moment and the distance between the two vehicles increased.

"Carl—" Schwarz said.

"Ironman, wait—" Blancanales protested.

Lyons slammed the pedal to the floor again. The Suburban rocketed forward like a battering ram. The bull bars mounted in front of the grille smashed into the rear of the Taurus, crumpling the trunk as the smaller vehicle shuddered beneath the impact. Lyons never let up, maneuvering the nose of the Suburban until it was scraping the rear quarter of the Taurus. Then he pitted the Taurus, slamming the sedan into the curb with tire-popping force. Maroon paint streaked the front fender of the Suburban. Lyons was out of the driver's seat almost before the two vehicles stopped moving.

"Out of the car, out of the car!" Lyons shouted. "Hands where I can see them! Hands!" A dazed Timothy Albert staggered out of the Taurus. His airbag had not deployed, and his forehead was bloody. He had something in his left hand. His other arm was behind his back.

"Drop it!" Lyons yelled. The barrel of the Python never wavered. "Drop it, now! Get your right hand where I can see it!"

Albert glanced at the device in his hand as if seeing it

for the first time. Something like recognition flashed across his face. Then his right hand came up. The Smith & Wesson's short barrel lined up on Lyons's chest.

The gunshot rang out. Crimson blossomed, soaking Albert's chest. The .357 Magnum bullet from Lyons's Python did its deadly work, dropping the politico-turned-gunman in a tangled heap. The body slumped against the creased rear fender of the Taurus and the .38 clattered to the pavement.

Lyons advanced, checking side to side and glancing to his rear as he kept the Python trained on Albert. When he was certain Timothy Albert wouldn't be shooting at anyone ever again, he spared a look at Schwarz and then at Blancanales. "We clear?" he asked.

"Clear," Schwarz replied said. He and Blancanales had taken up positions to form a triangle with Lyons around the damaged Taurus.

"Clear," Blancanales stated.

"All right," Lyons nodded. "Gadgets, grab a flare from the truck and direct traffic around us. We don't need any more rubbernecking than we're already getting."

"On it."

"Pol," Lyons said. "Give me a hand here." He knelt over the body. Blancanales, watchful for other threats and mindful of the traffic still streaming past, came to join him. The big former L.A. cop had picked up the device Blancanales had at first thought to be a phone. "Check it out," he said. "That's no phone. It's not a PDA, either."

"Strange," Blancanales said, taking the device and turning it over in his hand. "It almost looks like a miniature satellite link." The roughly square device had a tubular antenna running the length of its slim body, with a full miniature keyboard, a mike pickup and a tiny camera. It was much heavier than he would have thought to look at it. The device's heft made Blancanales wonder just how much microelectronic black magic was hidden inside it.

"What do you suppose it does?" he asked.

"That's Gadgets's department," Lyons said. "But I wanted you to get a look at it before he takes it."

"True." Blancanales laughed. "Once he's got his mitts on it, we'll never see it again."

"Why do you think I sent him to direct traffic?" Lyons cracked a rare grin.

"I heard that," Schwarz said over the earbud transceiver.

CHAPTER TWO

Stony Man Farm, Virginia

A bleary-eyed Aaron "the Bear" Kurtzman wheeled himself into the War Room at Stony Man Farm, cradling an oversize stainless-steel insulated travel mug in the crook of one hairy arm. He positioned his wheelchair next to where Barbara Price already sat, checking files on her laptop as she glanced up at the large plasma wall screens to which the slim notebook computer was connected. Stony Man's honey-blond mission controller looked up and raised an eyebrow at Kurtzman.

"Security blanket, Aaron?" she asked, nodding to the mug.

"Life support," Kurtzman said evenly. He took a long drink from the mug, the smell of his extra-strong coffee reaching Price from where the bearded, barrel-chested cybernetics expert sat. "Want some?"

"No, thanks," Price said, smiling. Kurtzman's personal blend was legendary for its power. "I don't want to burn a hole through my stomach."

"I haven't had any," a disembodied voice said over the War Room's speakers, "and I'm still working on an ulcer."

Price tapped a key on the laptop. The harassed face of Hal Brognola appeared on one of the plasma wall screens.

He was chewing an unlighted cigar and glanced repeatedly off camera to something that had to have been on his desk. The microphone on his end of the scrambled link picked up the sound of shuffling papers and then the tapping of computer keys. Brognola, as leader of the SOG, was one of only a handful of living human beings—apart from those operators working within Stony Man's ranks—who knew that the ultracovert antiterrorist operation existed. When it came to the Farm, Brognola answered to the Man himself, the President of the United States. But while Stony Man was the President's secret antiterror and security arm, it was Brognola's baby first. The stress, the constant worry, the basic wear and tear of heading SOG and the Farm were evident in Brognola's face, and had been for as long as Barbara Price had known him.

Price knew at a glance that Brognola was seated in his office on the Potomac, the gray-skies-and-white-marble Wonderland backdrop a stark contrast to the beauty of the Shenandoah National Park. The park ran along the crest of the Blue Ridge Mountains. Stony Man Farm—a real, working farm—was named for Stony Man Mountain, one of the highest peaks in the region and roughly eighty miles by helicopter from Washington. The natural beauty in which the base was located belied the brutal ugliness of the situations with which the Farm's staff so often coped. From the look in Brognola's eyes it was clear that this day would be no different.

"Good morning, Hal," Price said. On the other end of the scrambled connection, Brognola managed a smile.

"Barb, Aaron," Brognola said, nodding. Kurtzman grunted in reply. "Did you get what there was, Bear?"

Kurtzman swallowed and put the mug down on the conference table. "I've got Hunt and Carmen data-mining," he said, "but that's just to dot the eyes and cross the tees. I spent the night going through what they've pulled, organizing it and getting it uploaded to Barb for the brief."

Price nodded. "Hunt" was Huntington Wethers, the eminently refined black man who was one-third of Kurtzman's computer support team. Wethers had been a professor of cybernetics at Berkeley before Kurtzman recruited him. Carmen Delahunt, by contrast, was an old-line FBI agent until Brognola had gotten his hands on her. The vivacious redhead's personality made her an interesting counterpoint to Wether's quiet dignity. While Kurtzman hadn't mentioned him, Price knew that Akira Tokaido, the youngest member of Stony Man's team, was busy working on some hardware with one of the Stony Man team members. Of Japanese descent, Tokaido was never without an MP-3 player blasting heavy metal music into his much-abused eardrums. Price had no idea how he concentrated with that noise ringing in his brain, but he seemed to thrive on it.

"We almost ready?" Brognola asked.

"Bringing up Able now," Price said. She tapped a few more keys. A second plasma screen came alive with the out-of-focus image of a beefy palm. Price raised an eyebrow again, then shook her head with a smile as the hand was withdrawn. The image resolved itself into that of a very irritated Carl Lyons, obviously staring down into a Web cam of some kind. Schwarz and Blancanales crowded in next to him, their heads almost touching as they verified they were present for the meeting. Lyons shrugged them off, leaving only parts of their shoulders and torsos in view as he glared down at the camera.

"This," he said tersely, "is really annoying."

"You'll live," Price said evenly. "Can you hear us and see us okay?"

Lyons grunted. "Yes."

"Wideband scattering-noise projectors in place," Schwarz said, his face not visible. Price nodded; this would thwart electronic eavesdropping on their location, including directional microphones.

The door to the War Room opened again. Several men entered. Price watched them take seats around the conference table and nod to the images of Brognola and Able Team in turn. The new arrivals were Phoenix Force, the second counterterrorist team run by the Farm, responsible primarily for international operations. The greater scope of their turf was reflected in the larger size of the team—five for Able's three.

Slouching into his seat, nursing a can of Coke and appearing deceptively casual, was David McCarter, Phoenix Force's leader. The lean, fox-faced Briton had always been something of a hothead, which had brought him into conflict with Brognola more than once. He had proved a capable leader, however, through countless missions with Phoenix. The former SAS operative smelled strongly of cigarette smoke. Price assumed he'd just finished one before the briefing.

Next to McCarter, making a show of waving away the fumes, was the stockier, more heavily muscled Rafael Encizo. The Cuban-born guerrilla expert was a much squatter, blockier man, but his appearance, Price knew, concealed catlike reflexes.

Demolitions expert Gary Manning, sat on the other side of McCarter, sipping what Price assumed was coffee.

Tall and graceful, Calvin James slipped into a chair next

to Manning. The lanky black man, who'd grown up on Chicago's South Side, was the team's medic and former Navy SEAL who was also very talented with a knife.

Bringing up the rear was T. J. Hawkins. The youngest member of the team, Hawkins was a former Army Ranger. The Georgia-born southerner's easy manner and lilting drawl concealed a keen mind and viciously fast fighting abilities.

"All accounted for, Hal," Price said finally.

"All right," Brognola said. "Let's get started." Price took this as her cue and pressed a button on her laptop, bringing up a map of India.

"Bloody hell," McCarter muttered.

"Just under forty-eight hours ago," Brognola said, ignoring McCarter, "an armed raid was staged on a mining facility in the Meghalaya hills, north of Bangladesh, not far from the West Khasi Hills district headquarters, Nongstoin. The facility is jointly owned by UVC Limited and the Indian government."

"UVC?" Schwarz asked, his head still cut off on screen.

"Uranium-Vanadium Consortium, Limited," Brognola said.

"I thought India was relatively uranium-poor," Manning put in.

"Not anymore," Brognola said. "I don't yet have all the details, nor are they necessarily relevant, but UVC is using a new sonic-based technology to find and exploit previously untapped reserves of ore, including uranium. The deal they cut with the Indian government apparently stems to long before the ore was actually found in Meghalaya. Their surveyors gambled and construction began on an experimental laser enrichment plant well in advance of the actual mining operation."

"So just how large-scale is this?"

"Large enough to make India a much bigger player in the nuclear club," Brognola said. "The Indian government has long maintained a high level of secrecy regarding its nuclear power and weapons programs, but we all know they have nuclear weapons and have had them since the 1970s. A steady source of uranium ore and a steady production of enriched fuel will simply advance their program or programs, and significantly."

"So the issue is the standoff with Pakistan?" James asked.

"No," Brognola said. "That would almost be preferable. The issue is that the UVC facility in Meghalaya was relieved of several insulated drums of enriched, weapons-grade fuel. That itself is enough to get us involved. But that's just the beginning of the problem."

Price tapped a key on her notebook again. The image of a dark-skinned man appeared, a mugshot from an international criminal database. It was juxtaposed with a second image—that of the same man, eyes closed in death, lying on a slab in a morgue.

"This is Nilambar Chakraborty," Brognola said.

"It was, you mean," McCarter muttered.

Brognola spared McCarter a baleful gaze through his camera before continuing. "Chakraborty is a known member of the Purba Banglar Sarbahara Party, a terrorist group operating in Bangladesh. They've broadened their territory lately, moving farther and farther north into India and surrounding areas. The PBSP is a vicious, well-financed, anti-capitalist revolutionary group whose ideological origins stem from sympathy for the Chinese Communist movement. Their ultimate aims are vague, but coherent enough. They seek to bring about worldwide socialism, starting with their part of the world, through force of arms."

"These blokes have been around for years," McCarter put in. "Starting with opposition to the new Bangladeshi state. And last I knew, they spent most of their time and energy splintering off from one another to form different opposed sub-groups."

"That was true until perhaps two years ago," Brognola nodded. "The PBSP has since experienced a surge in growth, tied to global resurgence of various Communist and socialist groups."

"The political pendulum is swinging around the world," Encizo said sourly. "As it does, as people foolishly throw in with totalitarian ideologies, the fortunes of terrorist and agitator groups like these go up."

Price watched Encizo thoughtfully. As a native Cuban he was naturally sensitive to the evil that communist governments could wreak.

The door of the War Room opened. Akira Tokaido entered quietly, carrying what appeared to be a personal data device, and took a seat.

"But wait," Blancanales said off-camera, imitating a game-show host, "there's more."

"Indeed there is," Brognola said. "Akira?"

"This," Tokaido said, holding up the electronic device, "was recovered by a security guard who survived the attack on the UVC plant. The device was given to executives at Sugar Rapids Security, who forwarded it through channels to the U.S. Government almost immediately. We got word of and intercepted it before it could disappear into a Washington warehouse somewhere, crated up next to the Ark of the Covenant."

"Chakraborty was carrying that device," Brognola explained.

"And this," Schwarz chimed in, holding up a PDA-size device of his own, "is an identical unit, recovered from the now deceased director of the Illinois chapter of the World Workers United Party."

McCarter looked from the screen to the device in Tokaido's hands, then back. "Bloody hell," he said again.

Tokaido removed the earbud headphones attached to his MP-3 player. Heavy metal noise could be heard through the speakers, even from across the table. The young Asian blushed slightly and switched off the player. He pointed at the device recovered in India.

"This," he said, "is a sanitized communicator. It has been manufactured with parts that are supposed to be untraceable. It carries no identifying markings, but all I had to do was play with it and look at its internals to understand what it is. It's a Worldcom Transat Seever."

"A knockoff, you mean?" Hawkins asked.

"No," Tokaido said. "It is not a knockoff. It is a genuine WTS and uses the same satellite network and communications protocols. The only difference between this and a commercial WTS is the origins of the parts and the lack of serial numbers on them."

"Does somebody want to tell me what a WTS is?" Lyons asked, sounding irritated.

"The WTS is the flagship product of Butler Telecommunications," Barbara Price explained. "It's the next generation of secure, scrambled satellite phone."

"Like the units we carry?" James gestured with the secure phone he and all the Stony Man team members carried.

"Much more advanced," Kurtzman said, "in terms of the

bandwidth it can handle and the way the units interface with one another. Your phones connect with us at the Farm for security reasons, and we can transfer data, photos and so forth. The transmissions are coded and secure, yes, but most of that security stems from the fact that you're communicating with the Farm and not other points of transfer. The Seevers produced by Butler Telecomm are bulky and awkward compared to your duty phones, but they give an agent in the field a means of communicating with any other similarly equipped agent, completely securely, anywhere in the world."

"Not much need for such a thing among teams that are centrally controlled, such as ours directed by the Farm," James stated, "but perfect for terrorist cells to communicate and coordinate."

"Exactly," Brognola said. "The technology has been the subject of heated debate for that reason. Washington has pressured Butler Telecomm to provide access to the encryption used, for national security reasons. Reginald Butler, president and chairman of the company, has stonewalled the government at every step. He's become the poster boy for civil liberties in certain political circles."

"Why do I feel like something is tying all this together?" McCarter said ruefully.

"Able Team was sent to check World Workers United Party because of financial transaction warnings flagged here at the Farm," Price explained. "The party has received substantial funding from the Earth Action Front, an ecoterrorist group."

"What Able got, when they looked," Brognola said, "was three very trigger-happy 'workers' who were obviously expecting trouble. The director of WWUP in Illinois had one of these Seevers. We can't crack its encryption, but we do know that it is operating on the same subnetwork as the unit found in India."

"So uranium stolen by Bangladeshi Communist terrorists is somehow connected to environmental terrorists and also to an American Communist party," McCarter said.

"Yes," Brognola nodded. "Aaron and his team have been up all night sifting through the recovered drives from the WWUP office. Bear?"

"I'm uploading the files to all of your phones now," Kurtzman said, leaning past Price to tap a few of the keys on her notebook. "Following the money trail, and cross-referencing known associates with current records of terrorist actions that can or could be labeled 'green' in nature, not to mention cross-referencing these with NSA, FBI, and CIA files on various World Workers United Party members of interest, we have produced a series of potential domestic targets, ranked in order of priority."

"Able remains on-site in Chicago to begin local follow-up," Brognola said.

"Meanwhile," Kurtzman continued, "I have produced a similar list relevant to Purba Banglar activity worldwide, cross-indexing that with known coalitions of both international Communist and socialist terror groups, and 'green' agitator organizations. The trail starts in Nongstoin."

"And that," Brognola said, "is where I am sending you, Phoenix."

"Priorities?" McCarter asked.

"First, the recovery of the enriched uranium," Brognola said. "That is by far the most significant threat. Second, and this applies especially to you, Able, we need to know just how far and how deep the connection between the WWUP in the United States and these domestic and international terror organizations goes. American politics has long been ripe for infiltration by foreign elements. It looks like it's happening, and in a big way. I want to know the details—how, who, and why, in that order."

"On it," Lyons said.

"Coordinate through Barb to have the Farm deliver anything additional you'll need," Brognola said. "I'll arrange for a liaison with local law enforcement, both in Chicago and wherever the trail ultimately takes you."

"You sound like you have someplace in mind."

"I might," Brognola said. "Reginald Butler has long been a political activist. He's one of the richest men in America and he's got a lot to lose. If he's mixed up in any of this, or even if he's simply letting his company sell the Seever units to foreign nationals with ties to terror, I want him taken down. That means sooner or later you'll be paying him a visit at Butler Telecomm headquarters in Atlanta."

"And me, a local boy, stuck overseas," Hawkins drawled. "Let me know if you boys want a list of the local hotspots."

"Could get sticky," Blancanales said dubiously, leaning in so his face was visible. "Government operatives pressuring an American entrepreneur who's already complaining about governmental harassment."

"We don't exist," Brognola said. "We do, therefore, what we have to do."

"Understood, Hal." Lyons nodded.

"Every second that uranium is out there is a tick on the doomsday clock," Brognola said gravely. "If it's not recovered, we're looking at nuclear Armageddon in the hands of terrorists. On the next threat level, we have to look seriously at the idea our domestic political infrastructure is being compromised by violent terrorists with an international agenda. In either direction, the outlook is bleak, and the threat to the United States potentially terminal."

"Understood," Lyons said again. McCarter and the members of Phoenix Force nodded grimly.

"All right," Brognola said. "Phoenix, we're in touch with the Indian government and will have some of the red tape untangled before your boots hit the ground there. More information will be made available to you through secure data transfers as and if it becomes available. Get out there, people. Get it done. Hundreds of thousands of lives could ultimately ride on this."

"Bloody hell," McCarter repeated.

CHAPTER THREE

Nongstoin, West Khasi Hills, India

The old Range Rover was scarred and even boasted a small-caliber bullet hole in one rear side window, but the engine had turned over smoothly and the tank had been full when they boarded. For small favors like those, David McCarter thanked whatever higher power likely wasn't listening—fate, hope, karma, whatever—and brought the vehicle to a halt in front of the Deputy commissioner's office. The humidity hit him as soon as he exited the truck's air-conditioned cab. Across from the parking area, a low, round fountain—which was not running—sat full of stagnant green water. The fountain was surrounded by purple-red flowers that appeared almost to be growing wild.

The district headquarters squatted above them, a square, multistory, grayish-green building. An Indian flag fluttered on a flagpole jutting from the roof. In the distance, under gray skies and misty clouds, the hills for which the region was named loomed round and dark. McCarter paused to light a Player's cigarette. Inhaling deeply, he surveyed the area around the squat building. The rest of Phoenix Force climbed out of the Range Rover behind him.

"Bloody wonderful," McCarter muttered to himself, taking in the scene.

Jack Grimaldi, Stony Man Farm's ace pilot, waited with their plane at the airstrip, where Stony Man's logistics wizards had also arranged for a helicopter, Hughes OH-6A Loach which was in superb condition and came with a single Hydra 70 mm seven-tube rocket pod. McCarter had no idea how Brognola or Price had managed to wrangle that on Indian soil, nor was he going to look this particular gift horse in the mouth.

"Easy, David," Encizo offered, coming up to stand next to him. "It's a necessary evil."

"Don't I know it, mate," McCarter since, taking a deep drag from his cigarette. "It doesn't mean I like it any more. We should be moving directly on the first target."

"Proper form, my friend," Encizo said quietly. "Proper form must be followed." The target to which McCarter referred was a cement factory outside Nongstoin. It had been identified by the Farm's computer experts as belonging to an investor suspected of having ties to the Purba Banglars. It was too great a coincidence to ignore. Such a plant would be a great place to stage stolen uranium, it seemed to McCarter. He could not understand why they were wasting time appeasing bureaucrats, but Brognola had cautioned them against ignoring the district's deputy commissioner. They would need the cooperation of the locals if they were to operate without interference from the Indian government. While relations between India and the United States were not particularly strained, the presence of armed American operatives on foreign soil was always a touchy issue. Phoenix Force had been issued false credentials identifying them, officially, as U.S. Military advisers operating as security consultants. Each man had retained his first name, as this was not exactly deep cover, but any check on their fake last names would yield a Farm-produced piece of biographical fiction that would lead nowhere.

In the truck, in specially loaded gear bags, were the team's assault rifles. The Farm's armorer, John "Cowboy" Kissinger, had supplied them with his latest prizes—Israeli Military Industries TAR-21 Tavor assault rifles, space-age bullpup rifles chambered in 5.56 mm NATO and accepting STANAG M-16 30-round magazines. The incredibly ergonomic, compact weapons were modular firearms comprised of composite materials, each specially tuned to Kissinger's exacting standards. Each rifle had a cyclic rate of 800 rounds and was fitted with red-dot optics for fast target acquisition. James and Manning had been issued Tavors with the M-203 40 mm grenade launcher attachment, and their gear contained high-explosive, flechette and flare rounds for the weapons.

A padded, nondescript case in the truck also contained an M-24 Sniper Weapon System. The United States Army's version of the Remington 700 rifle, chambered in 7.62 mm NATO and boasting a Leupold Mark IV 10 x 40 mm telescopic sight, was nominally for Gary Manning's use, though any of the Phoenix Force commandos could deploy the rifle if need be.

Each of the men carried their pistols, nominally concealed in Kydex or leather holsters under the desert-tan BDUs each man wore. James, Encizo and Hawkins had opted for the standard Beretta M-9s. Manning carried an old favorite, his .357 Magnum Desert Eagle. For his part, McCarter could not forsake his Browning Hi-Power, which was as much a part of his identity as the pack of Player's cigarettes he carried.

Each member of Phoenix Force carried a few other

nasty surprises. Before they'd left, Kissinger had passed around a pile of long, black cardboard boxes, doling them out like candy. Each was marked with the slogan For Those Who Serve. McCarter couldn't care less for marketing, but he knew serviceable steel when he saw it. Each man in his command was armed with something sharp and deadly as a result. All of them had opted for fixed blades. McCarter carried a Triumph neck knife under his BDUs, slung under his shoulder on a paracord harness, that acted like a makeshift shoulder harness and allowed the knife to hang handle-down under his arm.

The team entered the building, leaving Hawkins with the truck. At the front desk, McCarter introduced the team only as the "U.S. delegation." They were ushered into the office of the deputy commissioner, Kamal Jignesh.

"Gentlemen, gentlemen," Jignesh said pleasantly in accented English, inviting them in from behind his desk. There were only two chairs. McCarter and Manning took seats, while the rest of the team stood behind them. "We of the West Khasi Hills district deeply regret the difficulty that the Consortium experienced. We will do whatever we can to cooperate in your investigation."

McCarter nodded, studying Jignesh. He was a short, somewhat plump man, wearing a lightweight suit that looked a size too big. His hair was receding over a wrinkled forehead and plump, deeply set features. While his face smiled, his eyes held something else. Fear? Suspicion? McCarter couldn't place it. He flashed his papers.

"Deputy Commissioner," McCarter said, doing his best not to sit on the edge of the chair out of impatience, "my men and I have urgent business. We were informed by our government that you would be assigning us a liaison."

"Yes, of course, of course." Jignesh nodded eagerly, waving the identification away. "I shall call him in. I know you must hurry. We are very concerned, of course, and wish for a quick resolution to this as much as you do. Our own forces have been alerted to the danger and are even now searching the countryside."

McCarter had no idea whether to take that seriously, but it didn't matter. He drummed his fingers on the arm of the chair. Jignesh used the intercom on his desk and spoke a few words—if it was Hindi, McCarter didn't know one way or another—before completing the call and looking at his office door expectantly. A second Indian man entered. He was tall and lean, with a beak of a nose and sharp, dark, darting eyes.

"Gentlemen," Jignesh said, "this is Sankara Gopalan, my aide. He will accompany you. If you must interact with any of our armed personnel, he will make sure your...autonomy...is respected."

The Briton noted that with interest. The Indians were either aware of just how potentially destructive the loss of the uranium fuel was, or they were getting heavy pressure from the State Department. Perhaps both. Brognola had definitely pulled some strings.

Gopalan nodded. "A pleasure to meet you." His English was more thickly accented than Jignesh's, but still quite good.

"This is potentially dangerous work." The former SAS operative eyed Gopalan hard. "Are you armed?"

"I am not," Gopalan replied, shaking his head. "Do not worry, sir. I am aware of the risks. But my government insists your activities be monitored."

"Meaning no offense, of course," Jignesh put in. "I'm sure—"

"Right, then," McCarter said, cutting off whatever other

blustering Jignesh might have been preparing to interject. "Let's get a move on, ladies." He waited as his teammates hustled Gopalan out of the room, following on their heels. Jignesh rushed from behind his desk and grabbed McCarter by the shoulder when the other men were through the door.

"He is not to be trusted!" Jignesh whispered. Gone was the mask of obsequious welcome. He was clearly terrified. "Your people were anticipated!"

McCarter nodded once, curtly, winking at Jignesh. Then he continued on so that none of the others, particularly Gopalan, could suspect that any words had been exchanged.

"Ears on, people," McCarter said as the team, with Gopalan tagging along, reached the Range Rover. With a tap, each man activated the earbuds that would provide them with a secure, local, and hands-free short-range communications link with one another.

The Briton waited for Gopalan to climb into the back seat of the truck between James and Encizo. Hawkins managed to squeeze in, too, while the larger Manning took the passenger seat. As he walked around the rear of the Range Rover, he spoke quietly, knowing his words were being transmitted over the earbuds.

"Right then, listen up. Jignesh has gone squirrelly and says we're headed for a trap. Keep a close eye on Gopalan. We've other targets to try, but I'm betting the most likely is also the deadfall. We'll trip their trap and take the battle straight down their throats."

He threw open his door and climbed into the vehicle. Manning was glaring at him, expressing what McCarter imagined was concern regarding knowingly charging a trap. He would get over it. He had before. He couldn't argue, either, not with Gopalan there to hear. That was almost amusing. McCarter glanced at the others. James looked cool and collected, as usual. Encizo was unreadable, while Hawkins looked like he might be waiting to take a nap. Nodding to himself and knowing that his team was more than ready, McCarter fired up the Range Rover. The engine caught easily and the British-made four-wheel-drive—surely that was a good sign—lurched from its parking spot.

McCarter drove, following Gopalan's directions to the outskirts of town, where the cement factory was located.

"There is parking near the supervisory shed," Gopalan said.

"Familiar with the plant, are you?" McCarter looked up at the Indian in the rearview mirror.

"Oh, yes, it is my job to meet with the local businesses," Gopalan said smoothly. "Encouraging trade and industry is the deputy commissioner's highest priority."

"I imagine it would be," McCarter said insincerely. He stopped the truck well short of the main cluster of buildings, stopping to turn it around so it was nose-outward in the middle of the access road.

"What are you doing?" Gopalan asked mildly.

"Parking," McCarter said. He motioned for Phoenix Force to exit the Range Rover. As they climbed out, Gopalan pointed up the road.

"You are blocking access to the factory," he said. McCarter couldn't be sure, but he thought the Indian was starting to look worried.

"Only for a moment," McCarter said, smiling.

His grin suddenly vanished and his tone turned hard. "Gary," he said. "Do it."

Manning, his face stern, produced his .357 Magnum

Desert Eagle. He cocked the hammer and shoved the massive triangular snout of the hand cannon under Gopalan's chin, grabbing the Indian by the back of the head to hold him in place.

"What are you doing?" Gopalan squealed. "I am a representative of—"

"Terrorists and murderers," McCarter finished for him. "Now, mate, you've got what I see as two choices. You can tell us what the ambush is all about, who put you wise to it, and who you're working for, or you can stand there quietly and my friend here will splash your brains all over this beautiful countryside. How about it?"

"You cannot... I... This cannot..." Gopalan sputtered. Finally he started cursing in his native language.

"Gary," McCarter said, "shoot him."

"No!" Gopalan shrieked. "I will tell you! I will tell you!"

McCarter smirked. "That's more like it." He shook a cigarette from his pack and lit it, feigning boredom as he took a long drag.

"Now—" he deliberately blew smoke into Gopalan's face as he turned to the man, "—get with it. He nodded to the other members of Phoenix Force. "Gear up." Encizo threw open the rear door of the Range Rover and began tossing gear bags to James and Encizo.

"I was told to watch for any searching for the uranium," Gopalan admitted. His words came out in a rush. "I monitored conversations with the deputy commissioner. I listened in when our government gave him his instructions to cooperate with the American advisers who were coming." He gave the Briton a meaningful look. Obviously he was smart enough to grasp that Phoenix Force was something other than what the Indian government had been told to expect.

"How did you know we would come here?"

"We didn't," Gopalan said. "But it was a likely spot. I was given a list of locations the authorities or the military might choose to investigate. I was to give warning as soon as I knew the destination, so that we could prepare."

"Who is 'we'?" McCarter asked. When Gopalan did not immediately answer, the Briton nodded to Manning, who pressed the Desert Eagle more tightly under Gopalan's chin.

"The Proletarian Party of East Bengal," Gopalan said.

"The bloody Purba Banglars." McCarter snarled. "What's their involvement?"

"We have the uranium," Gopalan said. "More I cannot tell you. I do not know where it is. I do not know what is to be done with it."

"How'd you know to hit the plant in the first place?" Calvin James said, walking up next to McCarter with his Tavor assault rifle in hand.

"I do not know," Gopalan shook his head, mindful of the Desert Eagle pressing against his throat.

"And the deputy commissioner?" McCarter demanded. "He in on this?"

"We have his family," Gopalan said.

"Bloody hell," McCarter whispered. "All right, then. He—" the Briton nodded to Gopalan "—has talked, and I want to see what shakes loose. We take the cement plant."

"What about him?" Manning nodded to the Indian.

"Oh, him," McCarter said. "Calvin, let me see your rifle a moment." He took the Tavor, unloaded it, and ejected the chambered round, handing both round and magazine to

James. "One second, mate." Then he walked around behind Gopalan. "Let go, Gary." When Manning did so, McCarter buttstroked Gopalan in the back of the head with the Tavor. The Indian fell, unconscious.

"A bit light," McCarter said, handing the rifle back to James. "But at least it did the trick." James winked coolly and reloaded the weapon.

"Now what?" Encizo asked evenly.

"That hill," McCarter nodded to a facing hill that overlooked the road leading to the cement plant. "A decent vantage. Gary, take the M-24 and get up there. Rafe and Calvin, you take the flanks. Skirt the plant and come at it from the rear quarters. T.J., you're with me."

"Y'all aren't going to do what I think you're going to do, are you?"

"Bloody well right," McCarter grinned, smoking his cigarette down to the filter and letting it fall to the dirt road. He ground it under the heel of his combat boot, picked it up and pocketed it. "We're going in the front."

The Phoenix Force leader helped Manning drag Gopalan into the Range Rover, where Manning secured his wrists and ankles with plastic riot cuffs. The burly Canadian took the M-24 and sprinted away. Meanwhile, McCarter saw to his own gear bag and prepared his rifle. It felt good to have the political games out of the way, however temporarily. Now it was time to see to business.

At a nod from McCarter, James and Encizo made their way left and right, moving quietly but quickly. Hawkins watched them go and then nodded up the dirt road, where the main cluster of buildings waited in the distance. "We walkin'?" he asked.

"We're walking," McCarter nodded. "Can you keep up?"

"I reckon I'll manage, hoss." Hawkins exaggerated his Southern drawl.

"Commo check," McCarter said, testing the earbud link.

"In position," Manning said. He wasn't even breathing heavily despite his fast climb.

"Moving," James reported.

"Also moving," Encizo called in.

"As are we, gents," McCarter said. He jerked his chin in the direction of the plant. He and Hawkins readied their rifles and started to march, keeping well apart from each other, using the road to maintain the distance between them.

"We're going to get shot at," Hawkins said.

"I'm counting on it," McCarter grinned. "Gary, be ready."

"On it," Manning called back.

The two Phoenix Force commandos, slightly crouched, moved from one piece of equipment to the next, closing in on the large main building that was the central point in the cement plant. McCarter was playing a dangerous game, he knew, but tripping a deadfall was never easy. They would have to strike a delicate balance, staying out of the enemy's direct lines of fire while nonetheless making themselves tempting targets. He paused near some kind of grinder, the mammoth machine showing spots of rust under peeling paint as it hulked in the humid climate.

The Briton caught movement in the corner of his eye and knew that the moment had come. The muzzle-flash, when it appeared in a window on the second story of the main building, was brief but plainly visible. Dirt churned near Hawkins's feet as a trio of bullets dug into the ground. The answering thunder from Manning's M-24 came half a beat later. One down.

McCarter and Hawkins ran for it, opening up with their Tavors. The chatter of the lightweight Israeli guns was met by the characteristic hollow racket of Kalashnikovs. The Phoenix Force leader, even as he moved, noted the positions of the enemy fire—and smiled with grim satisfaction. Almost lost in the chaotic din was the slow, deadly drumbeat of Manning and his sniper-tuned Remington 700, but wherever his answering call went, the muzzle-flashes marking the enemy suddenly ceased. By the time McCarter and Hawkins made the entrance of the big building, the Briton was confident most of the shooters were down.

Hawkins took the left and McCarter the right as they cleared the doorway. A pair of dark-skinned men wearing mismatched jungle camouflage and black bandanna face masks opened fire on them. The Tavors barked and the first man, then the next fell. Two more Kalashnikovs fell silent.

"Take the ground floor, T.J.," McCarter directed, confident his earbud would carry the words to Hawkins. "I'll take the high road." The structure was basically a corrugated metal warehouse boasting a single large, open factory floor. Heavy equipment, for grinding and mixing, was clustered in the middle at ground level. A metal catwalk ran the perimeter of the building's interior, and it was from there that the gunmen had been firing. McCarter scaled the nearest ladder and hoisted himself up onto the rickety, rusting framework, scanning for targets among the fallen bodies of the shooters.

"Anything, T.J.?" McCarter asked.

"No one left on this level at the front," Hawkins reported.

"No one at the rear," James said, unseen somewhere on the other side of the building. "We took out one gunner. All's quiet."

"All right," McCarter said. "Search the bodies. See if you can find anything useful. I'll make the rounds up here and then join you on the ground. Gary?"

"On my way back to the truck to check Gopalan," the big Canadian's voice came back.

"Good," McCarter said. "Not such a bad plan, now, was it?"

Manning grumbled something over the link. McCarter resisted the urge to laugh.

He checked each man in turn. The shooters carried guns and some ammunition, but nothing else—no identification, no clues, and no other personal effects. McCarter took a picture of each corpse with the camera built into his secure wireless phone. The other Phoenix Force members would be doing the same, he knew. The pictures would be sent to the Farm to see if an identification, and hence any records, could be pulled from across the vast computer networks to which Stony Man had access.

He was toeing over the last of the bodies when the man lying on the rusty catwalk opened his eyes.

The man screamed something and surged to his feet, a Kalashnikov bayonet flashing in his hand. McCarter leaned back in time to avoid the small bowie-shaped blade slashing at his gut, but the man lunged after him, and McCarter stumbled. The Tavor fell from his hands as the man tackled him. They rolled, coming up again, and the man charged with the blade before McCarter could take the initiative. The Briton had just enough to time to slap his hands down, knocking the knife aside, as he stepped in to slam the palm of his off hand up and under the man's chin.

The blow rocked the knifer onto his back. He rolled and came up again, shaking his head, his whole body trembling. McCarter saw the look of a true believer in his eyes, an expression he'd seen on many a fanatic and terrorist. The man came in again, close behind his knife, seeking McCarter's flesh with the needle-sharp clip point.

The Browning Hi-Power filled the Briton's hand.

"Drop the blade," McCarter ordered.

The knifer remained steady and focused.

"Look, mate," he said, trying to sound calm. "it's over. We don't want to kill you. We want to question you. Play it right and you could walk away from this." While that last was, strictly speaking, a lie, McCarter needed the guy alive. There were too many questions to be answered, and they had about all they were likely to get from Gopalan. Something was afoot, something big, and if the Stony Man teams were to get to the bottom of it, they needed to start producing more answers than questions.

The man lunged.

McCarter swore and fired, putting a single round between the man's eyes. There was no other choice; if he tried to play fancy trick-shooting games with a charging blade, it could mean his life. The would-be killer was dead before his body completed its fall to the catwalk, the knife clanging on the rusty metal.

"Bloody hell," McCarter said once more.

CHAPTER FOUR

The apartment building was as decrepit a structure as any the members of Able Team were likely to find in the area. Looking around, Carl Lyons shook his head. The buildings here had a sense of history. It was obvious this had once been a much better neighborhood. Now it was dying, rotting from the inside out, a victim of the animals who lived there and preyed on one another. Able Team had visited many such places in their battle against terror and crime. Still, even a hardened former cop and veteran counterterrorist like Lyons felt a pang of regret whenever he saw a place like this one, so badly gone to seed.

They were dressed casually. Lyons wore a bomber jacket over denims, while Blancanales and Gadgets wore slacks, polo shirts and windbreakers. Their nondescript attire did nothing to conceal the weapons in their hands. Lyons would normally have moved much more discreetly, but they had received a scrambled call from the Farm only minutes before reaching their destination that morning. Phoenix Force had taken down an ambush in India, and no one knew precisely how the enemy was a step ahead of what the Stony Man teams were doing. Given that, the former L.A. detective didn't intend to get blindsided. They were going in, yes, and they were going in hot.

The target was an apartment building, and specifically a unit on its top floor. The site was part of the list produced by the Farm's computer wizards. Each target on the priority-ordered list was linked to a person or persons of interest relevant to the WWUP or the ecoterror groups funding them, as Kurtzman had explained it. The fundamental mission had not changed. Both Able Team and Phoenix Force were shaking trees to see what fell out of them.

These trees, of course, often bore lethal fruit.

The shotgun Carl Lyons held in his calloused fists was a Daewoo USAS-12, a massive selective fire 12-gauge shotgun styled something like an M-16 and fitted with a 20-round polymer drum magazine. Lyons carried extra drums in the green canvas war bag slung across his chest. Schwarz and Blancanales carried similar bags. The rest of Lyons's armament consisted of his personal handgun, the Colt Python, as well as a Columbia River Knife and Tool "M-16" tactical folding knife. The blades carried by the other team members were of the same brand but in different styles. Blancanales had opted for a fixed blade CRKT Ultima, while Schwarz carried an "M-18" folder model.

Schwarz was armed with a Kissinger-tuned specialty, the silenced Beretta 93-R machine pistol, and several 20-round magazines were in the pouches of his web belt, under his windbreaker. Blancanales had opted for something a little less exotic, but no less effective—a short-barreled CAR-15 with a collapsible stock and vertical foregrip complete with flashlight unit.

The three men took the stairs leading up to the target apartment with practiced precision, covering one another with Lyons in the lead.

They had discussed the fastest way to breach the door

to the apartment. Lyons's first thought had been to use a portable battering ram of the type used by SWAT teams, but the warning from the Farm had nixed that plan. He did not want any member of Able Team to be vulnerable, even temporarily, if armed hostiles were waiting on the other side of the door. In the end he had simply loaded the Daewoo's chamber with a fléchette breaching round. The first shot from the awesomely powerful weapon would be to take down the lock, after which Lyons and his teammates would blitz the door and overwhelm whoever was waiting on the other side.

The hallways through which they walked were padded with stained, threadbare carpet, which softened the impacts of their combat boots. The hallways smelled of cooking food. Lyons could hear a baby crying through one of the doors on a lower floor; he signaled to Schwarz and Blancanales and frowned. His warning was clear. There were innocents nearby and they could risk no collateral casualties.

Their earbud transceivers were active, but Lyons didn't want to risk even a whisper as they neared the target doorway just past the top-floor landing. He signaled to his teammates, who took up positions on either side of the door to back him up. Lyons aimed the USAS-12 and braced himself. He looked to his teammates both of whom nodded.

Lyons pulled the trigger.

The shotgun blast disintegrated the lock. The big ex-cop immediately slammed the sole of his combat boot into the spot immediately left of the hole, slamming the flimsy hollow-core door open. He led Able Team into the apartment, his weapon sweeping the room for targets. Blancanales and Schwarz flanked him, taking opposite sides of the room as he advanced. They would sweep and clear in both directions, each man covering the other to prevent any nasty surprises.

"Clear!" Lyons shouted. The living room was empty save for a broken and half-collapsed flea market sofa and an ancient console television boasting a bent pair of rabbit ears. Pizza boxes were piled in a corner of the room, next to two blue plastic bins into which empty beer and soda cans had been piled. While the apartment itself was typical of the hovels third-rate scumbags occupied, Lyons thought to himself, it was surprisingly clean.

"Bedroom's clear!" Schwarz called from the next room.

"Bathroom!" Blancanales sang out. "Got a live one!"

His shotgun at a low ready, Lyons found Blancanales standing over a twenty-something male who was doing his best to look nonchalant—while sitting on the toilet. He had been reading a magazine when the team had busted down his door, apparently. It was crumpled on the floor at his feet, on top of the fuzzy blue bathmat that covered most of the floor in the tiny bathroom. The title *Earth Action* was emblazoned across it.

"Is there anyone else here?" Blancanales asked calmly, the stubby barrel of his rifle trained on the young man's face.

"No," the man shook his head.

"Your name?" the Hispanic commando asked in the same even, almost friendly tone.

"Ryan," the young man answered. "Ryan Pinter."

"Well, Mr. Pinter—" Blancanales lowered the CAR-15 "—I suggest you cooperate fully. You're in a lot of trouble."

"But…but…I didn't do anything!"

"We'll be the judge of that," Lyons said, easily playing bad cop to Blancanales's good.

"First things first," the Hispanic commando said. "Why don't you, well, pull your pants up. You'll be joining us in the living room."

"Is anyone else expected here?" Lyons snarled.

"No, no, not for hours," Pinter admitted readily. "Look, please, I haven't done anything wrong. I don't know what this is about, but—"

"Oh, you know," Lyons said, planting a beefy palm between Pinter's shoulder blades and propelling him into the living room as the young man left the bathroom, still hitching at his pants. Pinter almost collided with the couch and tried to crawl up into a ball on it, looking up at each of the armed men who had suddenly invaded his world.

"Look, you can't just break in here and… Do you have a warrant?"

Lyons, playing his part now, raised the USAS-12 menacingly. "This is my warrant," he said.

"You're a member of the World Workers United Party," Blancanales informed him.

"So that's what this is?" Pinter became indignant. "You're rousting me because of my political beliefs? Oh, man, I knew this *Patriot Act* thing was going to turn into oppression! You can't suppress my political beliefs at gunpoint! I'll sue, I'll sue and you'll be—"

"We'll be what?" Lyons asked. "You are aware, aren't you, that the director of the WWUP here in Illinois was killed while attempting to murder federal law-enforcement officers?"

Pinter looked down, the wind taken out of his sails for a moment. "I heard he was maybe in an embezzlement scandal." The young man shook his head. "That he tried to shoot his way out rather than get caught. That isn't right, man, but it shows you that capitalist greed can infect even those who—"

"Shove a sock in it," Lyons growled. "I'm not interested in your speeches."

"But look, man, you can't hold every member of the party responsible for what one guy does."

"Three guys, actually," Lyons said. "Or don't you read the news?" An officially scrubbed version of the events at the WWUP facility had been released to the media, complete with rumors of corruption as the official reason behind the shootings. The rumor mill had already started to manufacture plausible backstories, with the assistance of a twenty-four-hour cable news media desperate for unfounded speculation with which to fill its schedule. All of this put the public off the trail, as was intended. There was no point in starting a panic—though at this point, even the Farm didn't know enough to guess as to why the WWUP director had been so fast on the trigger—with the real story behind the events, and of course Stony Man's covert operatives had to be shielded. Lyons knew that Brognola's heartburn only intensified every time Able was involved in so public a shooting, but it went with the territory. The big former L.A. cop had been as surprised as anyone when the probe had turned to gunplay so fast. The fact that it had was just proof for Brognola's theory that big things were happening, or about to happen. The worm in front of Able Team now could well prove the key to unlocking some part of the puzzle. If not that, he might lead them to those who could.

"This is not about politics. At least, it's not about your public politics. You're also member of the Earth Action Front," Blancanales said calmly. "A highly ranked member, in fact."

"Look, man, you got it all wrong," Pinter said desperately. "I'm an environmentalist, sure. Green Party, a few other groups. I care about my planet, is that a crime? But I'm not in the Earth Action Front."

Lyons snorted and lowered the shotgun. He stepped away long enough to duck into the bathroom, grab the magazine Pinter had been reading and throw it at him. Ryan flinched as the dog-eared, glossy pages hit him.

"So what's that?" Lyons demanded. "A little light reading?"

"*Earth Action* is a reputable publication," Ryan almost whined. "Just because the Earth Action Front names themselves after a green magazine, you can't—"

Lyons snarled, set the shotgun on the carpeted floor and drew the Colt Python from his shoulder holster. He leveled the heavy barrel at Pinter's face. "Let's just stop dicking around, shall we?"

"Ironman," Blancanales said, sounding concerned. He, too, was playing a role for Pinter's benefit.

"Shut up." Lyons turned away from Pinter, to Blancanales, and winked. Then he turned back to the terrified young man. "You're a radical activist who uses saving mother Earth as an excuse for supporting violent causes, and you hang out with people who do the same, or worse. We're here because your activities aren't secret. You're on a list, kid. You're on a bunch of lists, in fact. When we cross-index those lists we get the profile of somebody we think is just screwy enough to firebomb a fast-food restaurant, or maybe, just maybe, take a shot at a federal officer."

"No way, man!" Pinter said vehemently. "Sure, I vote green. Sure, I want the EAF to succeed in bringing their voice to the people, man. But I'm, like, a pacifist! I wouldn't hurt anybody."

"You just support those who do," Blancanales said, sounding disappointed.

Pinter said nothing.

"You have one chance, kid." Lyons let Ryan Pinter contemplate the gaping maw of the Python pointed at his face. "If you know something that will help us, something that will take us to the EAF or the WWUP, something they're doing that's not on the up and up, you'd better spill it. Or so help me God, I will spill you."

Pinter seemed to deflate in front of their eyes. He looked down, shaking his head. "I told them… I told them this wasn't the way. I told them—"

"Told who what?" Blancanales prodded.

"My roommates, man."

"Roommates?" Lyons looked around skeptically. "In this one-bedroom dump?"

"They don't live here, exactly," Pinter said. "But they crash here a lot. Hang out, sleep on the couch, plan stuff."

"Stuff?"

"Direct action, man." Pinter shook his head. "Stuff we can do to save the environment and the country from the capitalists and from depoliation."

"Uh-huh," Lyons snorted. "And you're completely innocent in all this."

"I wanted to help the planet and change the country, sure," Pinter said. "But when they started talking about… well, I couldn't do it. Maybe I'm a wuss. They said I talk a big game. That if I'm going to be a facilitator in the WWUP or a field operative in the EAF, I gotta do more than talk big. I don't know, maybe they're right."

"Facilitator?" Blancanales asked.

"A recruiter, somebody who helps further the cause, volunteers in the offices."

"And your 'field operative' status?"

"Direct action," Pinter said again. "You know, go out and…do stuff."

"Terrorism," Lyons said flatly.

"It's not like that!" Pinter insisted. "We're not terrorists! We're just trying to…trying to get people's attention. Make them see that all this conspicuous consumption, all this crass commercialism, it's killing the planet!"

"Shut up," Lyons said. He lowered the Python, since Pinter seemed more than happy to talk. "What was it your friends wanted you to do?"

Pinter looked from man to man, turning pale.

"Don't make me change my mind about punching your ticket," Lyons snarled.

"Okay, okay," Pinter said, defeated. "Mogray Estates. It's a housing development. Full of bourgeois fat cats raping the land, pumping out too many kids. You know. In the suburbs, man. My roommates, they went to Mogray Estates."

"To do what?" Lyons asked, a sinking feeling in his stomach.

"What they always do in the suburbs, man. Fight the sprawl."

"Fight it how?" Blancanales asked.

"They're going to burn it down."

THE BLACK SUBURBAN'S engine roared as Gadgets Schwarz directed the big vehicle through the traffic of suburban Chicago. In the passenger seat, Carl Lyons was on his secure satellite phone, connected to Stony Man Farm.

"That's right, Barb," Lyons was saying. "Mogray Estates, a housing development in suburban Chicago." He rattled off the address Schwarz had pulled from the phone book in Pinter's apartment. "We need you to scramble fire and local police out there. Not sure how many we may be dealing with. Could be two or three kids, could be something else. But this Pinter character says it's happening today, now. Seems he chickened out of the party." He paused again. "All right, Barb. We're in transit now. ETA in… Gadgets?"

"Five minutes," Schwarz said.

"Five minutes," Lyons repeated. "Will do."

"What did she say?" Blancanales asked from the rear seat. Behind him, in the cargo area, Pinter was trussed up in plastic riot cuffs, blindfolded and gagged, with ear plugs in his ears. The plugs were held in place by a long strip of silver duct tape that was wound around his head and secured his blindfold. For his part, Pinter had not resisted and seemed resigned to his fate. No doubt he feared he was headed to someplace like Guantanamo. There had been no time to transfer him into appropriate custody for further questioning, so Able Team had simply bundled him up and taken him with them.

"She said to be careful," Lyons said as he closed the phone.

"We going to be careful?" Blancanales asked.

"Of course not." Lyons shook his head.

The entrance to the housing development reminded the big ex-cop of a gated community, except that there was no gate. It was an elaborate arch bearing the name of the development and boasting twin lion statues, their finishes painted to simulate verdigris. Why anyone would believe the statues and the development had been here long enough for the lions to look weathered was a mystery to the Able Team leader, given that the place was so new the lawns were still just dirt. He supposed those types of touches meant something to someone.

"Pulling up a satellite map of the complex now," Blancanales said, reading the scrambled feed from Stony Man Farm. "It should be transmitting to your phones, as well."

"What's the play, Ironman?" Gadgets asked.

"Take us in deeper, toward the center of the complex," Lyons said, watching the houses and parked minivans speed by. "We'll split up, head for three points roughly equidistant, then start sweeping clockwise from the perimeter. Sooner or later we'll find Pinter's little buddies."

"Let's hope for sooner," Blancanales said.

"That's right." Lyons nodded. "Otherwise it may be too late. Let's move."

Leaving Pinter trussed up in the SUV, the three Able Team commandos moved out. It was Schwarz who first called in over the earbud transceiver link.

"Ironman, Pol, I've got something," he said. He relayed the street address, which his teammates could check on the browsers on their secure phones. "Looks like one man, in an attached garage. I can smell gasoline from here."

"Move," Lyons instructed him.

"Moving," Schwarz responded. Lyons continued on it. He vaulted a low picket fence and rounded the corner of one of the many very similar houses. Parked out front was a panel van and emerging from it was a scruffy-looking, college-age youth with a gas can in one hand and some kind of electronic device in the other.

"Oh, shit," he said.

"Drop it!" Lyons ordered. The Daewoo USAS-12 came

up, its stubby barrel no doubt looking like the mouth of Hell from where the youth stood.

"Oh, God, man, don't shoot, don't shoot—"

Something, perhaps combat instinct, told Lyons to duck. As he did so, he could almost hear the bullet that burned through the air where his head had been.

The guy with the gas can never had a chance. His body rebounded against the panel van, leaving a red streak as he slid to the manicured lawn. Lyons was already turning, the Daewoo churning double-aught buck on full auto. The barrage stuck a man dressed in black BDUs and wearing a red bandanna over his face. His knees were chopped out from under him and he dropped his pistol.

"Don't move! Don't move!" Lyons shouted. Over the earbud transceiver, he could hear other gunshots, muffled through the automatic volume cutout the little units incorporated. There was no time to wonder what Schwarz and Pol had gotten into now.

The gunner was trembling, trying to remove something from inside the pocket of his BDUs. Lyons, ready to shoot again if the man's hand came out with a weapon, checked his fire when he saw the Seever unit. The man on the ground, broken from the buckshot and clearly in shock as he bled out, did not even seem to notice him. He brought the Seever device to his bandanna-covered face, coughed once, and died. The Seever slipped from his fingers onto the grass.

Lyons checked the man's pulse to make sure he was dead, then he went to the kid, finding no sign of life. The gas can was, well, a gas can. The other item was an electronic detonator with a stubby, rubberized wireless antenna. Lyons frowned. He and the rest of the commandos from the Farm were all too familiar with this kind of technology. Such a detonator could be used to set off a bomb by wireless phone, a tactic that had been used extensively with roadside bombs during the U.S. occupation of Iraq. He looked back at the dead, masked gunner, clearly much older than the young man he'd shot—accidentally or intentionally. A few kids with gas cans looking to burn down a housing development was one thing. It was ecoterror, yes, but it did not speak to some greater design. But high-tech wireless detonators, and additional personnel...now that was something else again. Lyons didn't like it, not one bit, and it was looking more and more like there was no fooling Brognola's gut.

"Pol! Gadgets!" Lyons said. "Report!"

"Two down," Schwarz reported. " I have firebombs and detonator gear here. If these guys are friends of Pinter's, there's an age gap."

"Meaning?" Lyons said.

"Meaning I'm willing to bet the Farm has dossiers on these two," Schwarz said. "They're way too old to be idealistic greens out for a night of arson."

"I've got another youngster here," Blancanales said. "DOA. I heard the shot, followed it in. Looks like his partner, another of our youth-challenged ecoterrorists, removed him from the equation. I engaged and he's out of the picture. I have a firebomb here wired to go, and another of those Seever units."

"Ditto here," Lyons said.

"What do you think, Ironman?" Schwarz asked.

"I think this is a synchronized terrorist attack with external coordination," Lyons said. "Get pictures and transmit them to the Farm, right away. I'll do the same. Then I'll talk to Barb."

"Then what?" Blancanales asked.

"We roll on the next target by priority, unless we hear otherwise. And we might. Guys, I don't like where this is heading."

CHAPTER FIVE

"Hal, I don't like where this is heading," McCarter said. "You don't mean to say you'd leave those people?"

"I'm saying," Brognola said patiently over the scrambled, secure satellite phone connection, "that we have mission priorities here. Will saving the deputy commissioner's family further the mission, or will it stop us from getting to the heart of this?"

"Bloody hell, Hal!" McCarter spit. He paced back and forth outside the Range Rover, which was still parked to block the dirt road to the cement plant. The rest of Phoenix Force looked on, weapons at the ready. Gopalan remained a prisoner inside the Range Rover.

"David, I'm not insensitive to the issues at play," Brognola told him. "But the reports coming in from Able only confirm that this goes as deep as we feared. We've cross-checked the IDs of the arsonists Able took down outside Chicago. Some are locals, young people with ties to environmentalist groups. The other dead are Russian-born mercenaries, one of whom is former military."

"What the hell are Russian mercs doing working with green firebombers in the United States?"

"We don't know the full extent of it yet," Brognola said,

"but it's clear that the operation in India to hit the uranium plant, the political activities of World Workers United Party, and the terrorist activities of the Earth Action Front and the Purba Banglars are all likely linked. It's the how and the why we don't yet have. What we *do* know is that somehow the Earth Action Front is alerted to our interdiction efforts."

"The Farm is compromised?" McCarter asked.

"No," Brognola said. "But by your own account, you were anticipated in Nongstoin. If they weren't waiting for you, they were waiting for someone, and they knew to mobilize fast. The question is, how? How deep does this go, and how far?"

"What are you saying, Hal?"

"I'm saying exactly what I said before. I'm saying that there is a conspiracy afoot here, David," Brognola said. "As we know, it is one that links international ecoterrorism to politics in the United States, generally. Specifically, the group or groups responsible for the uranium seizure, starting with the Purba Banglars and continuing with the EAF, are the same groups, or somehow working for the same groups, that are funding the WWUP in the U.S. They're using hardware in common. They're armed and they're obviously ready to use lethal force, which says they're no longer biding their time or trying to blend in quietly. We'd have to be blind not to see the potential."

"So you definitely think the uranium is coming to the States," McCarter said.

"I do," Brognola said. "We don't yet know who's orchestrating this. But the identifications of those you took down in Nongstoin have come back. With two exceptions, they're locals, all of them known Purba Banglars or mercenaries known to work for terrorist groups regardless of affiliation. Two of them, however, came back as Earth Action Front operatives. Both of your EAF specimens were last reported active in Europe, in fact."

"So the two terrorist groups aren't just fellow travelers. They're working in common."

"Yes," Brognola said. "And let's not forget that one is a green group, while the other is Communist. For them to be working together tells me there's some umbrella objective, something uniting them. And if they're importing assistance all the way from Europe, and the groups are sharing advanced technology here and in the States, that speaks to heavy financing. All of it means this operation runs deep and wide. Just as we feared."

"Not good," McCarter said.

"Not good," Brognola echoed. "And that is why we can't afford to assign priorities incorrectly. You're the field commander; it's your call. Will rescuing the deputy commissioner's family get us closer to the uranium? Will it help us stop it from coming to the U.S.?"

McCarter stopped and considered that. He trashed the cigarette he'd been sucking on, exhaling a plume of blue-white smoke as he retrieved the butt. "Yes," he said finally. "Yes, it will, Hal, and I believe that. I'll be straight with you. I don't want to leave them hanging. But we're dry here, and this was the most likely prospect. If we can take one or more of these blokes alive, we might be able to get ahead of the rest of this lot. They might be able to tell us where to look next, give us a better shot than an educated guess. I admit, I'm following my nose, Hal. But you know how it can be in the field. I want to see how deep this rabbit hole goes."

"Okay. Do you know where the family is being held?"

McCarter looked to the Range Rover, where Gopalan stared out from the side window fearfully. "Not yet," he said. "But I will in a moment."

THE SLUM TO WHICH an only too eager Gopalan directed Phoenix Force was as miserable as any the team members had seen in their extensive counterterrorist operations abroad. It had taken relatively little persuading to make the man talk. McCarter had simply leveled his Hi-Power at the Indian's head and thumbed the hammer back, then asked the question. Whatever loyalty Gopalan had for the Purba Banglars, it hadn't gone very far when his own neck was on the line. Whatever the man had been paid—McCarter would dearly have loved to know where the money was coming from, ultimately—hadn't bought much loyalty, either.

They'd dropped Gopalan with the local Indian military police. Whether that would do any good was anybody's guess. For all the Phoenix Force leader knew, Gopalan would be on the streets again in minutes, depending on how loudly money talked and how badly infiltrated with Purba operatives, or sympathizers, the local authorities were. Certainly the Purba Banglars had no difficulty placing an operative in the deputy commissioner's office, where their interests could be monitored district-wide. Silently, McCarter cursed the bureaucracy that worked to the advantage of terrorists like these. If Phoenix Force had just come in and made their hit on the targets identified for them, rather than tipping their hand by following through with all the governmental and diplomatic rigmarole, things might have gone differently. But there was nothing to be done about that now. As for Gopalan, he would unlikely amount to much and had given them everything he was likely to know. He probably deserved a bullet in the brain, but the members of Phoenix Force were not cold-blooded murderers. No, giving him to the local authorities was the best route. Whatever happened to him thereafter was irrelevant to the mission at hand.

What they found inside the hovel at the street address Gopalan had given up might change the Briton's mind. But he hoped not. There was actually a very good chance that Jignesh's family was alive and well, at least for now. They'd hardly be much use as leverage against the deputy commissioner if they were dead. Jignesh had a lot of stones, McCarter had to admit, cluing in the team despite the danger. McCarter hadn't told Brognola, of course, but he did feel a certain obligation to Jignesh for that. The man had put his own family on the line to stop Phoenix Force from walking blindly into a trap, knowing it was the right thing to do for his country. There was real courage there, and the way he'd done it had been fairly smart, too. A man like that was not likely simply to take the Purba Banglars' word for what had been done with the hostages. No, he'd more than likely insist on regular proof they were alive and well. So that meant there was a good chance they still were—though perhaps not for much longer now that their activities had been exposed.

They parked the Range Rover in a fetid alley a block from the target, after taking a route around the area to survey the neighborhood. James's sharp eyes picked out two different snipers on the rooftops. There were bound to be other guards, at ground level, but these were better hidden or simply not in evidence as the team made its recon of the area.

"Remember, mates," McCarter said, his voice low but

carrying over the team's earbud transceivers, "this lot could get word at any time that things have gone bad for them. Maybe they already have. Keep a sharp eye out for the hostages and do not hesitate."

A chorus of quiet acknowledgment greeted him, as each Phoenix Force member in turn spoke discreetly for his transceiver's benefit.

"Cal, T.J.," McCarter directed, "cut around the back of this building and retrace our route. Find those snipers and take them. See if you can spot any other guards. Remember, they may know somebody's coming."

"Right," James said.

"Understood," Hawkins said.

"Gary, you take the back," McCarter said jerking his chin toward the ramshackle house, little better than a shanty, that leaned precariously at the opposite end of the block. It was composed of equal parts scrap wood, corrugated metal and tarps. The entire neighborhood, a claustrophobic maze of narrow alleyways and stained, crumbling structures that looked to be falling down where they stood, stank like an open sewer. Rotting garbage was piled in some of the shadowed lees of the buildings. A man was lying against one of the closer hovels, and McCarter gave him a very careful look to make sure it wasn't a terrorist guard shamming as a drunk or a beggar. On closer inspection, however, he realized it was a body. The decay was unmistakable, even if the smell was lost among the other odors in the alley.

"Lovely," McCarter muttered.

Manning was already on his way. McCarter motioned to Encizo. "You're with me, mate. We'll take the front. Let's go."

"Right." Encizo nodded.

They kept their Tavor rifles low against their bodies as they went, but they made no real effort to hide the weapons. Any attempt to operate within the auspices of the Indian government had been fouled by Gopalan's interference and Phoenix Force's interception of him. McCarter was not about to accept another "liaison" he did not know and could not trust, so they were going to do things his way, and damn the consequences. If the Purba Banglars were sitting on the uranium and someone holding the Jignesh family knew where it was, there was no reason to delay and no point in playing bureaucratic games. McCarter preferred it that way. They passed plenty of locals, some of them dead-eyed, others alert enough to take note and hurry in the opposite direction. Places like this the world over shared a universal, overriding law. *Don't get involved.* The only resistance McCarter anticipated would come from the hostage-takers themselves. He was itching to bring the fight to them.

CALVIN JAMES WORKED his way along the alley, then forward, cutting around the sniper positions while keeping the miserable shacks between him and the enemy shooters. At the same time, Hawkins cut around the opposite side, staying low. The teammates did not have to exchange words to work effectively. They had been through scenarios like this time and again.

James had time to consider the sprawling debris around him. Slums were slums the world over. Grinding poverty like this made human life cheap and human beings desperate. It meant they were that much easier to turn, to buy off and to push around. Those they faced, be they Purba Banglar terrorists or just hired muscle off the streets of Nongstoin, would be capable of anything if the price was right.

When he had flanked the first sniper's position, he found a stack of crates spilling over with refuse. He used these to climb up onto the rooftop of the shanty facing them. On top of the rusted, corrugated metal roof, he found a maze of clutter. Everything from wooden crates to metal and plywood additions to the huts below dotted the artificial landscape. He took full advantage of the cover to carefully cross the ramshackle roof.

As he crept closer to the first of the sentries, he watched to verify that the target was still there. The man obligingly shifted in place, exposing his shoulder and head, as he looked through the scope of a Dragunov-type rifle. He was partially hidden in the lee of a precariously listing stack of rusting chicken-wire cages. These might once have housed some sort of livestock, maybe even birds of some kind. They were empty now and looked to have been for some time.

James got as close as he dared. When he judged that he, too, was partially obscured by the debris around him, from the perspective of the target house, he placed his Tavor rifle gently on the roof next to him. His hand went to the butt of the Desert Tan Columbia River M-60 fixed blade on his belt. The six-inch blade slid free quietly as James tightened his grip on the textured handle.

The sentry sensed death coming for him at the last minute. He turned, his eyes widening as James landed on him, his free hand clamping in a vise-like grip over the man's mouth as the M-60's blade slid between his ribs. James grimaced and worked the knife in and out to finish the job, making sure the sentry's cries went unheard under his palm. The man's death rattle was barely audible as his eyes lost focus and the light left them.

James rolled the sentry aside. He picked up the Dragunov knockoff, looked it over briefly and pulled the bolt back just far enough to verify that a round was chambered. Then he settled into the spot just vacated by the dead sniper. The front window of the target house was bright and clear through the scope, which was a surprisingly expensive German model. The scope and the rifle itself were covered in scratches that showed little regard for the weapon, but it felt solid and appeared to be functional. His Tavor was within reach if he needed it, which he might. Using an unknown weapon, which might or might be sighted in properly, which might not even fire when the trigger was pulled, was hardly something he was eager to do. But just in case others among the Purba Banglars were watching the sniper positions, it was important that there be a body up there behind the rifle. Unless they were using binoculars, James thought what little of him was visible would be sufficient to fool the enemy. If, however, they were keeping a close—and magnified—view of their rooftop shooters, he was made already, and there was nothing to do about it. The rest of Phoenix Force would deal with that, if those in the house grew suspicious and started shooting.

"This is Cal," he said quietly, knowing his earbud transceiver would pick up his words. "One down." There was no response from Hawkins, nor did he expect one until T.J. had his sniper neutralized. He could only assume the man had matters well enough in hand.

T.J. HAWKINS HAD MATTERS well in hand. While he never underestimated an enemy—he'd seen too many battles go south too quickly for that—so far he wasn't very impressed with the opposition. He'd located and skirted around his sniper well enough, where the man knelt hunched against a two-story shanty made of plywood and tarps. He was smoking, his cigarette smoke forming a plume that marked him as an amateur and served as a beacon to his location.

Hawkins found a foothold on one side, where several large holes had been punched, kicked, or otherwise pushed into the wood. A dirty blue tarp positioned inside the hovel protected the interior from wind and rain. As quietly as he could, mindful that there could be and likely were occupants of the slums in this building or in the nearby structures, Hawkins lifted himself up to the roof of the first story.

"This is Cal," came the voice in Hawkins's ear. "One down." That was the younger man's cue. He started to move forward, his hand going to the ergonomic grip of the Columbia River Ultima fixed blade on his belt.

His foot dragged against a piece of loose wood anchoring the tarp-covered rooftop.

The sniper spun in place, his head ducking out from behind cover, dark eyes wide and locking with the Phoenix Force commando. Hawkins did not hesitate. Crawling, crablike, on the roof, his Tavor was gripped in his left hand by the plastic stock. Instead of trying for it, he went for the Beretta M-9 in the inside-the-waistband Kydex holster behind his right hip. He whipped up the weapon, wiping the safety off with his thumb, and double-actioned the first 9mm round. The bullet snapped the sniper's head back.

The echoing crack of the gunshot was enough to set off the powder keg on which Phoenix Force—and presumably, Jignesh's family—waited. Hawkins wasted no time with the dead sniper. "Blown, blown, blown," he said out loud. "T.J., sniper down."

The audio cutouts built into each transceiver prevented them from amplifying and thus carrying deafening gunfire, but the answering shots ringing out from the target house were all the verification Hawkins needed. He shoved the dead sniper roughly aside and scooped up his weapon, a CZ-700 bolt action. Sighting quickly through the scope, he caught the outline of a gunner in the window of the target house. He couldn't be positive, but it looked like the enemy shooter had a line of sight to Encizo's position. He sucked in a breath, let it out halfway and squeezed the trigger.

The shot from the unfamiliar rifle, perhaps never properly sighted in, went low. It missed the gunner and clipped the window casing. "Shit," Hawkins said reflexively.

"Got it," James's cool voice came through his earpiece. The retort of the rifle James must have captured was loud from Hawkins's vantage. Through the CZ's scope, he saw the shooter in the window rock back.

"Thanks," Hawkins said quietly.

"No prob," James whispered back.

Encizo and McCarter made their entry through the front door of the target house, their Tavor rifles chattering. Hawkins bent his eye to the CZ's scope again. He saw a second figure, dressed in OD fatigues and carrying a Kalashnikov, emerging from an alley and moving toward the front of the house. Hawkins dropped the reticule over his head and then raised his point of aim, judging the differential.

His shot was echoed by James's own, some distance to his left and slightly behind him. The bullets took the enemy gunner in the chest and stomach. He hit the dirty, cluttered street hard, dead and dead again.

"Down, down, down!" McCarter's voice was urgent over Hawkins's transceiver. "Nobody move or you're bloody dead!"

RAFAEL ENCIZO FOLLOWED David McCarter through the opening after the Briton kicked in the flimsy, plywood door of the target building. Their Tavors spit military-standard 5.56 mm rounds in controlled bursts. The armed men waiting inside were all similarly attired in military surplus, olive-drab BDUs. They carried Kalashnikovs and, in a couple of cases, mini-Uzi subguns. Gunfire erupted outside the flimsy structure both in front and in back. The Cuban-born commando could only assume that the shots in front were from James and Hawkins, while Manning covered the rear.

Almost as if thinking of him had summoned him, the big Canadian appeared from the back room. From what Encizo could see past the ragged curtains in the doorway, that room was a makeshift kitchen and dining area. "Back's clear," Manning said softly.

"Clear, front," James's voice came over the transceivers.

"Clear, front, twice." Hawkins's normally relaxed drawl was more clipped than usual, the result of the firefight.

McCarter dropped the magazine in his Tavor and slapped home a fresh one. He motioned Manning to his left and pointed to Encizo before gesturing right. There was one room left, which had a heavy wooden door mounted on rusted but very sturdy-looking hinges. Manning and Encizo took up their positions as directed, flanking the sides of the doorway. They, too, took a precious moment to reload their weapons.

McCarter looked at both men, then nodded to Manning, bringing up one knee to make his point.

Manning nodded grimly. He stepped back slightly, then planted one big combat boot in the door just to the left of the handle. The wood around the lock splintered and the door flew inward.

MANNING FELT THE HEAVY wooden door give under his foot. Rifle at the ready, he charged through, scanning the room for targets. Each member of Phoenix Force had been trained and was experienced in making these split-second judgments: Gary Manning's job, as the first man through the door, was to find and fire on any hostiles without shooting any hostages.

The flash of recognition came through in moving images; there was no time to subvocalize or assign mental commentary to what he was perceiving. A woman and two children were bound and sitting on a sagging couch in the center of the room. The barrel of Manning's Tavor swept from right—that half of the room was empty—to left.

Target acquired.

The gunman held a small automatic pistol, which he was raising in Manning's direction. The burly Canadian did not hesitate. His rifle tracked the gunner and his left hand squeezed the trigger of the grenade launcher attached to it.

The 40 mm beanbag round Manning had preloaded for the assault thumped through the space separating him from the shooter, a bright yellow square of blunt force. Manning could hear the air being crushed from the man's lungs as the beanbag hit him and bowled him over. The man crashed to the trash-strewed floor. The small pistol sailed through the air, hit the wall and discharged before hitting the floor itself. Manning flinched slightly, but there was nothing to be done. The stray round had either hit someone or it hadn't.

He scanned the room a second time. The bound, gagged woman and the children with her began making muffled noises behind the silver duct tape sealing their mouths. Manning ignored them for the moment, other than to verify that they were not bringing weapons of their own into play. One never knew, in an unknown hostage situation like this one, if the story told beforehand was really true. Had this been a trap, had the "hostages" been armed and prepared to gun down the members of Phoenix Force, Manning would have been ready to take them, too, as would any member of the team.

Judging from the fear in their wide eyes, however, they were exactly what they appeared to be. He could detect no sign of wounds, and they did not appear, at first glance, to have been brutalized.

He retrieved the pistol from where it lay on the floor. It was an old Lorcin .22, something he had not seen in years. Most of its cheap finish had been worn away to bare metal. He found the bullet hole in the wall, too. As Manning checked, he was aware of McCarter covering him quietly from behind, making sure no one else crept up or was hiding inside the building.

"Clear," Manning said finally. He moved to stand over the stunned shooter, after first unloading the Lorcin and shoving it into a cargo pocket of his pants. The short muzzle of the Tavor and the cavernous maw of its grenade launcher loomed over the fallen gunman, who stirred and looked up fearfully as Manning toed him with one combat boot.

"Well, well, well," McCarter said, moving over to stand next to Manning. "You and me, mate, we're going to have ourselves a talk."

CHAPTER SIX

Atlanta, Georgia

Reginald Butler's eyes narrowed. He held the receiver to his office phone to one ear, while one of his own Seever devices waited on the expensive oak desk in front of him. He toyed with the Seever idly, rotating it on the desk blotter like a cat worrying a captured mouse.

"How many?" he asked angrily. "Working for who?" He paused. "Then find out, damn it. That's what I'm paying you for!" He waited again, listening. "They were doing *what*? Sweet mother of… That's over the line! What was done with them?" He stood and paced angrily back and forth across his well-appointed office. One wall was dominated by a large window that overlooked Atlanta. Another was covered in framed, signed photographs of Butler with various celebrities, politicians and world leaders. His wall of power, he called it. At the moment, though, he saw nothing in the room—not the pricy leather furniture, not the custom LCD televisions mounted to one of the walls, not the polar bear rug that had come from a bear he had taken down on a paid outing. No, he saw only the future, and the many and myriad ways it might just not turn out as he had hoped, unless he intervened.

"All right," he said finally, his resolve crystallizing. "All right, enough of that, we'll deal with it, that's all we can do. You know the appropriate people to contact. I want you to lean on them. Get the Chief involved. Get those men picked up. If they resist, so much the better. See that it happens. Do it now." He walked back to his desk and replaced the receiver in its cradle. Then he picked up the WTS device, keyed in a very long, very specific code known only to him and one other man.

"*Da.*" The Russian answered on the first buzz, as he always did. Butler wondered if the man never slept, though he was unclear on what time it might be in whatever corner of the world the Russian was hiding.

"We have a problem," Butler said without preamble. "Your environmentalist nutcases tried to burn down a housing development! This is not what we talked about. Mass arson? Possible mass murder? That's not what we're trying to do!"

"How many were killed?"

"My source inside the police department was unclear about that. It sounds like your people were shot, but no one else was killed."

"Technically, they are your people."

"Like hell they are!" Butler shot back. "Some of those punks may be Americans, but I know damned well your own men are advising them. We discussed this. You said you were just going to make sure they didn't get caught, give them the equipment they needed to make a nuisance of themselves."

"And they have done just that." The Russian's voice was oily, his accent fading in and out. "Your little would-be ecoterrorists are gaining quite a name for themselves.

What does it matter if a few are, how do you say, expended along the way? You must admit that the incident at the WWUP office went exactly as planned, yes?"

"I suppose so," Butler admitted reluctantly. "Though I never expected Timothy Albert to have armed security on the premises. Or to go for a gun like that!"

"He was…brittle," the Russian said, almost apologetically. "But what do you expect? For months you told him that the encryption technology and software you give him would shield him and his organization from any perception of wrongdoing. And at your instructions I continued to funnel illegal currency to him from groups that were certain to make him appear…quite devastatingly guilty. You should be pleased that he cracked as he did. He can answer no questions now."

"True," Butler said, mollified. "But how in the hell did he know to arm up like that? He was never that paranoid."

"Paranoia takes root quickly and grows like weed," the Russian said. Then he laughed. "I am profound today, *da*?"

"Damn it, Krylov, this is not funny!"

"Not for to use name on open channel," the Russian's accent grew more thick when he was angered.

"I keep telling you, the encryption we're using is impenetrable," Butler said. "The Feds can't crack it, and I'm not about to make it so they can. How else do you think your people and mine can stay in sync so easily, all over the world? It's the perfect network. Decentralized. Global. Totally secure."

"No doubt you gave Albert similar assurances."

"We both know that's different!" Butler cursed under his breath. The Russian almost always managed to turn things around on him like this. Reginald Butler despised being toyed with. He was a powerful man and this Communist old-guard son of a bitch was going to recognize that.

"Easy, my friend, easy." The Russian now sounded conciliatory. "I joke because we have understanding, yes? Our arrangement continues as before. You will continue to, how do you say, pull the strings on your end? I will continue to do the same. Your funding, it helps my brave ecowarriors worldwide. Your Seevers do the same. In turn I make sure things turn out as you wish them to United States. I send you more advisers. I make sure the WWUP left in your country do as you wish them to do. This is easy. So grateful for help of foreign experts they are. So willing to embrace ideas we share with them. We make socialist worker's paradise, worldwide. Yes?"

"Yeah, well." Butler himself slipped into the Southern accent he had tried so hard to eradicate for the sake of his image. He was Georgia born, after all, a local boy made good on the backs of countless lesser businessmen. "Of course I want to do what's right. Global capitalism is destroying the world. It only makes sense that we shift to the socialist model. Central planning is the only way to make sure people use their dwindling resources properly."

"*Da,* is good." The Russian sounded cheerful. "And of course we will require men like you, men who understand business, to help in this planning. Much influence will you have. You are to be commended, my friend. You do the right thing, in this, always. Calm yourself. In battle, many things do not go as planned."

"Battle?"

"This is war, yes?" The Russian's voice conveyed the smile Butler pictured on his face. "A war for the planet. A war for the future. Too long, the individualists, the capitalists, have exploited the people, and the planet herself. Together, we fix it. Some eggs must be broken to make cake, yes? But all is worth it. The ends, they justify the means. Yes?"

"Yes," Butler said. "You're right, Krylov. I just don't like to think some of these people are as ready to kill as they seem to be. I don't understand it. I mean, I thought the WWUP types were almost pacifists. And those Earth Action people, they're vandals, not arsonists."

"They do more of this, the arson, than you know," the Russian said, "but that is, as you say, not here, not there. Do not worry. Such people, the types easily used for your cause, are sometimes not so very stable. It is not something you should worry about, my friend. That is why you pay me. Let me worry about it. I am used to the type. I have seen it, fought it, fought with it."

"All right," Butler said. "But tighten the reins on these nutcakes, will you? We can't have them blowing people away, or burning people alive. That's going too far. I want to use them to an end, sure. But that end doesn't involve killing anyone."

"Remember, the breaking of eggs is needed for the omelet," Krylov cautioned. "Men of great power must be willing to do bold things."

"I know all about that," Butler said. "And we are doing bold things. But there's a line, Krylov, and we've got to be careful to stay on this side of it."

"Very well," the Russian said, sounding chastised. "I will do what I can."

"Good," Butler said. "Now, about the arrangements for the rally—"

"Mr. Butler," his secretary was calling him on the desk intercom. "Congressman Cross is on line one."

"I have to take this," Butler said into the Seever. "It wouldn't do to keep Cross waiting. We need to keep him happy."

"Indeed. Indeed we do. *Dosvedanya*." The Russian terminated the connection.

"Richard," Butler said as he picked up the desk phone, his tone immediately slick. "Thank you for returning my call."

"Before we get into that, I just wanted to make sure we're still on track," Cross said. "The news has been, well, good for us, in the long view. But I wanted to make sure the plan continues, what with the all the...violence."

"Don't worry about that," Butler said. "Yes, the WWUP has managed to give itself a reputation for instability. But that only helps us."

"True," Cross said. "And linking Senator Harrington to the WWUP and thus their unstable behavior will see to it that she loses the party's presidential nomination to me."

"Of course," Butler said. "The senator from New England is already widely known to be in bed, as they say, with the 'green' movement. She's hitched her star to groups like these. It's not a tie she can cut, not now. But you're sure she won't get cold feet?"

"And pull out of the rally?" Cross said. "Not likely. So far the WWUP is playing off its problems as the acts of a single rogue bureaucrat. That kind of thing plays well. It isn't likely to hurt her, not so far. But once the same group gets out of hand at the Green Coalition Rally, if their behavior is the riot you've been promising me, it will put her permanently in league with the radical element of the movement in the eyes of the voters. Then I'll step in. We're already poling well as a party. The voters want change. They want progressive action. They just don't want it to come too quickly, or too intensely. I'm the reasonable alternative, the happy middle ground."

"Richard Cross, the moderate's moderate." Butler laughed. "And of course someone with whom Butler Telecommunications has a certain...understanding. I'll see to it that your campaign continues to receive generous contributions. Within legal limits, of course."

"Of course," Cross said. "And I will see to it that those with whom I vote are made aware of the benefits of Butler Telecommunications' goodwill. I imagine the various investigations into your encryption technologies will go nowhere. I doubt any future actions will get beyond committee."

"That would be a relief," Butler said. "I would be grateful."

"Yes, I thought you would," Cross said. "Now, what was it you wanted?"

"Well, there are certain rogue elements operating against our interests in Chicago," he said. "My sources in the police department there said they, well, killed several deranged ecoterrorists in the midst of an arson attempt."

"Ecoterrorists of the same stripe as those with whom Senator Marcia Harrington is in bed, no doubt," Cross said, sticking to the playbook. Butler noted that the man was unmoved by the deaths. He was a cold fish, that one. No doubt years spent in Washington's halls of power could do that to a person.

Butler could only hope.

"Yes," Butler said slowly. "But there's a problem. Such men are outside the scope of my control or my influence. I don't need to tell you the trouble that might be caused if another government agency pokes its nose into our business out here. Surely local law enforcement in Chicago can handle any such incidents in the future. We don't need independent operators, answering to an unknown authority, blundering into what's being done. Do we?"

"No," Cross said. "We certainly don't. I'll make inquiries here in Washington. And I know certain law enforcement operatives, as well as a few people in the Bureau. I'll see to it that they get the message."

"What message?"

"Why, that there are rogue operatives acting out of control and murdering people in Chicago," Cross said with mock indignity. "Can you imagine? Of course if such people are removed from action by legitimate authorities, authorities who answer more directly and more regularly to the chain of command, the only persons to blame for anything that ensues would be these rogue elements themselves. Such things happen all the time, when one of the government's many elements goes off the reservation."

"I see," Butler said. "Well, that should work well for us, then."

"Yes," Cross said. "Yes, it should." He hung up without another word.

Reginald Butler allowed himself a tight smile.

"Dosvedanya," Fedor Krylov said. He switched off the Seever unit and set it gently back on the scuffed metal desk. Then he looked out the small window next to him, picturing the man Butler doing the same from whatever opulent monument to greed and industry suited such a person. It was all Krylov could do, in speaking with Butler, not to show openly his contempt of the billionaire. Such a

fool, this man. What was it they were called? "Fat cats." Yes, that was it. Butler was a fat cat who thought himself the puppet master when he was, in fact, the puppet.

Krylov, formerly of the KGB and late of the secret police in Russia, had no illusions himself. His eyes were not blinded like those of the greedy, easily manipulated Butler. No, Krylov saw the world as it was, not as he wished it to be. Such recognition was necessary if he were to remake the world as he wished it. That was the crucial quality men like Reginald Butler lacked. Already, for them, the world was as they wanted it. Only a few details remained for them to have what they desired. The rest was delusion, the type of delusion in which men who truly changed the world could not afford to indulge.

The Russian permitted himself a chuckle at the thought of Reginald Butler, safe in his office, believing himself to be in control. Little did the pathetic would-be power broker know that he was, like the rest of the pieces on this global chess game, simply another pawn, another piece for Krylov to move around the worldwide board. When the time came, Butler, too, would be sacrificed. Until then, he was useful.

Butler, Krylov reflected, was a peculiar breed of useful idiot, of the type one found so commonly in industrialized nations. He was a wealthy man who had benefited greatly from capitalism, yet he lived a guilt-ridden existence. He saw his money as almost a mark of shame and, determined as he was to right what he thought were the great and terrible injustices of capitalism, he was willing to finance the activities of men like Krylov—men who promised the global equity of communism, of socialism. Such was what Fedor Krylov promised, and of course he sought to implement it. That was, after all, the reason for everything he had managed to build to date. It was helpful that men like Butler were willing to devote themselves to such a cause. It was more helpful that the various and disparate environmentalist groups were only too willing to do the same, in the hope of seeing central planning and Marxist ideology shepherd through the types of controls and reforms they sought to save the planet.

That had been Krylov's most brilliant move, and he did not mind complimenting himself on it. The modern "green" movement was fast becoming a religion, of sorts, and that religion shared many tenets upheld by what Krylov's enemies might call "Communist true believers." Both groups, Communist and "green," saw thorough-going, all-inclusive government regulation as a means of social control and regulation. Both groups despised the exploitation of world resources, and world populations, by unfettered capitalism and the greed associated with it. Both groups were comprised, quite often, of wide-eyed idealists willing to take action to implement change. And both groups absolutely hated the established order, particular the established government of the United States, which both saw as the major obstacle to achieving their ends—even if those within the United States hoped to appropriate the reins of government for their purposes. This made perfect sense to Krylov, and had since become the linchpin of his overarching plan for the world.

Since the fall of the Soviet Union, many of his contemporaries had sought to find some means of reinstituting the greatness that the USSR had held, however briefly. Krylov had himself thought modern Russia might one day achieve the same goal, and so for many years he had worked within the system, as a highly placed agent of Russian's so-called "secret police." Unfortunately, it became clear that the current leadership was concerned with the mundane matters that concerned most world leaders—consolidating power, dealing with his enemies, and maintaining the tenuous status quo the once-great Russia now held. No, Krylov had finally decided, this was not the way. And so the former KGB agent and then-connected Russian political enforcer had embarked on what was to be the most ambitious socio-political scheme of his life.

The problem was not as daunting as one might first suspect. Given the worldwide acceptance of communism and its economic handmaiden, socialism, among certain portions of the world's population, how could those who understood the necessity of global collectivism implement their vision across the planet? The key was in uniting the disparate groups. Krylov, who had long been a student of communism and related socio-political movements and economies, had seen the possibilities where violent groups like the Purba Banglars were concerned. From there, he had realized, it was not so great a leap to entice those who saw saving the Earth—through the socialist-Communist mechanisms of collective economics and central planning—to join him.

Using his contacts within the former KGB, and the network of intelligence operatives to which his past within the Russian secret police had linked him, he had begun building his ties. Never one to fail to borrow a successful model rather than reinvent the wheel, Krylov had happily appropriated the al Qaeda organization framework and methods. Cell by cell, he built a global network of Communist operatives and their would-be ecowarrior counterparts, uniting them under a shared goal. That goal was a world with a central Communist government, which of course Krylov or his handpicked operatives would control. It was not so absurd a notion, nor so high a pinnacle to achieve in only a few years. Had not the mighty Soviet Union fallen from global superpower to fragmented paper tiger in only a few short years at the height of the cold war? He could implement similar change, and in what so many called the "post 9/11 world," he would do so through united, coordinated terrorist action.

The fact that violent action was required was, of course, a foregone conclusion, and he had at first worried about whether it would be possible to agitate the various environmentalist and worker's party groups—particularly in the United States—to actual violence for the cause. He had been pleasantly surprised. Most of them were only too willing to resort to violence. They were eager to see their utopian vision of the future.

This was what a fool like Reginald Butler could not see. Butler lived in a fantasy world in which global communism could be achieved with a minimum of actual violence. Great men had, long before Butler, explained quite plainly that political power stemmed from the barrel of a gun. Krylov had identified Butler early on, when he realized that the obstacles faced by his global Communist network included some very real logistical handicaps. Many of those handicaps could be dealt with through money, and rich, self-hating, would-be communist ideologues like Butler happily provided that money. Krylov had, in fact, cultivated many corporate donors, especially among American entertainment and business luminaries whom one might think would be ardent capitalists.

The Russian had been amazed at just how many of these

wealthy business tycoons and Hollywood personalities were only too happy to work against their own success, to volunteer a portion of their own fortunes, for the optimistic hope of "saving the world." Knowing that Krylov or his operatives were less than entirely legally legitimate in their activities had not harmed the plan. Far from it; the element of danger had added a mystique of which Krylov's wealthy donors were excited to partake. He had shaken his head at their foolishness even as he had taken their money.

For Krylov's global Communist network to operate, however, it was necessary for them to communicate. That communication had to be efficient, widely available and resistant to penetration. It was for this reason that Krylov had originally targeted Butler. The man's socialist sympathies were a big help, yes, and made Butler a willing accomplice, which was good. First above all else, however, was the fact that Butler's WTS communication units made it possible for Krylov to communicate with his cells. It also allowed the cells to trade information with one another, when needed, and to share personnel. This rapid communication was what made Krylov's plan feasible, in fact what made it possible at all.

As long as he had the precious Seevers, his own samples of which Butler's people had been manufacturing of cleansed components in a secret location for Krylov's special project, he could keep all of his units operating together toward the common goal they shared. As long as the U.S. Government's demands for encryption transparency were held at bay by the country's own Constitution, by its courts and its civil liberties groups, Krylov's communications could remain secure in a terrorism-fearful world of increased wire-tapping and public surveillance.

Krylov's ultimate goal, the goal Butler believed he

shared with the Russian, was to own the United State's presidency. To do this, much complicated maneuvering was involved. Krylov was no stranger to political chess, or of the "long game" that required thinking many steps ahead through convoluted and complex machinations that would eventually put the persons he held in the positions where he needed them. Butler fancied himself a master of such chess, as well, which suited Krylov. Let the man think he controlled the pieces, while the Russian himself directed the game.

Butler's weakness regarding the levels of violence required would be his undoing. Integral to their complex political plan was making sure that the World Workers United Party and the Earth Action Front were painted as dangerous terrorist groups. This could not be done with a few acts of vandalism or some unruly protests. Butler refused to see this. He was not willing to go as far as was necessary. That was fine. Without Butler's knowledge, it had been easy to speak directly to the various groups and their operatives, encourage their revolutionary fervor. And of course while they maneuvered Timothy Albert to discredit the WWUP and link it to terrorism on the world stage, Krylov had seen to it that Albert was provoked. It would not be enough for a stunned Albert to be arrested and hauled away, complaining that he had no knowledge of the financial transactions that had led to his arrest, to suspicion leveled at the WWUP. No, he had to react violently, as would a man steeped in guilt and accustomed to terrorist action.

Krylov had placed two calls to Timothy Albert. The first had been to warn him that a right-wing extremist group planned to assault the WWUP building with firearms, and that to avoid a massacre on the order of an abortion-clinic bombing, Albert should hire armed guards and be prepared for the worst. Once Krylov had verified that Albert had, in fact, hired such guards, he had called again, this time telling Albert that the federal government, in league with the paramilitary group targeting the WWUP, had grown impatient. He filled Albert's head with visions of being detained and water-boarded, of being left to rot in a terrorist prison camp such as Guantanamo for the rest of his life, without trial and without appeal. Albert, already nervous, had not even thought to question his anonymous informant's motives. Krylov had, both times, pretended to be a low-level government employee and WWUP sympathizer.

The plan was moving forward and doing so quite quickly. The only thing that vexed Krylov was the loss of his "advisers" during the arson attack he had helped orchestrate. He had not anticipated this level of resistance from the American counterterrorist authorities, even after he was tipped off to their pending interference both domestically and in Nongstoin. He had taken what preventive measures he could, but these were proving inadequate. He would, therefore, have to redouble his efforts, unless Butler managed to do as much. While the American businessman lacked a certain amount of resolve, he was cunning and he was not stupid. He had influence among the Americans and would take the steps needed. It would simply be left to Krylov to follow up from there.

The Seever unit on his desk chimed, indicating an incoming transmission. He picked it up and activated it.

"*Da*," he said.

"You were right," said the voice on the other end. "You

said he'd call on me, and he did. He doesn't know I'm already keeping you informed on the same issue."

"You can do something about these government men?" Krylov asked.

"I have influence among the local authorities, and of course in Washington. The same people who tipped me that something was being done at the highest levels, something going as high as the President himself, can help us here. I still can't get a handle on who these people work for. You can bet it won't be whoever they say they're working for. I've seen enough black bag ops run through here that I know when I'm going to get a brick wall or a bullet in the head if I ask too much more."

"But you can take action nonetheless? You still have inside information?"

"Of course. I warned you about India, didn't I?"

"*Da.* Of course. Does Butler have any idea of the true extent of your involvement with me?" the Russian asked.

"Of course not. He's as clueless as you said he was. But useful enough."

"Indeed," Krylov said. "Very well. Do what you can, and I will see to it that our interests abroad are similarly protected. Have you any more information about the operation in Nongstoin?"

"Only that it will continue. The President knows full well the sort of threat that uranium represents."

"And well he should," Krylov said. "For it is the threat of the uranium in the hands of one of America's enemies, or one of his proxies, that will hand America's future president—how do you say—carte blanche when it comes to enacting his emergency powers. Such a president would make FDR look like a do-nothing, yes?"

"And of course such a man would have the power to make certain corrections to an economic system long over-due for alignment with the rest of the enlightened world."

"Just as you say," Krylov said. "I go now, make calls to cover certain bases. I must have certain evidence cleared away, just in case these government men come."

"Of course. I'll double-check my own files and computers, just in case."

"Until next we speak, Congressman," Krylov said, and closed the connection.

CHAPTER SEVEN

"Right," Carl Lyons said into his secure phone. He grabbed an indelible marker and began writing on the palm of his hand. "We're rolling, Barb," he said. Snapping the phone shut, he glanced back at Blancanales, then to Schwarz in the driver's seat, as he pulled a map of Chicago and its suburbs from the glove compartment of the Suburban.

"We have a GPS unit, you know," Schwarz said.

"Yeah, yeah, yeah," Lyons muttered.

"Not to mention a pad of paper."

Lyons read the address out loud, which Schwarz punched in to the GPS unit one-handed, bringing up a route from their current location.

"I want to check out what's in the area, though," Lyons said, unfolding the map. "You never know."

"What are we looking for, exactly?" Blancanales asked from the rear seat.

"It's a storage company," Lyons explained. "Barb says they've been doing more detail work combing through the WWUP computer data, specifically their accounts receivable and payable, and they tracked down a couple of holding companies used as cutouts between the storage place and the WWUP. Apparently it went a lot deeper than the other points of contact on the priority list Aaron's people put together for us, which is why they've only just now found it."

"Which means it was considered a lot more important to hide," Blancanales said.

"Exactly." Lyons nodded. "We're looking for units 24 and 25, apparently. Barb says they're the biggest lockers the facility offers, as big as two-car garages."

"Just imagine the prizes that could be hidden inside," Gadgets said, his eyes scanning back and forth between the road ahead and the route on the GPS unit.

It took them perhaps half an hour to reach the storage lot on the outskirts of the suburbs. It was an unremarkable cluster of single-story, prefabricated metal buildings surrounded by a barbed-wire-topped chain-link fence. The gates stood wide open, which was not unusual for such a site. Typically, Lyons imagined, the gates would be unlocked early in the morning and then shut again sometime in the evening, giving clients access to their lockers during the day. Schwarz brought the Suburban smoothly through the gate and then began cruising up one row and down the next, following the numbers painted on the faces of the metal garage doors.

As they rounded the corner to the last row, they spotted the van.

"Heads up!" Gadgets said. "Company!"

The cargo van was backed into position directly in front of two very large storage areas. Lyons did not believe in coincidence. Those could only be units 24 and 25. They had apparently gotten there just in time. He turned to give instructions to his teammates.

"All right, let's hit the pavement and secure the—"

The bullet starred the windshield just under the rearview mirror. Schwarz slammed on the brakes and threw the big truck into reverse. The Suburban roared and lurched backward. At the first break in the buildings, the Able Team electronics wizard whipped the wheel sideways, throwing the SUV around the corner of the metal structure and out of the line of fire.

"Go, go, go!" Lyons ordered. Able Team leaped from the Suburban. Schwarz unlimbered his 93-R as he dropped to the pavement, while Lyons jacked a round into his Daewoo shotgun. Blancanales retrieved his short-barreled Colt CAR-15 from its place under his seat. Each man activated his earbud transceiver as his boots hit the asphalt. With reflexes born of long training and many hours together in the field, the members of Able Team spread out, each taking a different route through the maze of storage buildings.

There had not been time for more than a glimpse of the enemy, but Schwarz, behind the wheel, had seen enough.

"Five men, one vehicle," he said into his transceiver. "Doors to both units open. Van doors open. Cardboard boxes and other items waiting. No positive IDs."

There would be plenty of time for identifications later. For now, the hostile nature of the enemy was more than confirmed. Lyons preferred it that way. He grew impatient with the endless posturing and pussyfooting around that characterized some operations. Better to get the hostilities out in the open, the lead flying through the air. That way the right tickets could get punched and they could all get on with things.

He did not need to tell his teammates to spread out and attempt to get around and behind the shooters. Able Team had faced countless enemies in their time together, and while Lyons and his men would never underestimate their foes, they had so far not been terribly impressed by the operatives they'd encountered. Lyons, with the Daewoo's stock tucked into his shoulder, took the next corner wide and worked his way past the next row of corrugated metal buildings.

SCHWARZ HELD the suppressed Beretta 93-R machine pistol in both hands, his support hand using the enlarged trigger guard and snap-down foregrip to steady the machine pistol. The weapon, specially tuned by Cowboy Kissinger and loaded with twenty rounds of 9 mm hollowpoint ammunition, remained one of his favored tools for the varied operations on which Able Team embarked. It provided him with a great deal of firepower in a small, portable package. These were essential characteristics for the electronics specialist, who never knew when he might be called on to defuse an electronic detonator or unscramble a computerized lock while on the run or balancing on top of a building. Lyons favored his automatic elephant gun, and Blancanales was a little more conventional. For Schwarz, though, the select-fire handgun was just right.

Like a metal hedge maze, the storage facility extended in each direction, providing ample concealment. Schwarz hesitated to call it "cover" because he did not trust the thin metal buildings to actually stop a bullet of any significance. In a half crouch, he moved quickly and quietly from one to the next, checking each path between blocks of buildings for the missing shooters. He supposed they were WWUP operatives, but that was not necessarily the case. They could just as easily be EAF or some other fringe group. Certainly this mission had demonstrated that there were a few not-so-strange bedfellows operating in concert.

Schwarz felt rather than heard the shot that almost tagged him. The bullet struck the metal building behind him, raising sparks and punching a neat hole through the steel. As soon as he sensed the shot, Schwarz was rolling forward, throwing himself out of the path of the bullets and making himself as small a target as possible. He came up with the Beretta leading, searching for targets, and found one. A young man wearing a T-shirt, denim jacket and jeans was aiming a revolver in Schwarz's general direction. He punched a 3-round burst into the middle of the gunner's chest, sprawling him on the asphalt. The revolver went off a second time, punching a hole in a nearby garage door.

"One down," he said quietly.

He moved forward in his half-crouch, gliding heel to toe to maintain a stable shooting platform should another gunner present himself. When he was close enough, he dropped to one knee to check the body. The dead man still gripped a Smith & Wesson 637, a stainless-steel snub-nosed revolver. Schwarz pried the man's lifeless fingers from around the rubber grips and checked the weapon. Searching through the corpse's pockets, he found a wallet with an ID and pocketed it. He also found a cheap metal-handled folding knife and a pair of speed strips bearing standard 158-grain lead, round-nosed cartridges for the .38 Special.

He took a moment to eject the spent rounds from the .38's cylinder as well as the still unfired cartridges. Moving quickly, he snapped the cylinder shut, aimed the empty gun at the pavement some distance away and pulled the trigger double-action. It fell with a satisfying click. The aluminum frame was scuffed from the fall to the asphalt, but the weapon was still functional. Schwarz reloaded it using the loose rounds and two from one of the speed strips, then tucked the little .38 in his waistband. There was no sense leaving a weapon behind.

As he stood, a second man rounded the corner. He was in his early twenties, like his counterpart, dressed in a sweatshirt and jeans. A fashionable clothing line's name was emblazoned across the front of the sweatshirt. When he saw Schwarz, he hesitated just a moment too long before bringing up the pump-action shotgun he carried.

There was no time to get fancy, not against a shotgun at that range. Schwarz fired another 3-round burst, stitching the man across the trendy logo. He fell on top of the weapon.

"Make that two," Schwarz said.

BLANCANALES HELD his CAR-15 in the low ready position as he moved from building to building, sweeping each gap and watching for movement. The shooters were here, somewhere; it didn't matter if they were EAF "greens" or more trigger-happy WWUP gunmen. Either way, they were going down, and whatever they were protecting or trying to move was going with them.

He nodded to Lyons as the big man broke off and headed left. Schwarz had gone right. Blancanales, for his part, went straight forward, retracing the hasty retreat they'd made in the Suburban. Specifically, he was headed for the vehicle, to make sure that none of the shooters currently running through the storage complex circled back around to take the vehicle.

He checked the vehicle, the muzzle of his CAR-15 leading the way. He found no one. There was no time to check the boxes inside or the contents of the two open storage areas. Rooting among the goods would only get him shot.

He did, however, have time to make certain the van was going nowhere soon.

Blancanales slid his knife left-handed from its sheath, his fingers wrapped around the textured, ergonomic handle. The big fixed blade felt reassuring. Holding his CAR-15 in front of him in one fist, he backed up to one of the front tires, reversed the knife in his hand and plunged it backward into the tire as hard as he could. The blade lodged in the sidewall. He wrenched it free, and the balding all-season radial hissed itself slowly flat. He took out the rear tire on the passenger's side in the same fashion, then sheathed the knife.

That took care of the van. Now it was time to see after the men who'd driven it here.

He heard a shot—the crack of a handgun. Then, through his earbud transceiver, he heard the answering slap of Schwarz's 93-R, the sound from which was mitigated enough that the transceiver's cut-out relayed it as below its safety threshold.

"One down," Schwarz's voice was calm. Well, that figured. Blancanales had known the man for a long time, and he was as cool under fire as any soldier in the Stony Man teams. The savvy electronics expert downplayed it, but he was a combat veteran of years' experience.

Blancanales circled wide around the corner of one the buildings, catching a glimpse of a running figure two buildings down. He pursued, cautiously but quickly. So far the men they faced hadn't proved terribly creative, but they were deadly enough, and walking into a bullet wasn't something Blancanales intended to do.

"Make that two." Schwarz's voice sounded in his ear. All right, that left three, total, and Blancanales was chasing at least one.

A bullet cracked through the air to his left.

The man he'd been chasing was now braced against one of the building corners up ahead, using the metal storage unit for cover. Obviously he'd gotten far enough ahead, or so he'd thought, to take the shot in relative safety. Blancanales judged the distance, dropped to one knee in a shooter's crouch, and leveled the short-barreled CAR-15. The shooter's head disappeared behind the corner.

Blancanales fired once, then again, then a third time.

The three 5.56 mm bullets tracked neat holes into the metal, each drifting farther left in pursuit of the hiding gunner. Blancanales waited, risking quick glances left, right, and back to make sure no one was flanking him. There was no answering fire. He moved up on the shooter's position and found a middle-aged man with a craggy face and a shaved head. A Ruger Mini-14 lay on the ground beside him. Blancanales quickly frisked the corpse, finding nothing but an extra magazine for the rifle and a stainless-steel wristwatch. The watch had Cyrillic lettering on its face. He turned it over and looked at the back of the casing. It was of Russian manufacture.

Clipped to the dead man's belt was another WTS device.

"One down," he said aloud. "Another Russian operative, possibly. I've got another Seever here."

"Ironman?" Schwarz said softly, his voice clear over the transceiver link. "You okay?"

Blancanales wondered the same thing. Neither of them had heard from Lyons since the shooting started, and both had been busy, he presumed, taking down their own targets. There were two left somewhere in the facility, unless they'd fled. Blancanales took both magazines for the Ruger, ejected its chambered round and took that, too.

Without ammunition it was useless. They could police it up later. For now, his pockets bulging with the captured magazines, he moved out, looking for Lyons. Whatever the enemy was likely to throw at the Ironman, he was confident Able Team's leader would see it coming.

That's when he heard automatic gunfire from somewhere in the facility, followed by 12-gauge thunder.

LYONS ALMOST DIDN'T SEE it coming. The machete blade whistled through the air as he neared the edge of one of the storage units, the blade's owner neatly hidden from view until it was nearly too late. With nowhere to go and no other options, not even time to raise the barrel of the Daewoo between Lyons and the sharpened steel, he simply threw his own legs out from under his body. He landed on his shoulder in a modified fall and brought up his combat boot. He managed to tangle up the machete-wielder's legs, bringing the man down in a heap on top of himself.

The man swore under his breath in a foreign language.

Another Russian, Lyons realized, like the men on the arson team. Whomever these bastards were, this was starting to look like a pretty broad conspiracy. The Russian tried to push his way into a sitting position, mounted across Lyons's stomach. Lyons took the butt of the Daewoo and slammed it across the Russian's jaw. The man was knocked clear and hit the pavement hard.

"Artur!" someone shouted. Lyons pivoted to target the voice, his finger on the Daewoo's trigger. Bullets scored the asphalt next to Lyons, who found himself suddenly under attack. He flipped the Daewoo shotgun's selector from semi-automatic and cut loose with a monstrous burst of double-aught buck, tearing apart the enemy shooter before the gunner could track and kill Lyons. As he unleashed 12-gauge hell, Carl Lyons was dimly aware of a voice in his transceiver, but the mighty automatic shotgun drowned out whatever was being said. He checked his flanks and his six while the echoes from the USAS-12 were still dying away. It was an old habit that saved his life.

The Russian, presumably Artur, had recovered sufficiently to draw a pistol. The muzzle of the old Smith & Wesson 645 looked impossibly large as he leveled it at Lyons's head from close range. Lyons simply reacted. He brought up the barrel of the shotgun and swung it around in a tight arc that slapped the barrel of the .45 out of the way. The Russian pulled the trigger and the deafening blast immediately set Lyons's ear ringing.

The shotgun's barrel ended its arc in front of Artur's own face.

Lyons pulled the trigger.

The Able Team leader was standing over the nearly headless corpse when Blancanales and Schwarz joined him. They held their weapons at the ready, but all of the enemy shooters were accounted for.

"Russians," Lyons said as they moved up.

"Mine was, too," Blancanales said. "At least his wristwatch was."

"Unless that's what the kids are wearing these days," Gadgets said. He moved around Blancanales and got a good look at the body nearest Lyons. "Holy shit, Ironman."

"Yeah," Lyons said. "Let's run a perimeter check, sweep the buildings one more time." He slapped a fresh magazine into the shotgun. "Report back to the van when you've run your check. Do it on the run. We've got to get a look at those storage units before there are cops crawling all over the place. I don't want them getting in the way."

"Got it," Blancanales said.

"Right." Schwarz nodded. Both men moved off, leaving Lyons with the gory task of searching his two downed opponents. When he found nothing significant, he moved back to the storage areas and the van with its two flat tires. Removing the flashlight clipped to his pocket, he flashed its beam through the cardboard boxes sitting in the back of the van. The small light made it easy to check each carton as he opened it, sometimes ripping the flaps free rather than cutting them open. There was no time to waste on finesse.

Several of the boxes contained paint, pieces of wood and poster board. He was momentarily confused by this—what about these craft products was worth killing for?—when he found the first cardboard carton of explosives.

The blocks were Semtex, relatively small, but big enough to do serious damage. There were only a few. He pocketed one; you never knew when such a thing might come in handy.

He found, in the back of the cargo van, a sandwich board bearing the relatively generic slogan, One Earth, One Cause. On the inside of the front of the sandwich board, however, he found a detonator screwed to the lightweight fiberboard. The wires were trailing loose. There was no explosive, though any of the blocks of plastique could have been fixed in place there.

A second cardboard carton contained pipe bombs, nasty-looking lengths of iron pipe to which nails and screws had been glued with some sort of thick, yellow adhesive. Leaving these for the moment, he checked the two storage areas, which still stood open as the shooters had left them. Most of what was inside was just trash, cardboard boxes full of packing materials and wadded-up papers. There were several crates, however, containing campaign literature.

Lyons removed from one of these a stack of bumper stickers. The name on them was Marcia Herrington, whom Lyons recognized as a prominent New York senator. In the other boxes were vinyl parade banners and quite a few printed signs proclaiming support for Harrington. A few more carried environmentalist slogans.

Yet another box contained hardcover books. Lyons, curious, lifted one of these out and looked at it. It was called *Earth's Last Hope*. The picture on the dust jacket matched the author's name: Senator Marcia Herrington. According to the copyright page it had been released only two months previously.

Interesting.

"Gadgets, here, all clear. Coming in."

"Pol, here. The same. I've gathered up the shooters' weapons."

"All right, guys," Lyons responded. "We have some explosives here, and we're going to have to make apologies to the local cops." He could hear sirens approaching, as if on cue. "Let's pack it up and hope we can wrap this sooner rather than later."

CHAPTER EIGHT

"Rodro Begum," McCarter recited, listening to his secure satellite phone as he watched the captured gunman's eyes. Begum flinched when he heard his name, looking up in a split-second's recognition before steeling himself again. It was enough for McCarter. Manning had snapped a photo with his own phone and transmitted it to the Farm, where Kurtzman and his team had run the man's identification through various international databases. He was a confirmed member of several terrorist groups, most recently the Purba Banglars. This was all the confirmation Phoenix Force needed that it was up against the Purba Banglars there in Nongstoin, but McCarter wanted more.

"You," he said to Begum. "You speak English?"

"I speak none to you," Begum said, his face hard with false bravado.

"Oh, okay, chap," McCarter said amiably. "Gary? Shoot him in the head."

Manning drew his .357 Magnum Desert Eagle and put it to the side of Begum's head. He thumbed back the hammer of the big pistol.

"Wait!" Begum shrieked. "Wait, wait, do not kill me!"

"Hold on, Gary," McCarter said. "But best to keep the

gun there. Just give me a second to move back, mate, so I don't get splattered."

"I will tell you what you want to know!" Staring into Manning's unflinching gaze, Begum no doubt saw that the big Canadian was deadly serious.

"What do I want to know?" McCarter asked.

"The…the uranium," Begum said, looking down for a moment. "I know of it."

"And who are you?"

"Rodro Begum," Begum said.

"Yes, I know that, mate." McCarter rolled his eyes. "I mean, *who* are you?"

"The Proletarian Party of East Bengal."

"Right, then." McCarter glanced at Manning and then at the other members of Phoenix Force in the room. "We knew we were dealing with the Purba Banglars, didn't we?" Begum, his wrists bound behind his back with plastic riot cuffs, had taken the place of Jignesh's family on the couch in the Nongstoin hovel where the family had been held. McCarter imagined that, in the time it had taken the Farm to run Begum's identity, the deputy commissioner had been reunited with his wife and daughters. There might be no love lost officially between their respective governments, given everything that happened, but Jignesh was probably grateful. Seeing the man's family safe, after the courage he had displayed in alerting Phoenix to the trap, did McCarter's heart good.

"Yes." Begum nodded, unnecessarily. McCarter was beginning to wonder if international terrorists were all going soft these days. He was glad not to have to waste a lot of time in an interrogation.

"The uranium," he said, nodding at Manning's pistol.

"Give me a location, or he splatters your brains all over that old settee."

Begum rattled off an address.

"T.J.," McCarter said to Hawkins, "call Jignesh. Run that by him, ask him if he's familiar with it. I suspect he'll be happy to help."

"You got it," Hawkins drawled.

"Now, then—" McCarter turned back to Begum "—what's going on? What's the plan for the uranium? Who's calling the shots?"

"I do not know."

McCarter, looking annoyed, glanced at Manning.

"I swear I do not know!" Begum shouted. "Our cells, they are kept separate. I only take my orders from my...my cell leader. You have killed him. He died when you entered. I know only the location, nothing else!"

"Don't know much, do you?" McCarter shook his head. "Why fight for the Purbas at all? Greater glory of communism, worker's paradise, something like that?"

Begum frowned. His eyes were those of a fanatic, though apparently not a particularly brave one. McCarter dismissed him mentally.

"David," Encizo reported from the door, "the locals are here to take charge of the prisoner."

"Good," McCarter said." Let's get moving, then, as soon as T.J. talks to Jignesh."

"Done and done," Hawkins said from outside, his words still carried by his earbud transceiver, which he had deactivated during his call. "Jignesh said the area is well-known. It's a shipping and receiving center for something called New India Textile. Basically another warehouse."

"Then let's load up and get on the move," McCarter said.

"T.J., get on the radio to Jack. Tell him to load his toys and give him the coordinates."

"You got it," Hawkins responded. Behind McCarter, Manning chambered a round in the Desert Eagle prior to making it safe and holstering it.

Begum looked up at the big man, comprehension dawning on his face.

"What can I say, mate?" The Briton almost laughed. "Neither of us wanted to get any of you on us."

THE DRIVE TO THE TEXTILE warehouse took half an hour on poorly maintained roads. As standard operating procedure, Encizo parked their vehicle some distance away. There was good cover leading up to the facility, consisting of stands of small trees and scrub dotted by what appeared to be vacant trailers.

"What's with these?" Hawkins pointed to one of them.

"Probably lodging for seasonal labor," Encizo said. "They don't look occupied now."

The area was, in fact, strangely deserted, especially after the teeming streets of the Nongstoin slums. David McCarter didn't like it one bit.

"On your guard, mates," he said. "Something about this smells." He put through a call to Grimaldi on his secure satellite phone. "Jack, it's David," he said, still employing first names only for the sake of their cover identities—not to mention the discretion he knew Brognola preferred. "Get on the move. I don't like this. I think it feels like it's going to get hot."

"On my way," Grimaldi confirmed. McCarter closed the phone.

"Full weaponry," he said to the other members of the

team. "T.J., you take the Range Rover. Calvin, you follow him in. I want one of the grenade launchers at the front. Gary, your M-203 and Rafe, go left and cover the flank. I'll take the right, see if I can work my way 'round to the back. Once we see how it breaks we can figure it from there." He looked at the textile warehouse in the distance and shook his head. "This smells," he said again. "All right. Go."

The members of Phoenix Force moved in.

McCarter shook off a sense of déjà vu as they stalked ever closer to the building. "Stay alert," he said unnecessarily. "Our new mate Begum confirmed these are the Purba Banglars, and they've proved damned bloodthirsty to now. Expect resistance."

McCarter cut right when the timing and the distance to the building seemed appropriate. Behind him, Hawkins drove the Range Rover in, as James walked behind him and covered him with his Tavor's grenade launcher. McCarter expected gunfire to explode from the building at any moment, but nothing came. He found a vantage relative to the corner of the building and watched tensely, as the other members of Phoenix Force reached their own positions.

The Range Rover stopped some distance from the front entrance. Hawkins waited with James, but nothing happened.

"David? What y'all want me to do?" Hawkins asked over his transceiver.

"You and Calvin, take the front," McCarter directed. "The rest of us will follow you in. I'm not at all sure there's even a door on this side, but I'll find a window or something. Move!"

A chorus of affirmatives sounded in his ear. McCarter hefted his Tavor and, just as he'd thought, could not find a doorway the length of the right side of the building. He found a window that was already broken, saving him the need to smash one and possibly alert those inside with the noise. It was an easy matter to climb up and over. He came up on the other side, bracing himself on the cement floor on one knee, the muzzle of his Tavor sweeping the room.

Still nothing.

"Clear, front," Hawkins's voice sounded in his ear once more.

"Clear, left side," Manning reported.

"Nothing here, either," McCarter said. "Let's hope this is not a dud, ladies. All right, we'll go high and low, assuming this structure has a basement. T.J. and Calvin, down. Gary and Rafe, up. I'll join you two on the high road."

The Briton joined Manning and Encizo as they worked their way up the stairwells to the second, then the third floor. There was no one to be found, and nothing of interest except textiles, raw and processed, in containers of various sizes. McCarter was beginning to think their man Begum had led them seriously astray. Either that, or the man had not been party to as much information as he thought he had.

The three Phoenix Force members reached the top floor of the building. McCarter cocked his head to one side, speaking for the benefit of his transceiver. "You boys down there got anything?"

"Negative, David," James said. "We...wait. Yes, we have something. There's a secure door down here. Heavy steel, some sort of electronic lock. Looks very new compared to the rest of the building."

"Right, then," McCarter said. "We're on our way. Gary, guard the entrance at ground level. Let us know if any surprises come our way."

Manning took up his post as McCarter and Encizo double-timed it down the stairs to the basement level. Once there, they took a short, badly lighted concrete corridor to its termination, where they found James and Hawkins looking over the door. James looked up.

"I've got a lock-busting round for the M-203 that could probably penetrate this," he said, indicating the electronic lock.

"What happens if the door doesn't open once the lock is disabled?" McCarter asked.

James shrugged. "We pry it open, I guess."

"Any chance we can circumvent it without destroying it?"

"Probably not," Hawkins put in. "We don't have the gear needed to slice it."

"Then we blow it, and hope for the best," McCarter nodded. "Everyone back off a bit, give Calvin some room."

James gave himself some distance from the lock, chambered the lock-breaker in his M-203 and aimed. The noise didn't seem to bother him when the round exploded, fragmenting the electronic lock in a shower of sparks.

Hawkins moved in and tried the door. "It's loose," he reported.

"Go, go, go," McCarter directed. Covering each other, two by two, Phoenix Force entered the doorway.

Two dozen men with Kalashnikovs waited for them.

"Bloody hell," McCarter whispered.

The men, dressed in olive-drab fatigues and wearing scarves or pieces of black cloth over their faces, were arrayed around the perimeter of the room on three sides. They had just been waiting for Phoenix Force. A man whom McCarter singled out as the probable leader strode forward. Even from several paces away, the Briton could see the WTS unit clipped to his belt.

"You are prisoners of the Proletarian Party of East Bengal," the leader said from behind his scarf in accented but fluent English. "You will surrender, or we will be forced to make your deaths painful. Put down your weapons and you shall have a clean death."

"Well—" McCarter looked the Purba leader in the eye "—isn't that a fine kettle of fish?" He turned to James, who held his Tavor carefully lowered. "Calvin, how do you like that? We're surrounded by more than twenty men and they say we either surrender and die, or resist and die painfully. How's that for a rock and a hard place?"

"Understood," Manning said over their transceivers, listening in from ground level. "You'll be pleased to know that help is here. G-Force is inbound, visual."

"G-Force" would be Jack Grimaldi, and that meant the chopper had made it here. McCarter took a quick glance around, getting his bearings. He looked at the Purba leader. "Do we have time for this?" he asked, glancing down at his wristwatch. The small compass also strapped around his wrist was what he was really looking at. He checked the directions and glanced to the three sides of the room that held armed men.

"Enough," said the Purba Bangla leader. "Lay down your weapons now, or die."

"All right," McCarter said. "I just have a few words to say."

"Yes?" The Purba Banglar looked at him quizzically.

"Jack," McCarter said, "aim low. Avoid the north wall. Now."

STONY MAN PILOT Jack Grimaldi, a veteran of countless operations and a master of every machine with wings or rotors, brought the helicopter in low and fast, expecting trouble. He caught sight of Manning, waiting out front near the target building. Tapping the earbud transceiver he wore, he listened as the device kicked on in a buzz of quiet static.

"...inbound, visual," said a voice he recognized as Manning's, now in range of the earbud unit. He frowned, then, as he listened to McCarter's voice, speaking with someone who was obviously an enemy.

"Jack, aim low. Avoid the north wall. Now." McCarter's direction made Grimaldi smile.

He brought the chopper in and across the building, swooping laterally across its face. Activating the Hydra rocket pod, he swung the aircraft around to target the south wall, right at ground level. Then he triggered the pod.

Seven M-151 high-explosive, point-detonating 10-pounders shot through the air on streamers of thick smoke, tearing into the building and cracking it like an egg. The explosions sent fragments in every direction and caused part of the building to crumble inward.

"Gotcha," Grimaldi said out loud.

JAMES WATCHED the basement wall shatter and fly inward as if the hand of God had slapped it. Several pieces of concrete struck him, none hard enough to cause damage. He coughed in the sudden cloud of dust, attempting to take visual stock of his teammates, make sure none of them was hit. As far as he could tell, all of them were functional.

Grimaldi was up there, not far away, their heavily armed guardian angel. This random thought had time to flash across James's mind as fragments of concrete crashed into the line of Purba Banglar gunmen in front of him, sending several of them sprawling. The members of Phoenix Force did not wait. They opened up with their Tavors, spraying the assembled gunmen, concentrating on those at the flanks of the south wall group. The confusion and the carnage acted to their advantage as they, in the eye of the storm, unleashed a deadly maelstrom of flying lead before the Purbas could rally or even cope with their sudden losses.

Each man moved, gliding heel to toe, staying low amid his enemies as he stalked among the dying. The constant movement was part of their advantage, a product of their training. To stop moving was to die. To stay mobile, acquiring and firing on targets of opportunity, was the only way to survive.

James emptied yet another magazine in his rifle and reached for what he counted as his last spare. It was gone, ripped free from his gear somehow, possibly by a flying chunk of debris. He slammed a lock-buster round into the M-203 grenade launcher under his weapon, targeted and pulled the trigger, tearing apart two men and wounding a third as they bunched up in his field of vision. Then he let the Tavor fall on its tactical sling and drew his M-9 pistol, firing several 9 mm rounds into the last of the Purba Banglars as the other Phoenix Force fighters performed similar mop-up.

As suddenly as it had begun, it was finished.

The Purba Banglars lay dead or dying on the cracked basement floor. McCarter looked in James's direction. "Calvin, check these men. Look for survivors, and make sure there are no grenades or other nasty hidden surprises clutched in eager hands. Jack, assuming you've spent your rockets, get up and out of range of small arms fire. I'll call you when I need you. The rest of you secure the building perimeter with Gary. I don't want anyone sneaking up on us while we're occupied with this."

James nodded and headed from corpse to corpse. Shells, fragments of concrete and torn bodies were strewed everywhere. In seconds the empty space full of more than two dozen living men had turned into a charnel house boasting only a fraction as many people. Battles were like that.

"What do you think, David?" James said as he checked each dead man, McCarter looking on.

"I think Begum set us up," McCarter said. "The Purbas were already waiting for something. Somebody'd tipped them to the fact that they could expect a force or forces to come looking for the uranium. So they, or whoever's running them, set up a little welcome committee. All it took was somebody willing to tell us what we wanted to know. Hang on, mate, let me check something."

The former SAS commando took a small device from his pocket, something James knew Kurtzman had given him for just an occasion such as this. The miniature Geiger counter immediately began clicking.

"The uranium was here," McCarter concluded. "But obviously it's gone now. Bloody hell!"

Somewhere among the bodies, a man began to laugh weakly.

James found him immediately. It was the man who'd spoken to David. His scarf had been pulled from his face, revealing a craggy, weathered face with dark skin. Blood stained his lips. He'd been gut shot, and badly, during the carnage. He started coughing up more blood as he tried and failed to laugh again.

James stood over him, covering him with the Beretta M-9. "What's so funny, man?"

"El…" The man struggled to get the word out, wheezing through bloody teeth. "El…Hombre. El Hombre Fuerte…"

"What's that he's saying?" McCarter came to stand close by.

"El Hombre Fuerte." James shrugged, still holding the M-9 on target.

"He…will…show you…" The terrorist laughed again, then started to cough, his eyes bugging out of his head. He stopped abruptly, his cough ending in a death rattle that rasped out of his throat as half a laugh, a sound unlike any James had ever heard a dead man make.

"What in several bloody hells is that supposed to mean?" McCarter groused. "'The Strong Man?' Who's that, then?"

"The Farm will know," James offered.

"If anyone will." McCarter looked around the basement. "Let's search them, see if we can find anything. I'm not optimistic. Damn it all, the uranium was here. It was *here*." He smacked a fist into his open palm. Then he removed his secure satellite phone. "I'm headed to ground level. I'll call this into the Farm and see what they can tell us. Take as many pictures as you can, and upload them. They might or might not make a difference."

James nodded.

The uranium was still out there. The mission wasn't over, not by a long shot.

CHAPTER NINE

Suburban Chicago

Fred Fleisser sat in the black Ford SUV, one of several identical vehicles his company owned, and press-checked the Kimber Warrior 1911-pattern handgun in his thigh holster. Satisfied for the third time in twenty minutes that a .45-caliber round was chambered, he hunkered down in the passenger seat and tried not to fidget. He couldn't help the anxious feeling in the pit of his gut. It had always been this way. He was used to it. Fred Fleisser was a combat veteran, after all.

He'd tell anyone who'd listen, and he'd found plenty of people who would do just that. Since serving in the Gulf, going on to get his Criminal Justice degree and founding Black Bag security, Fleisser had always made a point of telling everyone he met that he had been there and done that. He had, after all, unlike all these other jokers in the security field who had never once fired a shot in anger. Why, Fleisser had fired an entire magazine in anger, once, not so very many miles from Baghdad, and while there were no confirmed kills to his credit, well, he was certain he'd seen a man go down. Probably Iraqi military, maybe Republican Guard. Who could say for sure? When the drinks flowed and the tales got taller, among friends, well, that one Iraqi soldier sometimes turned into two, or three, or four. Who was to say? There was no one there to remember the incident but Fleisser himself, and he was happy to tell people about it.

He left out details, of course. Left out his court-martial. The details were so complicated, and he'd spent so much time drunk, that he wasn't exactly sure how he'd skated on the rape charge. All he knew was that the servicewoman with whom he'd had less than consensual intercourse had eventually been discharged, or been transferred out, or wherever the hell it was that people went, and when it was all over, he still had a clean record and nobody'd ever know the difference. Go figure.

When the time came, though, he was happy to get out. He'd done his time in the Army. He'd been there, he'd done that, and he was damned well going to cash in on it. Black Bag Security was the result, a consulting firm specializing in armed bodyguard work. The problem was, the security consulting business just didn't pay as well as he'd thought it would. He didn't know if he just didn't have a head for business, or if other hardened veterans of combat now employed in private security were having similar problems. But the issue had been pretty stark and the choice pretty clear. If he didn't want his business to go belly up, if he didn't want to end up selling cars on his uncle Ray's lot in Ohio, he'd damned well better make a go of it. That meant seeking less conventional means of making ends meet.

What he'd discovered had been a gold mine, really, if you just weren't too picky about where your money came from. The up side was that he never had to declare the income he got from these extralegal sources, so it was like a big fat raise on top of the extra income stream. It seemed the world was just full of people who needed private security, who were not themselves the most upstanding of citizens. These were people who valued discretion. Sometimes, when they were particularly desperate, they paid extra to see to it that hammers got dropped on people they needed gone. To a professional like Fleisser, well, that was no problem. After all, he was no stranger to killing, having taken out an entire Iraqi Republican Guard squad in the Gulf. Was he, now? No, Fleisser discovered, there were plenty of people in the world who wanted done what he could do for them, and they had money. They also tended to defer to Fleisser's obvious combat experience, which made him happy. Yeah, he would admit it to himself. It made him feel cool. But what harm was there in that?

He'd been thinking thoughts not very far from those lines when the phone in his office had rung that morning. Reginald Butler had been trying to get hold of him since the previous day, but the billionaire had been using go-betweens. Fleisser had insisted that if the big man wanted wet work done by Black Bag Security, then he could damned well call Fleisser in person. He didn't work with go-betweens. Fleisser wanted no misunderstandings. That was why, he was happy to tell those who called him, he had installed the very best scrambling and monitoring equipment on his office lines. If anyone ever tried to listen in on his conversation, why, he'd know about it before they did, and he's see to it they got a bullet before they knew it was time to run.

Butler had been pretty agitated, and apparently his problems had gotten worse since he'd started trying to make contact. It seemed, a reluctant Butler had finally explained with a minimum of euphemisms, that he had highly paid private soldiers, probably working for a competitor, trying to knock over his business interests and intimidate his executives. He couldn't have that, no, but he couldn't really do anything legally other than call the police and bitch about it. And how did that make him look? Why, it made him look weak. So he'd taken matters into his own hands, asked the appropriate questions of the appropriate people, and finally been referred to Fleisser and Black Bag because they were local. Above all, Butler needed somebody local, because he needed the problem dealt with *right now*.

He told Fleisser that he had a good business friend, a nice lady named Melody Forest, who was likely the target of one of these intimidation attacks, maybe even of murder. Butler hadn't been sure, but he had been very firm about what he wanted done. He wanted the three men responsible, whom he said were reported traveling in a Chevy Suburban, brought down, and but good. If Fleisser could make it look like an accident, there'd be a bonus. If he couldn't, as long as he didn't get caught, well, there would still be a little extra for a job well done. That had been all Fleisser had needed to hear. He'd assembled a team of employees he knew he could trust to keep their mouths shut—men who themselves had criminal records, in many cases, and weren't afraid to get their hands dirty—and staked out the most likely access route to the Forest woman's home. Then he and the three men he'd brought with him, two of whom were in the second Ford SUV parked next to this one, had settled in to wait.

He almost froze when the Suburban they were waiting for cruised by at several miles under the speed limit. The driver was obviously looking for a specific address.

"Let's hit 'em," he said to his driver.

NOT MORE THAN HALF AN HOUR earlier, Hermann Schwarz had been listening on his secure satellite phone as the Suburban rolled through the Chicago suburbs. Blancanales and Lyons were discussing whether the next several properties on the priority list, some of which were storage sites, were any more or less likely to yield material of the type they'd just found. Meanwhile, Schwarz had called the Farm to report on everything they'd discovered. Kurtzman and the team had been running the data and Schwarz was waiting to see if Price had any comments on the results.

Price had finally picked up her end again. "Okay, Gadgets, I have it here. Senator Marcia Harrington, junior senator from New York. She's been growing in popularity over the past several years. She's gotten particularly big lately, after the book you found was published. It's made her a rising star in the environmentalist movement, the poster politician for fighting global warming, promoting conservation, and so on."

"And the link to Chicago is…?" Schwarz asked.

"There's a huge national environmentalist rally scheduled for the end of the month, at McCormick Place in Chicago. Marcia Harrington will be the keynote speaker. Rumor has it that she'll announce her intention to seek her party's nomination for a presidential run come the next election. It's a very big deal. Political speculation for months has had it that Harrington and her frequent ally, Congressman Richard Cross, are looking to form a ticket."

Schwarz quickly repeated what Price had told him to Lyons and Blancanales. Then he put the phone on speaker so the others could hear. "So what we're looking at," he concluded, "are the components of a political rally massacre."

"But why?" Blancanales asked. "If Harrington is an environmentalist candidate, why would she be targeted for assassination by a political coalition of greens and communists? Aren't they the fringe end of the same side of the political aisle that she's on?"

"You'd think," Price said. "We're not certain why. Harrington leans more center than left, though, which might mean she's not radical enough for them and they're hoping to spread the word through violence. Or there may not be any real logic to it. The rally is huge, covering the whole country, with foreign guests. Some of these are dignitaries of nations hard hit by environmental problems, not to mention a few representatives from industrial nations who see the environmental movement as a threat to their forward progress. We're not really interested in the politics of it, apart from determining possible motives. Whatever message your terrorists hope to send, it looks pretty obvious they intend to send it at this rally."

"You said the end of the month." Lyons spoke up from the driver's seat. "That means we've got some time to work."

"We're catching them in the planning stages, yes," Price said. "But what worries me is that you caught them in the process of unloading the explosives and accessories. Why do that now? The more you move something like explosives, the greater the chances you'll be caught. You remember the would-be terrorist who was planning a major bombing in an American city, who was caught when he was pulled over for a traffic offense? They caught him simply because they found the goods in his car when he was stopped. The chances of a critical error like that go up whenever you move around contraband. So why are they risking it now?"

"Almost as if they were worried we might be stopping by," Blancanales said.

"It's a concern," Price said. "At any rate, this information changes our priorities. I'm relaying an address through your phone now, Gadgets. It's the home address of a woman named Melody Forest. She's the event coordinator for the rally. We've tried calling her and gotten no answer. We had local law enforcement cruise by, but they reported nothing out of the ordinary. So we're sending you to take a look, see what you can find, maybe take a look inside her place if she's still nowhere to be found. She might know something, and even if she doesn't, she can give us more details, discreetly, about who and what is going on at that rally. Since the rally is the target, at least eventually, she's the logical next stop."

"Agreed," Lyons said. "But what happens if we find her and she's already been gotten to?" He put in words what they were all thinking. "What if the reason you can't get hold of her is because she's dead?"

"Then we're back where we started, more or less," Price admitted. "But we have to know for certain. She has an office downtown, but I called there and was told by her answering service that she's almost never there, that she does most of her work from home. If there's anything that might give us more insight into the rally or the attendees, and she can't give it to us in person, it's likely to be in her house somewhere."

"If the place hasn't been tossed already," Lyons said.

"Exactly. The locals didn't see any evidence of a break-in and didn't want to risk breaking in without a warrant."

"Then I guess we'll do just that, if she's not home," Lyons said.

"Good luck, Able."

"Thanks, Barb," Schwarz said.

"I THINK IT'S AT THE END of this block," Schwarz announced, looking at the GPS navigation unit. "I—" He paused. "Carl? What is it?"

Lyons had slowed, looking in the rearview, and then pressed his foot nearly to the floor. The Suburban surged ahead.

"Two matching SUVs," he said. "Dark Fords. They pulled onto the road behind us when we passed."

"Could be coincidence," Blancanales said innocently.

Lyons glared up at him in the rearview mirror. "And it could be the tooth fairy's driving," he said.

"What have you got against the tooth fairy?" Schwarz said.

Then a bullet smashed the side mirror next to him.

"Was that a quarter?" Blancanales offered.

Lyons swore. He stood on the pedal and the big Suburban roared down the road, only to slow as he came to a four-way stop. Pausing to verify that there was nothing coming, the Able Team leader powered through the intersection.

"They're still on us," Schwarz said. He had turned somewhat awkwardly in his seat belt to watch behind him, rolling down his window. The suppressed Beretta 93-R was in his fist. He took careful aim as the two Fords shifted back and forth behind the Suburban. The passenger in the lead vehicle was firing from his window, but except for the lucky bullet in the side mirror, he wasn't hitting anything he intended to hit.

"Nice," Lyons said, disgusted. "Spray lead all over a residential neighborhood, why don't you?"

Schwarz said nothing. He waited, aiming the Beretta,

and Lyons did his best to hold the Suburban steady to let the electronics expert aim. Schwarz held his breath briefly, waited for the lead Ford to swing back across the rear of the Suburban, then stroked the trigger.

A 3-round burst stuttered across the windshield. The Ford faltered and started to fall back.

"We need someplace to take this off the road," Lyons said. "Someplace away from all these houses."

"There!" Blancanales shouted, pointing to the left. "Left, Carl, left! That parking lot. It's empty!"

Lyons nodded grimly and threw the wheel left, bouncing up over a curb and across a median. He narrowly missed a taxicab minivan as it shot across his path. Schwarz couldn't hear the curses Lyons was uttering, but he knew the man possessed an impressive vocabulary of profanity.

The Suburban rolled into the parking lot of what had once been a fairly good-size grocery store. The low, brown building was faced with artificial stone and bore a vinyl banner proclaiming it For Sale Or Lease with a contact phone number. The front of the building was almost entirely plate-glass windows, which had been papered over from inside with newsprint.

Lyons hauled the wheel over and aimed the Suburban's nose at the front of the vacant store.

"Ironman, no!" Schwarz looked up, momentarily horrified.

"Yes," Lyons said. His lips curled upward in a tight grin as he floored the accelerator again.

The Suburban crashed through the windows into the thankfully empty space within. Lyons switched on the headlights and foglights, bringing the Suburban around and almost managing to make the big truck fishtail. Schwarz, through his open window, could smell burning tires and brakes. He was jerked in his seat as Lyons threw the SUV into reverse and brought it nose out facing the opening he'd just made.

"Gadgets! Blancanales!" he prompted.

Schwarz brought his 93-R once more to bear as he leaned out his window. Blancanales did the same thing from the driver's side, from his window behind the driver's slot. He braced the muzzle of the CAR-15 against the side of the vehicle, angled outward, trained on the approaching Fords.

"Incoming," Lyons said unnecessarily. Rather than put himself in the path of Pol's bullets, he allowed himself to slide down in his seat, putting the engine block between him and the enemy. Schwarz did his best to minimize his forward exposure, too, while still aiming the 93-R machine pistol. There was a good chance the enemy would fire into the windshield.

The gunners opened up from the Fords as they came closer. A couple of bullets ricocheted off the roof, but none came very close. Blancanales and Schwarz returned fire. Lyons, from his position cramped against the dash, gripped the steering wheel with both hands.

"That's enough to make it look good," he announced. "I'm going for it!"

"Got it," Schwarz said. He pulled his gun arm inside the vehicle.

"Roll, roll, Ironman!" Blancanales shouted, slapping the roof.

Lyons tromped the accelerator again.

When the Suburban came rolling out of the storefront like a freight train, the two Ford drivers lost their nerve. The trucks broke away from each other, giving Able Team just enough room to push between them. Metal scraped on metal as the driver's-side mirror traded paint with one of the Fords. Then the two vehicles were past and Lyons was bringing them around for another pass.

"Blancanales!" he shouted. "Take them out, each for each!"

Blancanales rapped the roof, leaning farther out of his window and bracing himself on the low roof rack atop the truck. He emptied the CAR-15 into the flank of the closer Ford, which Lyons was circling like a shark. The 5.56 mm bullets tore through the tires and the lower portions of the doors between them. Then the Suburban was wheeling in the opposite direction, performing a deadly, tire-squealing, rubber-burning doughnut around the other Ford. Blancanales reloaded his CAR-15 and gave it the same treatment. Both of the enemy vehicles were rolling on sparking, raw rims when they managed to come to a stop.

"Out!" Lyons ordered.

The Suburban lurched to a halt and the men of Able Team jumped clear. Lyons jacked back the cocking handle on his massive Daewoo shotgun as his boots hit the pavement, with his teammates close behind. They spread out, Lyons and Schwarz taking one vehicle, Blancanales taking the other, using the body of the Suburban for cover. Lyons put the truck's flank between them and the other two vehicles, the only barriers in the otherwise empty lot.

The shooters in the Fords bailed out of their vehicles. They were carrying handguns and AR-15 rifles. They opened up on semiautomatic, which made the ARs civilian models—unless, Schwarz thought, they were just practicing rather severe fire discipline. He scooted around the body of the Suburban, which was taking bullet holes at an alarming rate, and lined up on the nearest gunman.

For a brief moment, the shooter and the man next to him were lined up in Schwarz's sight picture. The other pair of shooters, one with an AR-15 and one with a .45, were on the far side. They had bunched up rather nicely. While Schwarz couldn't believe his good luck, he was not about to look a gift horse in the mouth.

He unleashed a fusillade of 9 mm fire in 3-round bursts from the Beretta. As his bullets tore into the nearest targets, the thunder of the Daewoo 12-gauge echoed across the parking lot. The shooters, who had moved to stand in a firing line in front of their vehicles were toppled by Able Team's counterfire, sprawling across the parking lot. The last man, the man with the .45 farthest from the shooting, was running for it.

"Gadgets!" Lyons ordered, his voice carrying through the earbud transceiver and also across the lot. "Go after him!"

Schwarz was, of the three of them, arguably the fastest, and his 93-R made him more mobile than the heavier weapons Lyons and Blancanales carried. He dropped the 20-round magazine in the machine pistol as he ran, slamming a fresh one home. His legs pumping, he skirted the far Ford, raced past, around the corner of the grocery store, where the running man had sought cover.

Two bullets cracked through the air, raising chips from the vacant building's artificial stone facing. The gunfire didn't come close enough to Schwarz to cause him to break stride. He poured on the speed, hoping to get close enough to the runner to bring him down without killing him.

The man sprinted into traffic, looking back at Schwarz as he crossed the road. The Able Team operative had enough time to drag in a startled breath. Then an old Buick station wagon slammed into the man's body as he darted into its path. The driver hit the brakes and squealed to a stop, shedding some of his momentum before slamming into the runner, but it was a bone-cracking impact nonetheless. Schwarz jogged up, his eyes scanning the pavement for the fallen .45.

"United States Justice Department!" he announced to the driver, who was starting to get out of the car. "Stay in your car, sir."

Cars began to back up behind the Buick, some of them honking. Schwarz ignored them, making sure the gunman was really down for the count and not just shamming. He found the .45, scuffed from its impact with the asphalt, and thumbed its safety on before tucking it into his belt.

"Is he dead?" the worried driver asked. "I don't wanna get sued."

"Don't worry, sir," Gadgets informed him. "I am apprehending this man on behalf of the Justice Department. Just stay in your car, please, and everything will be fine. You won't see him again."

"I gotta call my insurance company," the man said.

"That's all right." Schwarz nodded. He recited one of the cutout contact numbers Brognola kept in place for liaisons with civilians. "Just call that number if you need some sort of paperwork." Resolving issues like this quickly was far better, in the long term, than leaving Americans to wonder why they'd encountered a random shooting on which local law enforcement never followed up. For Stony Man Farm to stay covert, it was necessary to dot an occasional *i* and cross an occasional *t*.

The gunman groaned. Schwarz knelt over him, securing his arms behind his back with plastic riot cuffs. "Iron-man, Blancanales, I've got him," he reported. "He had an accident. Bring the truck." He poked and prodded, not un-gently, trying to assess the man's injuries. "Doesn't look like anything serious, though I couldn't say if he's got internal damage. I don't think his ribs are broken, though, and he didn't dent the car too badly. Odds are he's just stunned."

"On our way," Lyons responded. "This is about to get complicated."

In the distance, Schwarz could hear sirens.

CHAPTER TEN

Central America

The heat and humidity were as oppressive as those of the West Khasi Hills region. As the rest of Phoenix Force stood guard with their Tavor rifles, McCarter and Manning consulted the portable GPS device the Briton carried. In it were the coordinates of their destination, a reasonable hike from the landing zone. They had buried their HALO gear and the rest of the equipment, including oxygen masks, that they'd used for the high-altitude, low-opening drop over this disputed piece of Central American territory. Now it was time for the trek overland to the target. McCarter paused in switching from screen to screen on the handheld electronic map, wiping sweat from his brow.

"Bloody hell," he muttered.

"But it's a dry heat," Hawkins drawled.

"T.J., mate," McCarter said, "shut up." He could only hope that their current target was the right one. He had to admit that all of the information that the Farm had managed to pull together pointed in that direction.

"El Hombre Fuerte," Kurtzman had explained via the secure satellite phone, "is Jorge Jiminez, the Strong Man. He's made a minor religion of using that tired old title. You say The Strong Man in geopolitical circles today, you're talking about Jiminez. He's built himself a private army, whose name translates to The Sons of the Strong Father. The Man has had people keeping an eye on him for a while, but in the absence of any overt actions against the United States, and with our own armed forces spread pretty thin across the globe, he hasn't been a high enough priority to deal with before now."

Kurtzman had transmitted a map of Central America, on which a small zone was highlighted. "That area," he had explained, "is under dispute. It's not officially claimed by any single country and, apart from being a rather miserable little stretch of jungle, rocks and more jungle, it's never been of much interest to anyone. That was until a few months ago, when Jiminiz came to power. He came out of nowhere, really. Staked off the territory and claimed it was now his, since the national interests in the region couldn't be bothered to take decisive action. He started establishing military bases to hold and control it, and then sent media releases to the neighboring countries' television and radio outlets, declaring the spot a no-go zone. Nobody wanted to fight him for it. I think word has gotten around, behind the scenes, that Jiminez is sponsored by somebody powerful, somebody who'll step in to back him up. So until further notice, he's the local warlord."

"A warlord who's not at war with anybody?" McCarter had asked.

"Not yet," Kurtzman said, "but State thinks he's part of somebody's long-term plan. He's been linked to dictatorships who aren't exactly our friends, but nobody's claimed him officially. Whoever's sponsoring him, though, is using him as a proxy."

"A proxy for what?"

"Well, word is he's got his hands on some surplus Soviet missiles. NATO calls it the SS-24t, a variant of the Scalpel RT-23 Molodets ICBM. The 24t is smaller than the Scalpel, which could be driven around on mobile rail-based launching platforms. These are small enough to be launched from trucks but still have the range to reach the United States."

"Which means…"

"Which means that if someone were to equip Jiminiz with weapons-grade-enriched uranium, he could be lobbing nuclear weapons across the U.S. border."

McCarter swore. "And then we're staring down the barrel of a bloody Cuban missile crisis all over again," he said.

"Exactly," Kurtzman confirmed.

Barbara Price had broken in with more. "I can't stress enough, David," she said, "that El Hombre Fuerte is more than just a paramilitary leader, and more than just the pawn of anti-American political interests. He's an almost religious figure who's known throughout Communist and socialist movements worldwide. They're touting him as the next Che Guevara. We're guessing that's why your man thought the name would mean something to you, that it would be a potent threat. They're wearing El Hombre Fuerte T-shirts at global Communist rallies. Intelligence sources noted what may have been the first of them during the last May Day demonstrations. The man and his supporters are very dangerous."

"I'm glad to know he wasn't a priority until now," McCarter groused.

"You know as well as I do that there are endless hot spots and areas of concern," Price said.

"More importantly," Kurtzman added, "satellite tracking records indicate that a plane with sufficient cargo capacity to carry the enriched uranium left the West Khasi Hills area not long before your raid on the textile facility. It took a roundabout route, and we had hell trying to verify its location on each leg of its journey—I had Hunt up practically all night backtracing and cross-referencing satellite imagery from two different NSA birds. But that same plane, as near as we can figure, eventually made its way to Central America. It didn't land in the Zone of Dispute, as the UN calls it, but it got close enough. The uranium could have been trucked in from there. Our Strong Man could be fueling nuclear warheads right now."

"Do we have any reason to think action against the United States is imminent?" McCarter had asked.

"When is it not?" Price asked. "We're a big target, David, and you know as well as I do that the only thing holding back most of these militant factions is opportunity, not motive or will. Once they have the weapons, we have every reason to believe the threat of nuclear missiles flying our way is very real. Even if El Hombre Fuerte is somebody's pawn, which he likely is, and even if they're using him as leverage in a long game, you can bet the threat is real. If we didn't believe it, the threat itself would have no value."

"So what's our target?" McCarter asked.

"We're going to HALO drop you guys over the Zone of Dispute," Price had informed him. "There you'll meet a local guide, one of our intelligence assets in the area who'll be dispatched to meet you. He's equipped with a GPS tracker and you'll have the appropriate beacon. Our man in Central America is part of an advance intelligence team whose job it's been to keep an eye on El Hombre Fuerte. That's why we know as much as we do. The Strong Man may not have been a military priority, but State has been nervous about him since he first appeared, and that means they were more than happy to have boots and eyes on the ground to monitor his activities."

"And once we're there?"

"Once there, your guide will take you to El Hombre Fuerte's headquarters, an armed camp that is his primary center of operations. If the missiles are there, you know what to do. If not, perhaps you can find them. We're assuming you're going to find the uranium. If it was in Nongstoin and now it's not, there aren't too many other places it could be."

"Could it have been offloaded along the way? That plane didn't fly straight from India to South America, did it?"

"From what we can determine from its rather circuitous route, based on satellite photo analysis," Price said, "it did not offload anything of significance, no."

"Right, then," McCarter said. "It's all or nothing time. We're away, Barb."

"Good hunting," Price told him. Kurtzman had then provided him with more necessary details, including the arrangements for them to meet their plane and receive the needed gear.

And that was that. Now they were here, checking the coordinates the Farm had provided, and speculating on the route they might take. The man who approached them was quiet, but he still didn't manage to get close enough to take them by surprise. It was Calvin James who picked him out of the brush and ordered him to come in. When he did so, McCarter greeted him warily.

"It's cold at night," he said.

"Not as cold as in the early morning," the man said in accented English, finishing the code exchange.

"David," McCarter introduced himself.

"Javier," the lanky visitor replied. He smiled, revealing crooked teeth. He had stringy, shoulder-length brown hair. The eyes under his heavy brow were bright and alert. The face was dark and well-lined. He was tall, almost gangly, and he carried a copy of the ubiquitous Kalashnikov with a folding wire stock. He wore only sandals and what looked like the remains of an olive-drab flight suit, the legs and arms of which had been hacked off, leaving frayed edges. On his belt was a large machete. The handle of the big blade was worn with much use.

"You're to take us to El Hombre Fuerte's base camp, eh?" McCarter asked.

"*Sí,*" Javier nodded. "Though 'base camp' is not sufficient to describe it. The operations camp of El Hombre Fuerte is like a fortress. The camp is surrounded by a wooden palisade made from local trees, sharpened at the tips, like your cowboys, no? Many men, much equipment, waits inside."

"How far by foot?" McCarter asked. He was well aware that the distance in miles as the crow flew meant nothing in the jungle.

"Not far," Javier said. "Come."

They picked their way cautiously through the jungle. Javier was able to identify footpaths that they'd not have found on their own. He quickly earned McCarter's respect; he knew what he was doing and he went about his business quietly and efficiently. Machete in hand, he removed a few obstacles here and there, but generally made his way with a minimum of fuss.

Javier called a halt after nearly two hours. "We are nearing the camp," he said. "Through there, and beyond the small rise." He pointed to the trees beyond. "The palisade starts there. Armed guards watch from a raised wooden platform running the perimeter of the gate. Inside are large tents. Most of the facility is of canvas or tarping on wooden frames. The Strong Man has a large building of wood that serves as his command center, in the center of the camp. Many rooms, many men inside and outside. There are machine-gun emplacements within rings of sandbags. The men guarding the perimeter will have rifles and a few grenade launchers. Perhaps a LAW rocket or two."

"Lovely," McCarter said.

"I will assist you," Javier said. "Long have I watched and waited for this opportunity. The rest of my team has been recalled. I was retained to show you the way. I was told to report to my handlers when I was finished. This I will not do."

"Handlers?" James asked. "Who might they be? CIA?"

Javier shrugged. "It makes no difference. The Strong Man is a curse on this area. I was born not far from here. I love this land. It has been a long journey for me, finally to be here once more. Men like El Hombre Fuerte are a curse. I will help you. Darkness fast approaches, and it will be under cover of night that we make our approach. This is perfect." He grinned, showing his less than perfect teeth.

"All right." McCarter nodded. "Rafe, take Javier with you. Work your way around to the west side. Gary, take the east end of the perimeter, with T.J. Cal, see if you can get around the back. I'll take the front. Ears on, fast and quiet. Move out, mates."

RAFAEL ENCIZO WORKED his way through the undergrowth, the perimeter of the Strong Man's palisade looming above him. He had been a little wary of having an unknown ally along, at first, though of course the members of Phoenix Force had teamed with more than their share on many missions. His concerns were quickly allayed by Javier's conduct, however. The man moved like a ghost, and saw things even Encizo, an experienced guerrilla fighter, did not. At one point Javier motioned for a halt, then pointed to his nose and pointed up. Encizo smelled it a few moments later: tobacco smoke. A sentry behind the palisade above was smoking and had moved within range. The two men waited until he moved off, then continued.

A probe like this was fairly straightforward. Each member of Phoenix Force or, in this case, Phoenix Force plus one, would be responsible for helping to scout out the weak points of the enemy facility. Every base had certain vulnerabilities, even if these were only momentary, even if such gaps in the security of the site could only be identified after extended observation. The commandos of Phoenix Force would wait all night, if they had to. Encizo doubted that would be necessary. While it was obvious Jiminez had himself quite a fortress, at least by local standards, there were plenty of points of entry.

They had spotted one already, and Encizo intended to use it. The west wall of the palisade included a wooden watchtower. While the ladder to the tower was on the inside of the wall, the struts of the tower's legs had enough crosspieces to afford them purchase even without grapples or other climbing tools. Encizo made sure no one but Javier was around to hear, then whispered for the benefit of his earbud transceiver.

"Rafael," he said softly, identifying himself. "I have a tower here. I intend to climb it and penetrate the perimeter."

"David. Go," McCarter responded.

"Gary," Manning said. "I have same, over."

"David. Proceed," McCarter instructed. Somewhere on Manning's side of the perimeter was an identical tower, and McCarter was giving his go-ahead for the big Canadian and Hawkins to use it as a point of entry.

"David," McCarter whispered. "Have no entry, repeat, no entry. Move with caution. Out."

Encizo slung his Tavor and scrambled up the tower, mindful of his exposed position once he was silhouetted against what little of the night sky was visible past the surrounding tree line. Behind and beneath him, Javier moved up effortlessly, his Kalashnikov across his back. They paused at the top of the tower, just beneath the lip of its edge. There was a guard there.

Javier grinned at Encizo as he drew even with him. He rapped on the edge of the guard tower with knobby, calloused knuckles, in an SOS pattern—three short, three long, and three short.

"¿Que?" The guard, confused, moved to look over the lip of the watchtower.

Javier reached up, grabbed him by the collar of his olive-drab fatigues and threw him over the side.

The guard didn't even have time to scream as he hit the ground with a sickening crunch. Encizo traded glances with Javier, and then the two men pulled themselves up into the watchtower. From there they had a good view of the rest of the compound. They crouched, behind the watchtower enclosure, so that no one below would see two men in a space previously guarded by one.

"It is as I said," Javier whispered. "There, in the center of camp." He pointed. "The Strong Man's main building. Arrayed about him, the tents of those less worthy."

A few men, all wearing a variety of different military surplus fatigue patterns, moved around in the camp below. There was a call from the front gate, which was a heavy wooden affair moved aside manually by the gate guards. Encizo stretched a bit to get a better look and saw that a four-wheel-drive vehicle had approached. It was an ancient jeep with multiple auxiliary lights attached, all of them blazing brightly.

"That," Javier whispered, "is El Hombre Fuerte himself, or at least his vehicle. He has a lieutenant, named Hector Socaras who sometimes takes the jeep out."

"Where do they go?" Encizo whispered.

"To a second camp," Javier said. "It is just outside the nearest village, a place with no name. The village is, for all purposes, owned by Jiminez. All within it live because he permits it."

"What is this second camp?"

"I do not know." Javier shrugged. "It is heavily guarded. It has been difficult enough to maintain watch over Jiminez, who rarely leaves the camp, or does so under heavy guard. My people and I were told not to pursue, and we dared not attempt it without support from our handlers. It could be nothing."

"Or it could be very important," Encizo said. He watched the gates open slowly under the gate guards' manpower.

"David here, attempting entry behind the truck," Mc-Carter's voice said quietly over Encizo's transceiver.

Encizo removed a pair of compact portable binoculars from a cargo pocket of his pants. He used them to focus on the front gate. He saw the jeep coming in, bearing only the driver. He couldn't see the driver's face, though he wouldn't know El Hombre Fuerte from this Hector Socaras at this distance; the binoculars simply weren't that powerful. Stony Man's files had images of Jiminez on file, and the man was no prize. But at this distance, a man-size figure was a man-size figure, even in the lenses of the binoculars.

Encizo saw the shadow that was McCarter, moving in behind the jeep. He could only hope that the other members of Phoenix Force had neutralized all the watchtower guards, as anyone this high up could conceivably be watching activity around the gate. If only friendly eyes watched McCarter as he slipped past the front gate security, there was a very good chance that—

"David!" Encizo whispered. "You're blown, you're blown!"

He'd caught the motion almost too late. Someone had been waiting outside the gate, either a straggler or perhaps someone walking on foot with the jeep, far behind. That man was now moving up behind David. Encizo could just make out the shape of the Kalashnikov coming up as the enemy drew a bead on McCarter from behind.

Encizo didn't think. He aimed the Tavor. It was a long shot for the red-dot optics, but there was no choice, and no time.

The gunshot rang out, followed by several more as Encizo poured it on. The man targeting McCarter went down.

The rest of Phoenix Force opened up from their positions in the watchtowers, as did Javier with his own Kalashnikov. Each man, Encizo could only assume, was picking up targets of opportunity. They had the high ground, the tactical advantage. Encizo started tracking and picking off running men as fast as he could. Next to him,

Javier's AK banged away in single-shot mode, as the savvy jungle fighter picked his targets.

The rattle on the floorboards of the watchtower would have gone unnoticed, in the gunfire, if not for the fact that whatever had just landed in the tower bounced off Encizo's foot. He looked down in time to see the stun grenade and recognize it for what it was before it burst.

Everything went white, then black, and then there was nothing.

WHEN THE FLASH-BANGS and stun charges started going off, David McCarter didn't stop to wonder what was happening. The Strong Man's people were smart enough to be prepared for a sudden incursion, all right. That made sense. The man was anything but stupid. There was no reason for McCarter to concede defeat, however. He would simply have to keep moving forward, find his next options and push through, rallying Phoenix Force with him.

He rounded a corner between two tents and buttstroked a charging paramilitary soldier as he ran past, not realizing that McCarter was not one of El Hombre Fuerte's own. The man dropped like a sack of potatoes and McCarter helped himself to the AK-47 he carried. In the darkness the profile of the weapon might help him blend in. He slung the Tavor and made sure the Kalashnikov had a round chambered.

He decided to work his way across the compound to the far tower, where James had made his entry. He'd seen the stun grenade go off up there, and the gunfire around the camp was starting to die off. Could all of the men be down? He didn't want to picture it. No, he'd climb his way up there.

"Stop right there," a voice behind him said in Spanish.

McCarter froze. "My Spanish is limited," he said.

"So. Your men are very good," said the man, whose deep, sonorous voice carried only a hint of an accent when he switched to English. "They killed quite a few of mine. But I am no stranger to a war of this type. We have contingencies for your invasion. Place the rifle gently in the dirt, yes? No need to harm a perfectly serviceable rifle, or risk an accidental shot, would you not say?"

The Briton turned and looked. A man in neatly pressed OD fatigues, wearing a cap that made him look like Fidel Castro—which, McCarter realized, may well have been the point—stood holding a .45-caliber pistol, directed his way. Several soldiers with Kalashnikovs stood around him, covering McCarter warily. The man in front of them, obviously their leader, was unmistakable. Even if McCarter hadn't seen file photos of him, he'd have known.

"El Hombre Fuerte, I presume," he said.

"You have the pleasure of an audience with me, yes," he said pleasantly. He stood tall and broad-shouldered, one hand on his hip as the .45 pointed steadily at McCarter's center mass. He had a full, bushy beard and eyebrows to match, with a misshapen, florid bulb of a nose that spoke of too much drink and more than a few punches to the face. His eyes were small and dark, but they burned with an inner fire that might have been cunning or might have been simple bloodthirstiness. Here was a man, McCarter had time to think, who would rip out your tongue as soon as speak to you, who employed his elaborately overpolite manor to conceal his animal nature. His forearms, exposed below the rolled-up cuffs of his fatigue blouse, were enormous and well-defined. His hands were massive, the sort of ham-size mitts that could crack walnuts—or skulls. The Strong Man, indeed.

El Hombre Fuerte spoke a word in Spanish. The rifle butt came out of nowhere and cracked McCarter in the temple. The flash of pain and light brought darkness.

CHAPTER ELEVEN

Suburban Chicago

When Fred Fleisser realized he was again awake, he opened his eyes to find himself on his back with his hands strapped together. His whole body hurt like hell. With his eyes closed, he tried to wiggle his toes and fingers, flex his muscles as best he could. He didn't think anything was too badly busted up. That car had hit him hard. He remembered seeing the grille in the last instant, and the face of the guy behind the wheel. Fleisser figured he was lucky he hadn't bought it right there. Sucking in a deep breath, he let it out again. No real pain. His ribs didn't seem to be broken, but damn, did he hurt.

He was aware that he was being bounced around pretty good. He realized he was in the rear cargo area of a truck, obviously the Suburban he and his men had been pursuing. Damn, but they'd taken him by surprise with that storefront trick! He'd been certain they were losing it when the driver crashed through that window. He'd never anticipated the truck flying out at him like that, and neither had his drivers. They'd scattered, and lost it, and the only thing he could think to do was get them all out there and shooting. It should have been obvious that they were dealing with people who knew what end of the gun was what. They'd had him for lunch. He'd never seen it coming, and the boys definitely hadn't, either. Now they were dead or down, and he was...

He was a prisoner. He wasn't just a prisoner, he was the prisoner of violent terrorists or *mafioso* or something! He turned pale with fear when he imagined the types of horrors that might await him at the hands of such people. God, the things he'd heard they did to people...

"Oh, hey, you're awake," said the slim guy kneeling over the back seat. He sounded cheerful, which for some reason disturbed Fleisser all the more. The gun in his hand was a Beretta 93-R machine pistol. Fleisser couldn't imagine what manner of criminal would carry a piece like that. A variety of scenarios, ranging from jihadist sleeper agents to Colombian drug cartel killers, ran though this head. He was way past whatever scenario Reginald Butler had tried to describe on the phone.

"Pistol whip him if you have to," a deeper voice said from up front.

"Ironman, come on," said the slim guy. "I'm sure there's no need for that."

"Need, hell," the one called Ironman shot back. "Our truck is all shot up, I've got no side mirror, Hal is going to chew me out but good for those windows, and now we're being chased by the police."

That was when Fleisser realized he could hear sirens. It explained the rough ride, too. "Ironman," who was driving, was apparently piloting them at a rapid pace away from the cops. The cops! That meant they were coming after these guys. Maybe Fleisser could hope for rescue.

"Don't get your hopes up," said the gray-haired Hispanic man who came to lean over the back seat with his partner. "Gadgets, I agree with Ironman. Pistol-whip him."

"I will not, Pol." Schwarz made a production of sounding offended. "What sort of brute do you take me for?"

"Police," Lyons said sternly. "We are being chased by police. Could you two stop screwing around back there and find out what he knows?"

"I'm afraid my grumpy friend has some very valid points," Schwarz said. "Look, pal, we're all happy you weren't splashed all over that Buick back there, but the fact is, you tried to kill us, and, well, we don't have a lot of time, as you can probably tell." He grew suddenly stern. "That's why I'm going to shoot you in the head if you don't tell us who hired you."

Fleisser saw no reason to lie. Apart from the fact that he didn't want to eat a bullet, these were dangerous terrorists. They'd either be caught or they wouldn't, but he needed to buy time.

"Reginald Butler," Fleisser admitted.

"Let's be clear on that," Schwarz said. "Reginald Butler, the billionaire? Reginald Butler, the telecommunications mogul? *That* Reginald Butler?"

"Yeah," Fleisser said. "He said he wanted to send a message. Said you boys had been harassing his people, said it was an under-the-table business thing. Figured if you could play hardball, he could, too."

"He did, did he?" Pol said.

"Pull over!" an electronically amplified voice said from behind them. "This is the Illinois State Police! Pull over right now!"

"That," Schwarz muttered, "is not good."

"Look, I know where it's at," Fleisser said.

"Who are you, by the way?" Schwarz turned back to Fred Fleisser, almost as an afterthought.

"Fred Fleisser, Black Bag Security," Fleisser said. "Look, I'm a combat veteran. I've been there, man. I've done that. I'm a United States combat veteran. I—"

"Uh, yeah, whatever." Schwarz waved his free hand dismissively. "You can shut up now. We'll turn you over to the police and you can explain it all to them."

"You think they'll buy the Butler thing?" Blancanales asked.

"No, but it won't matter," Lyons said from the driver's seat. The Suburban began to lose speed. "Who do you think has them on our tail in the first place?"

"You think Butler's pressuring somebody to come down on us?" Schwarz asked.

"Of course," Lyons said. "Why else would the state troopers be chasing us? If it was just the disturbance of the peace, the locals would have been called, and they know to cooperate. Presumably Stony Man has pulled all those strings before the fact. No, this has big money written all over it. Butler has called in whatever favors he's owed by those with some pull, and they've got the cops out after us. That's why I didn't stop when they came up behind us. I wanted to get what we could out of the Greatest American Hero here before they hauled him off."

"And us," Schwarz said.

"And us," Lyons nodded.

"Hauled me off?" Fleisser sputtered. "But…you're criminals! Terrorists! I was trying to stop you!"

"We—" Schwarz smiled down at him "—are the good guys. You're going to prison, Fred."

CARL LYONS SAT in the interrogation room, so very much like so many other rooms used for the same purpose in police stationhouses across the country. He sat, and he seethed. Blancanales and Gadgets sat with him. Blancanales had his eyes closed and was leaning back in his chair as if he were sleeping. Schwarz was staring off into space, probably building clocks in his mind, or something. Lyons, who was neither particularly calm nor particularly patient, was seriously thinking of picking up his uncomfortable wooden chair and hurling it through the mirror that separated the interrogation room from what he knew would be the observation room beyond. They had no reason to believe anyone was watching—nobody had asked them any questions beyond the obvious—but it would have satisfied Lyons nonetheless.

They were wasting valuable time. There was no telling where the lead they had been trying to follow might take them, or how cold it might be going while they sat and twiddled their thumbs in this room. And all because it never failed, no matter how many times he had seen it play out: the feudal lords of these little bureaucratic fiefdoms never got tired of throwing their weight around, playing the big fish in their respective small ponds. He was mixing his metaphors as he worked himself into a fit over it, and he didn't care. Every minute they wasted was one that the WWUP and EAF coalition, and whichever other nutjob tangoes and agitators might be joining them, could be using to squirrel away more explosives.

If they couldn't get to the Forest woman, if her place had already been tossed or some critical clue to the planned hit had since gone missing, they were back where they started. The state troopers had surrounded them and, rather than engage in a gun battle with the good guys, Able Team had gone quietly. They'd been taken, not to a state trooper facility, but to this local stationhouse. Lyons suspected that somebody in power wanted an audience, and he was not disappointed. They were all alike; when someone like that got the chance to make others toe the line, it was impossible to resist the urge to make a speech about it.

The door to the room opened. Lyons had to restrain himself from charging forward as soon as the first crack of outside light could be seen. The man who walked in was short, round, and balding, with wire-rimmed spectacles perched on the bridge of his nose. He carried himself like a man who thought a lot of the power he possessed. In other words, he waddled like a pompous stuffed shirt. Lyons immediately disliked him and again stopped himself from doing something he knew he would regret. As he'd told the others, he was already going to get an earful from Brognola. There was no point in making it worse.

"Gentlemen," the newcomer said with obvious disdain. "I'm Marlon Kincaid."

"The state legislator?" Blancanales asked, opening his eyes and bringing his chair back down on all four feet. How he managed to keep all those details in his head was a mystery to Lyons, but it was obvious that being recognized soothed Kincaid's ego somewhat. He preened before their eyes, straightening himself and tugging at the lapels of the dark blue pinstriped suit he wore with a conservative red tie.

"Yes," he said, clearly starting what was probably a much-practiced diatribe. "You've caused considerable trouble. I've been speaking with the attorney general's office about this issue and—"

"Save it, you little turd," Lyons said.

Kincaid looked as if he'd been slapped. "Now, see here," he started.

"No," Lyons said, standing to grab Kincaid by the front of his suit and slam him down in the chair he'd just vacated. "*You* see here. We are representatives of the Justice Department, you self-important little troll. We're federal officers following a federal case, and we're now being impeded in its pursuit because you and your cronies have to get in on the act! When will these territorial pissing matches be less important to you than national security?"

"Let go of me right now!" Kincaid squealed. "I will see to it that you—"

The phone in Kincaid's jacket pocket began to ring.

"You won't see to anything," Lyons said, releasing him and stepping away. "That is what I've been waiting for. Answer your phone, Mr. State Legislator Kincaid."

"What?"

"Answer it!" Lyons took a threatening step forward.

"Kincaid here!" The man couldn't get the phone open fast enough. He listened, his expression angry at first. Then he grew very, very pale. "Yes, of course," he said. "Yes, Mr. Brognola, I understand. Oh, of course, Justice will have full cooperation from the State of Illinois. Yes, Mr. Brognola. Yes. Yes, Mr. Brognola. Of course. You…you do? Well, okay." He turned rather sheepishly to Lyons. "Are you Carl?"

"Yeah."

"He wants to speak to you."

Lyons took the offered phone and put it to his ear. Brognola's pained voice was unmistakable.

"Carl," he said, "while I understand the position you are in, and while the mission is of course critical, you would not believe the phone calls I have been getting. It has taken me longer than you can imagine to straighten these out."

"Oh, I can imagine," Lyons said. "I used to work with people like this all day, remember?"

"Never mind that," Brognola said. "This is an open line."

"I got you," Lyons said. "We're free to go?"

"Yes," Brognola confirmed. "I've talked to the appropriate people. They know not to interfere. You'll be interested to know that I've followed the trail back. The state troopers were called in by a few very important persons in the state, among them the attorney general's office, and of course State Legislator Kincaid there."

"By whom?"

"By Richard Cross, if you can believe it."

"Harrington's political bosom buddy?" Lyons asked. "The guy who's going to be her veep?"

"None other," Brognola said.

"So he's dirty somehow," Lyons said.

"Possibly. We're looking into it."

"All right," Lyons said. "We're rolling."

He hung up and handed the phone back to a shaken Kincaid. "I suggest," he said, "that you get the hell out of my way."

The team's equipment was returned to them by an Officer Wright, who walked with them as they left the station. "Hey," he said as they headed for the glass doors fronting the stationhouse, "I just wanted to tell you, I heard what you said. I agree with you. We spend too much time worrying about territory and not enough actually getting things done. I gotta say it was refreshing to see somebody like that Kincaid rocked on his heels." He stuck out his hand.

Lyons looked down and then at the officer. He grinned.

"Hell," he said, shuffling his heavy gear around and taking the offered handshake. "Thanks."

"No problem," Officer Wright said.

The bullet that killed him hit him between the eyes, knocking him down like a bowling pin. Lyons, shocked despite all he'd seen and done, hesitated for the briefest fraction of a second before his teammates tackled him. The three men hit the steps in front of the stationhouse. Automatic gunfire strafed the front of the building. The shooters were spraying automatic weapons from the side windows of a Chrysler sedan passing slowly by. As the shots echoed and the gunmen paused to reload, the sedan started to speed up and move off.

Lyons looked back at the dead cop, then at the shooters, and snarled in anger.

He jacked back the cocking lever on the massive Daewoo shotgun he carried, putting a round in the chamber. Running as fast as his big legs could pump, he raced for the Chrysler. The driver or one of his passengers saw what was going on and the Chrysler started to accelerate. Lyons, determined not to let them get away, leveled the Daewoo at waist level and held back the trigger. The shotgun sprayed double-aught buck across the lower portion of the Chrysler, shredding its tires like tissue paper and peppering the body with holes.

The Chrysler rolled to a slow stop. The doors flew open and the men inside, three in all, leaped out. One man in the rear seat stayed where he was, slumped against his door. Apparently, Lyons's fire had penetrated the body of the vehicle, in his case; he was dead or at least out of the fight.

"Back, back, back!" Lyons ordered. Schwarz and Blancanales scrambled, bringing up their weapons, backing up into the police station to take the only cover available. The shooters, insanely, closed in instead of running, intent on their targets. There was no doubt they were gunning for Able Team.

They were shouting to each other in Russian.

"Great," Schwarz said. "More Russian mercenaries."

"Looks like it," Lyons said, swapping box magazines in the shotgun. Gunfire from the submachine guns the Russians carried hammered away at the building's facade and shattered the safety glass of the doors.

"I…am in…a very bad mood," Lyons said through gritted teeth.

"Uh-oh," Schwarz said.

"Cover me," Lyons said, holding his automatic shotgun against his chest.

"Ironman," Schwarz began.

"Don't you 'Ironman' me, Gadgets!" Lyons said angrily. "I said cover me!"

"You got it," Schwarz said, Blancanales nodding.

"Three…" Lyons counted down. "Two…one…now!"

Blancanales and Schwarz cut loose with their weapons. Under the aegis of their fire, Lyons surged forward, once more holding down the trigger of his shotgun, riding out the recoil as the weapon pumped shell after shell at the Russians. He chopped the knees out from under the first man and then blasted him in the chest. Still moving, he shot the second man in the face. The third man was starting to bring up his weapon to cover Lyons, so the big ex-L.A. cop brought the butt of the shotgun up and around and smashed the Russian across the jaw.

The gunner's Uzi hit the pavement and discharged, spraying into the sidewalk and raising a cloud of debris.

The ricochets came dangerously close but did not manage to strike anyone or anything that Lyons could see. He swung the shotgun around once more, bringing the weapon on target, the muzzle black and huge as it pointed at the Russian's face.

"Hold it right there," Lyons said through clenched teeth.

"I surrender," the man said, his English heavily accented, his Russian heritage obvious.

"Who are you working for?"

"I will not tell you," the Russian said. Lyons could see that one of the dead men nearby had a WTS unit on his belt.

"We already know you've got something going with Reginald Butler," Lyons said, fishing for information. "You might as well tell us."

"You know nothing." The Russian laughed. "I am one of many. You may kill me, but others will take my place."

"Why don't we find out?" Lyons said angrily.

"You will die," the Russian said. "Probably now."

The engine noise tipped them off. A second Chrysler, identical to the first, was roaring down the road in front of the stationhouse, weaving in and out of traffic, two men hanging out the rear windows. The gunners held pistols and began shooting, one from each side, as the Chrysler neared.

Blancanales and Schwarz took evasive action, shooting as they backed away. Lyons looked down at the Russian, who smirked. Then he went for something hidden under the polo shirt he wore.

Lyons pulled the trigger, ending the grinning Russian's life with a single 12-gauge shell. He looked up to see Schwarz and Blancanales riddling the approaching Chrysler with bullet holes, flattening the tires and spiderwebbing the windshield before causing the vehicle to smash into a parked van across the street. The two Stony Man fighters moved in, their weapons at the ready, and the gunshots that cracked across the space between the van and Lyons were all the former cop needed to hear. Blancanales and Schwarz executed their would-be assassins. The Hispanic commando then stood guard, the CAR-15 at the ready, as Schwarz checked the second Chrysler.

Police officers were streaming out of the building now, first surrounding Lyons to make sure he was not injured, then swarming over the dead hit team members, and finally moving out across the street. Traffic was beginning to back up, and a couple of the officers started directing it around to alternate routes. Schwarz walked back across the street, changing 20-round magazines in his Beretta as he went.

"At this rate," he said, "we're going to need to resupply on ammo. Something about you brings out the best in people, doesn't it, Ironman?"

Lyons began to laugh.

"I don't get it," Schwarz said. "What's so funny?"

"I was just looking around at this mess," Lyons said, loading another fresh magazine into his well-used shotgun.

"Yeah, and?"

"Hal's really going to get some phone calls now."

CHAPTER TWELVE

The cells beneath the main building of the Strong Man's compound had been dug from the earth and faced with wood. The doors were heavy planks held in place by external bars. It was a low-tech prison, but an effective one. There were three small cells, with two men in each one: McCarter and Manning were in one, Encizo and Javier the next and Hawkins and James in the last. Their weapons had been taken and they had all been stunned or gun-butted into unconsciousness, awaking with throbbing heads and sore bodies in the dark, damp cells.

Their earbuds had not been taken, however; apparently the Strong Man's people had not been thorough enough to recognize the tiny pieces of technology. The communicators could not do anything for them at this point, but it was something. Their satellite phones had likewise not been taken, probably because the Strong Man's men thought they were ordinary cell phones. Still, the point was the same: whom would they call? It was not as if the Farm would HALO drop in a rescue. By the time such a rescue could be fielded, it would all long since be over. No, there was no point in calling anyone. Frankly, Phoenix Force was right where McCarter wanted it to be…apart from some unpleasant preliminaries, which they were about to go through.

Outside the cells, there was a simple rough wooden plank set on sawhorses. Next to this, a crate with a car battery and a pair of jumper cables sat ominously. It was an old technique, but a crude and effective one. And of course, McCarter reflected, making them sit here and stare at the thing was a psychological tactic meant to start breaking them before the first clamp struck flesh. He was not looking forward to that part.

"All right, mates," he said quietly. There was the possibility they were being recorded or otherwise listened in on, but he did not think the setup here was quite that advanced. "We're going to be in for it. There's no way around it. Any man will break, given enough pressure, and nobody's asking you to play hero. Just remember that while they're working on us, the break we want will come. Let that sustain you. That, and the sure and present knowledge that we're going to wreak bloody hell on them once we have the chance."

It wasn't much of a pep talk, but it would have to do. There was little else facing them. There were few other options. Each man knew, likewise, that calling for help would do them little good, except to amuse their captors. Let the Strong Man's men continue to think that the phones were useless, ordinary phones, in an area where service for the devices was nonexistent.

Jiminez came swaggering in not long after. He was accompanied by two soldiers and another man about his height and build, but younger and far less weathered. This man has a scar across his face and a wild-eyed look that McCarter thought did not bode well.

"You are back among the living," Jiminez said. "That is good. I trust there was no permanent damage done to you during your capture? We wish you healthy and strong, after all." He laughed, and the soldiers with him laughed artificially, as if they were long used to parroting the Strong Man's amusement when prompted.

"Who's your girlfriend, mate?" McCarter asked. He did it deliberately, knowing there would be consequences. Calling attention to himself was one way to keep their captors focused on him, rather than the other members of his team. If anyone had to get hooked up to the juice, he'd rather it was him, and if they were all in for a session with the cables, he wanted to go first. Better to get it out of the way and set a reasonably good example for the others, he tried to persuade himself. In truth he did not consider himself a particularly "tough" guy, at least by the standards of the SAS. He was merely average as far as he knew. The enemy did not need to know that, though.

"This," Jiminez said, his eyes narrowing, "is Hector. Hector is one of my most trusted men."

So this, McCarter decided, looking the man over, was Socaras. Stony Man's briefing files had made mention of the man. Little was known about him, other than basic statistics. The Farm had little enough to go on in terms of a psychological profile, for example. Well, from the eager look on his face, it seemed McCarter would be able to add "sadist" to that data. He only hoped that before it was over he could also recommend that the file on Hector Socaras be closed, permanently.

Socaras wore a 1911 pistol in a flap holster on his belt. He also had a machete on his hip, which looked oddly familiar. McCarter realized that this was Javier's machete, apparently taken from him after his capture. It had to be a good blade, indeed, for Socaras to bother with it. Then again, maybe the man just enjoyed stealing things. Who could say?

"I will leave you in Hector's capable hands," Jiminez said. "I have business to attend to. Good day, gentlemen." He tipped his cap with a flourish and then strode out of the room. One of the soldiers went with him, while the second, a fresh-faced youngster barely out of his teens, stayed behind. The young guard carried a Kalashnikov that Mc-Carter eyed covetously. He wanted that weapon. He didn't need to look at Javier to know that the man was himself especially interested in the machete now on Socaras's belt. Javier struck McCarter as a machete man at heart, from what he'd seen of the fellow. Well, he hoped Javier would get his chance.

Two more guards appeared, also relatively young, also armed with AK-47s. That was the beauty of Central America and points south, McCarter thought. You were never far away from one of the bloody things. The rifle was sloppy and cheaply made, but it worked and kept working under conditions that would destroy more modern weapons. It was also simple enough to be user-friendly to a wide array of conscripts, terrorists and military units, ranging from Russian special forces to the most illiterate of Third World troops and underage African child-soldiers.

Socaras licked his lips hungrily. "Let us start with you," he said, pointing to McCarter. "You, who have such a big mouth. Come, let us get you comfortable." He cackled, and McCarter's ears grated with the sound. When he pointed, the two new guards moved forward. They unlocked the wooden door facing McCarter's cell, the small window of which he had been using to watch what was going on and communicate with those outside. Securing it again behind them, they dragged the Briton out to Socaras. The sawhorse and plank arrangement boasted no straps that he could see. When Socaras pulled on a pair of heavy rubber gloves and handed two more pairs to the guards, McCarter understood. They pulled on the gloves as if they'd done this before, which they probably had.

"Hold him," Socaras said.

The two guards pulled McCarter to the plank and held him by the arms. Socaras took the jumper cables and slapped the two clamps together, raising sparks. "This is going to be unpleasant," he said. "You can make it less so by answering all of my questions. I will not lie to you. I intend to make you hurt, no matter what you say to me. But you can stop it from being very much worse by answering truthfully and quickly."

"Hell, mate, I'll tell you what you want to know. You don't have to spark me up."

"Do I not? Good." Socaras laughed. He placed the clamps down for a moment and slowly opened McCarter's BDU shirt. He whistled in surprise when he found the CRKT knife on its paracord harness.

"The men missed this when searching you?" He looked genuinely surprised. "I shall have to find those responsible and discipline them." He examined the fixed blade with its cord-wrapped handle. "I give you full credit for doing nothing stupid while this was in your possession." He placed the knife on the plank after pulling one end of the harness loose. "It is a fine blade. I believe I shall take it."

"You're making yourself quite a collection there," McCarter said.

"I suppose I am." He picked up the clamps then, touching them to McCarter's bare chest.

The jolt traveled through his body. He closed his mind to the pain, letting it wash over him.

"Good," Socaras was saying. "You are not weak. You do not scream and cry and beg the second the electricity touches you. That is good."

"Well, I'm here to impress you, mate," McCarter said. "If you go to bed tonight telling yourself you met one tough as nails Briton, my work here is done."

Socaras did not respond to that. He put the clamps to McCarter's flesh again, watching his back arch as the pain hit him.

"You may cry out," Socaras said. "There is no shame in it."

"No," McCarter said, breathing heavily. "I don't suppose there is."

Socaras pressed the clamps against McCarter's body once more. This time he did scream, as the Central American torturer left the clamps in place just waiting for a reaction. McCarter roared in agony, quite content to lose himself in the maelstrom of agony that coursed through him.

"Now, we understand each other," Socaras said. "We understand the dimensions of pain that I can bring to you. This is good, yes? It is good to understand. It is good to know. Now you can make decisions with the full knowledge of what awaits you."

"Decisions…mate?" McCarter breathed.

"Yes, decisions," Socaras said. "I want to know who you are. I want to know who you work for. Are you Americans?"

"All day long, mate," McCarter said. "Born and raised in the deepest South, y'all. Shop at the Wally World and watch professional wrestling on the tube while drinking Budweiser, that's me."

Socaras rewarded McCarter's attempt at humor with another long jolt of electricity. "Please," he said, sounding disappointed. "I wish real answers, not more jokes. Who are you working for?"

"The bloody Purba Banglars," McCarter said. "We're card-carrying members. Proletarian Party of East Bengal, that's us."

Socaras frowned. "Are you CIA?"

"Sure, mate," McCarter said. "NSA, too. And also the FBI. And the IRS. Did you file this year?"

"Enough!" Socaras said, growing angry. He touched the clamps to McCarter and left them there, watching the Briton struggle. "You will tell me what I wish to know or I will bring you pain, nothing but pain, and then I will kill you! Your last moments will be begging me to let you die!"

"I will talk!" Javier said. "Please! I will tell you! Do not hurt him any more. I will tell you everything!"

Socaras turned to eye Javier, looking at him curiously. "You will, will you? You are not unknown to me."

Javier said nothing.

"Yes, we are well aware that you have been watching us." Socaras nodded. "Do you think there is nothing El Hombre Fuerte does not know? We allowed you to monitor us because it did us no harm for you to think we were reasonably secure. What other reason could there be to let you persist in your futile efforts? As long as you believed you knew our affairs, no action would be taken. And now we know that the time for looking is over, and the time for action is here. That is good, for our leader has plans of his own, and the time is ripe for them to move forward."

"Plans?" McCarter said weakly.

Socaras turned back to him. "Oh, yes. But of course that is why you are here, is it not?" He frowned again. "You will tell me what you know. We are done with the pointless questioning."

"He does not know anything," Javier lied. "He is just playing brave so you won't question the rest of us. I...I cannot watch this any longer. I will tell you. Strap me to your board if you must, to see that I am telling the truth. I will talk."

Socaras looked at Javier as if he did not quite believe him, but the temptation was more than he could resist. He motioned for the third guard to take Javier from his cell, then looked down at McCarter and spoke to one of the two holding the Briton down.

"Help him." He jerked his chin to the guard taking Javier from the cell. "This one is not likely to resist."

McCarter lay limply on the board, sweat covering his body. He managed to look at Socaras with glazed eyes. Socaras laughed. "No, not likely at all."

The guard who released McCarter took a step away. For a moment, only one of the Briton's arms was held. The guard who remained moved to place one of his hands on McCarter's free arm, to take over for his missing partner.

That fraction of a second was all the former SAS commando needed.

McCarter's hand shot out with the speed of a rattler. He snatched up the CRKT knife on the plank, placed the sheath in his teeth and ripped the blade free. In the same motion, he slashed the blade across the neck of the man holding his other arm. The guard managed a wet, strangled cry and went down, his hands clutching at the deadly wound.

Javier, in the process of being removed from his cell,

struck a vicious blow with one foot, planting it in the groin of the lead guard. He snatched the man's Kalashnikov and, as the young guard who remained tried to bring his weapon to bear, he buttstroked the kid in the face. Then he reversed the rifle and slammed it down on the face of the guard he'd kicked.

Socaras clawed at the flap holster on his belt. McCarter surged forward and slammed into the man with his shoulder, knocking him into Javier across the small space of the interrogation chamber. Javier, whooping in triumph, snatched the handle of his machete and drew the blade from the sheath on Socaras's belt.

The barrel of the .45 came up.

The blade of the machete came down.

Socaras screamed, an inhuman sound, as the blade of the machete cut deeply into his arm, all the way to the bone. The .45 fell from suddenly nerveless fingers. McCarter snatched it up with his free hand, covering the fallen guards. Javier drew the blade of the machete across Socaras's throat.

The Central American looked up and grinned his uneven grin again. "There. Was that adequate?"

"More than sufficient, mate," McCarter said.

"We should make our way out of here now." Javier nodded. "It may be necessary to kill quite a few of them as we go."

"Somehow, mate," McCarter said wearily, picking up one of the Kalashnikovs his captors had set aside while holding him, "I think I'll be able to bring myself to do it."

"The second base, the one near the village," Javier said. "This is the likely location of the missiles."

"Agreed," McCarter said. He looked to the members of Phoenix Force. "We'll equip as we go. Let's move."

Javier took his captured Kalashnikov and smashed its wooden butt into the padlocks on the other cells, freeing the rest of Phoenix Force. He seemed to take a grim satisfaction in his work.

"There was a key," Encizo said. "I think one of those guys has it." He gestured to one of the fallen guards.

"This way is more fun," Javier said.

McCarter searched Socaras's body and found a WTS unit, coded and useless. He also found several magazines for the 1911, which he appropriated. He took a moment to wipe clean the blade of the CRKT knife that had helped secure their freedom, resheathed it and pocketed it.

They took a set of rough plank steps up the corridor that had been dug as part of this underground chamber. The temperature grew steadily warmer as they moved up. There was something to be said, McCarter reflected, for having your electrical shock torture take place below ground level, where things stayed cooler.

They moved quietly into the ground level of the Strong Man's main building. A lone guard sat at a desk in a little anteroom off the entrance to the stairs. He was asleep with his feet up on the desk. Javier put his finger to his lips, then took his Kalashnikov and slammed the butt into the man's head. He folded and did not move.

"Y'all are getting entirely too much use out of that gun butt," Hawkins drawled with a smile.

"There is no such thing," Javier replied, smiling.

"Site assessment," McCarter directed. The men of Phoenix Force, all business again, moved silently from the room, threading their way through the building. McCarter thought he could hear, as the Phoenix Force commandos spread out, the sounds of other guards being taken down.

They would be well equipped by the time they left, though he hoped they could get their hands on some of the heavier weapons. A few grenade launchers to replace the ones taken with their Tavors would be nice. Perhaps the LAW Javier had mentioned. They searched the building fairly thoroughly, but no evidence of their missing weapons was uncovered. That was unfortunate. He would miss that handy little Tavor.

Still, the .45 now in his belt and the Kalashnikov in his hands were old friends. The equipment did not matter; it was the men using it that made all the difference.

They swept the building, neutralizing the guards in residence. McCarter halted them near the front entrance.

"It occurs to me, mates," he said, "that getting out of here may be tricky. At least, it would be if we were trying to elude those still in the camp. However…"

"David," James said, "are you thinking what I think you're thinking?"

"We take the camp." McCarter nodded. "We take it all."

"Let's do it," Encizo said.

Using their earbud transceivers to coordinate—Javier did not have one, but he simply stuck with Encizo and followed along—they broke up and spread out, moving like wraiths among the camp. Each man moved into a key position. A watchtower here, a tent full of fuel drums there, the entrance to a tent full of sleeping soldiers of El Hombre Fuerte over there…it was not hard to identify the camp's vulnerable points. Presumably the Strong Man himself was not in residence; the business to which he'd referred was probably going on at the second camp. They would catch up with him soon enough.

"Now," McCarter said out loud.

Kalashnikov fire ripped the night. The 7.62 mm rounds carved through the Strong Man's guards, some of them walking the perimeter, others moving around the camp, still others as they slept. The men of Phoenix Force were merciless, knowing that each and every one of the Strong Man's soldiers was a terrorist, an enemy combatant, who was facilitating a major threat to United States security.

When the last of the green steel casings hit the packed earth of the compound, McCarter, looking back on it, was surprised by just how easily accomplished it had been. While the Strong Man's forces had contingency plans in place for an attack, it would seem they had no such plans in readiness for escaped prisoners. Destroyed from within, the camp had folded easily. The grip of fear in which the Strong Man held those in the region was just possibly more about psychological intimidation than physical reality. If they were lucky, this would be true when they reached the second camp.

"Calvin here," James reported in. "I have secured a pair of four-wheel drive trucks near the front entrance. Old jeeps, ugly but functional."

"Gents," McCarter said, "we have our ride. Rafe, ask Javier if he wants to come along."

"I don't think he'd have it any other way," Encizo responded.

"Then let's get going, mates," McCarter said. "We've still a long row to hoe."

CHAPTER THIRTEEN

Suburban Chicago

Melody Forest's home did indeed look normal enough from the outside. Schwarz took a look through one of the living-room windows and saw furniture in place, with nothing out of the ordinary. Blancanales rang the bell several times and then tried knocking. There was no answer.

"Let me take care of that." Lyons, with the Daewoo shouldered, started to haul the weapon into position.

"No, no," Schwarz said. "Hal's got enough headaches." He removed a small pick gun and retention tool from his pocket. "Let's finesse this."

Lyons moved back while his teammate went to work on the lock and popped it only moments later.

"Open, says me," he quipped.

Weapons ready, they entered the home and spread out, each taking a different direction.

"Guys," Blancanales said. "Bedroom. I've got a body."

"The living room may be fine," Schwarz said, "but the rest of the rooms have been trashed. Somebody was here, looking for information. There's a second bedroom that's been converted into an office. The computer's been wrecked."

"She was the coordinator," Lyons said, joining Gadgets

in the bedroom. The woman lying on the bed matched the file photos the Farm had uploaded to Able Team's secure phones. Her eyes were open and staring at nothing. "Her computer would have all the details the terrorists would need. We've got to assume they've cooked up plenty for that rally."

"Now what?" Schwarz asked.

"Call the Farm," Lyons said. "Inform them of what's happened here. And find out where we can find Marcia Harrington."

"Harrington herself?" Schwarz asked.

"Yeah." Lyons nodded. "I don't know about you guys, but I'm sick and tired of dicking around. Let's go to the source. If Harrington's the target, we'll just flat out tell her she is. Maybe she can shed some light on all this. We've confirmed that the rally is compromised. That's what we were trying to do, wasn't it? Well, it's all downhill from here, as far as I'm concerned."

It did not take Schwarz long to get the name and address of the hotel where Harrington was supposed to be staying. It was right in the area.

"She's local," he concluded, closing the phone. "But why would she be here already if the rally's not until the end of the month?"

"For the same reason that our boys were moving their bombs and other toys when they were, and not later," Lyons said. "Isn't it obvious? The rally's been moved up and no-body's telling us when. I'm guessing it's a security mea-sure, intended to keep Harrington and especially the visiting dignitaries safe. It's not unusual. The Man often doesn't reveal his schedule until the last minute, to prevent assassins from planning something out ahead of time. I'm betting that's why Melody Forest was targeted and murdered. She or her computer had the confidential date and time of the rally, the *real* date and time."

"You're good at this, Carl," Schwarz said, deadpan. "You should have been a detective."

Lyons gave him the evil eye.

They took the bullet-riddled Suburban to the hotel, parking it in an alley behind the hotel where it hopefully would not attract attention. Lyons had reluctantly left his Daewoo secured in the locker in the back of the truck, and Blancanales had done the same with his CAR-15. They could not meet the senator in her hotel, or even walk through the lobby, carrying such weapons. Lyons didn't like it one bit, with all the action they'd seen on this outing, but there was nothing to be done about it.

"Nice place," he commented. The lobby had polished marble floors and the front desk looked about a mile long.

"Your tax dollars at work," Schwarz joked.

"Actually I think something like this would be paid for out of contributions to the senator's campaign fund," Blancanales put in quite reasonably.

"You used to be fun, Pol," Schwarz said sourly.

They passed the elevators and took the stairs. Harrington's room was on the seventh floor. For security reasons, her stay at the hotel was strictly confidential, though of course the Farm was able to ferret out her itinerary and gain cooperation from her staff. Lyons reflected that Brognola's government connections were getting quite a workout.

Lyons was easing open the door to the seventh floor when he heard hushed voices in the corridor beyond. He stopped with the door open only a crack, peering through.

Several men, wearing the white shirts and black slacks

of hotel employees, were standing outside the door to room 703, which they'd been told was Harrington's room.

They held pistols and submachineguns in their hands. One of them knocked on the door. A muffled voice from inside answered.

"Room service, ma'am," said the man who'd knocked. His Russian accent was thick.

Lyons turned back to his teammates, raised his fingers to count off the number of men they faced and pointed back toward the door. He drew his Colt Python. Blancanales and Schwarz drew their Berettas.

Much as Lyons didn't want to engage in a gun battle in a hotel hallway, where a stray bullet could penetrate a wall and go into another room, any room, there was no choice. This was clearly a hit team, just like the men at the police station.

The only way to put them off their stride was to brazen it out, take the initiative.

Lyons pushed the fire door open and stepped into the hallway.

One of the assassins looked up. *"Nyet!"* he yelled.

More Russians.

Lyons raised his massive Colt Python and double-actioned a single .357 Magnum round in the man's head. The rest of the hit team was raising their weapons. Lyons had time to put a second bullet into the closest man, then a third.

War broke out in the hall.

Automatic gunfire ripped the air. One of the assassins hosed the corridor with his micro-Uzi, sending Schwarz and Blancanales back behind the fire door of the stairwell. Sparks flew off the metal surface of the doorway. Lyons, with nowhere to go, threw himself under the hail of fire, landing on the carpeted floor at the feet of the gunman.

He glanced down.

Lyons pumped a .357 Magnum slug up through his jaw and into his brain.

He fired into the remaining assassins. On the first empty click from the Python, he let it fall to the carpeted floor and snatched up the fallen H&K MP-5 K one of the now dead hitters had carried. He pulled the trigger and burned the last of the magazine into the two men who were still moving. They danced briefly and then toppled to the carpet.

"Gadgets, Blancanales, go, go," he said, unable to hear his own words for the temporary ringing in his ears. The two Able Team commandos came up behind him, flanking the door to room 703.

Blancanales rapped on the door with his fist. "Senator Harrington?" he asked quietly. "United States Justice Department, ma'am. We've just killed several men who were here to hurt you. Could you let us in, please?"

"I've called the police," said a woman's voice from inside.

"That's good, ma'am," Blancanales said reassuringly. "We would have asked you to do that ourselves."

Lyons gave him a look. He wasn't eager to interface with any local authorities at the moment, though everything should be squared away.

"How do I know you're not with them? The killers?" the woman asked.

"Because, ma'am, we'd have kicked in the door and shot you to death by now," Blancanales said calmly.

There was the sound of an interior bolt being moved. Then none other than Senator Marcia Harrington opened the door. "Come in, gentlemen," she said.

"Hermann, Rosario, check the adjacent rooms, and one of you talk to the front desk. Make sure everyone is on the same page when the cops get here. Call an ambulance if needed. I want to make sure nobody in any of these rooms nearby, or on the floors above and below, caught a stray bullet."

"That's admirable of you, sir," Harrington said.

"Call me Carl," Lyons said. He waved his Justice Department credentials at her before replacing them in his pocket. "As I said, we're with the Justice Department, ma'am. These men are assassins. We're not exactly sure why, but we believe them to be part of a plot to disrupt and possibly terrorize your environmental conference."

"Oh no," Harrington said. She was a distinguished-looking woman in her forties, wearing a tailored pantsuit. Her hair was silver-gray and her eyes bright. She looked for all the world like a senior model, Lyons had to admit. In this world of camera-ready politicians, it should not surprise him, but she seemed earnest enough. Her next question clinched his opinion. "Does this…does this have anything to do with poor Melody? I haven't been able to get in touch with her."

"Your campaign coordinator?" Lyons said. "I'm afraid it does, ma'am. Ms. Forest was killed. She's dead, ma'am."

"Oh no. She was so full of life…wait. Killed, you say? It wasn't an accident?"

"No, ma'am," Lyons said. "I'm afraid she was murdered."

"Oh no," Harrington repeated. "No." She looked down. "Melody…" Then she looked up, and there was steel in her gray eyes. "Did you get the men responsible? The men outside… Did you kill them?"

"We killed the men outside, yes," Lyons said. There

was chatter in his transceiver but he was focused on the senator. "And there's a good chance we got those who murdered Melody. But we don't know for sure. There could be more of them."

"Carl," Schwarz's voice was clear over Lyons's transceiver. "Carl, can you hear me? Carl."

"I'm here, I'm here," Lyons said. Go ahead."

"There *are* more of them. We've got half a dozen men coming up the east stairwell, armed Blancanales spotted them and is following. I'm on the west, covering the opposite side, but I don't see anyone. Looks like Blancanales's got them covered, but he's outnumbered and then some."

"Weapons?" Lyons said.

"What?" Harrington asked, unable to hear the other end of the conversation. Lyons waved her off, placing a finger to his ear. She grasped it then.

"I've got the 93-R and Pol has his pistol," Schwarz said. "Plus he picked up a Beretta 12s subgun from one of the dead Russians."

"Why isn't he telling me this?"

"He can't answer," Schwarz said. "He's still shadowing them."

"All right," Lyons said. "I'm going to take the senator out of here, then contact the…contact Justice to see about a safehouse."

"But I have to go," Harrington said. "I have to be there."

"Be where?" Lyons asked.

"Why, the rally," Harrington answered. "The rally at the McCormick Place."

"When?" Lyons asked, his eyes widening.

"It's this evening," Harrington said. "It was moved up for security. Everyone's been informed."

"The rally is *tonight*?" Lyons said. "Did Melody know about this?"

"Of course she did," Harrington said.

"Come with me, Senator," Lyons said. "We've got to leave. More men are coming, men who most likely mean you harm. Can you use a gun?"

"No, no, I've no experience with them," Harrington said honestly.

"Good enough. Come on now. We need to move. Stay close, do as I tell you when I tell you, and we'll be okay."

"I understand."

BLANCANALES CREPT down the corridor, keeping the corner between him and the approaching hit team. They emerged from the stairwell on the seventh floor, but at the opposite end. Lyons, as he could hear through his earbud, was already moving with Harrington in the opposite direction. The two would not even cross paths. To stop that from happening, however, it was necessary to stop the hit team from pursuing. The logical search pattern was across the floor, hitting Harrington's room to verify whether she was there, then down the opposite stairwell. If they moved fast enough they'd eventually encounter Lyons, and that could not be allowed to happen.

The Hispanic commando was within earshot of the hitters, who were now checking Harrington's room. He slipped his secure phone out of his pocket, hit the quick dial for Schwarz's phone and tapped out a text message *Meet me, opposite side.*

Schwarz made it not a moment too soon. The fire door behind his teammate opened as the shooters were starting to move from Harrington's room, having not found their

target. They did, however, find the bodies left behind by
Able Team's counterattack and were now alerted to the
presence of opposition. It would also be only moments before local law enforcement showed up. They had to stop
the gunners now.

Blancanales nodded to Schwarz and hefted his captured
Beretta 12s. The subgun had an ergonomic foregrip and felt
good in his hands. Schwarz switched the Beretta 93-R he
carried to 3-round burst and nodded back.

The first of the shooters rounded the corner.

"Pazhalusta!" he exclaimed.

Schwarz shot him.

The 3-round burst caught the Russian in the chest and
dropped him. The suppressed burst sounded like hands
clapping in the hallway. The next Russian around the corner, curious, stopped and froze. His eyes grew wide and
he brought up the sawed-off shotgun he carried. Behind
him, the other four gunners were also aiming weapons.

Blancanales cut loose. He pumped neat bursts of 9 mm
bullets from the Beretta 12s, taking a second man and
wounding a third. The others ran for it, one risking a shot
from his own Glock that narrowly missed the Able Team
warrior.

"Go!" Schwarz urged.

They took off down the hallway, gliding heel to toe,
maintaining their shooting stances as well as their mo-
bility. Schwarz finished the wounded one as he passed by,
placing a single bullet in the assassin's head. That left three.

One of the trio of Russian killers kicked open a door and
ducked inside. Blancanales and Schwarz hurried after
them. Schwarz covered the door as his partner dived
through the opening, rolling, avoiding the gunfire that

ripped into the floor near him and creased the air where he would have been had he entered on his feet. He fired the Beretta subgun empty into the first target, let it fall, and ripped his Beretta handgun from its holster. He fired a single time into the second man, putting the bullet between his eyes.

The third man was not alone.

There had been a woman in the bathroom; the room had not been vacant. She was in her early thirties, maybe, pretty, with straight brown hair and delicate features. The Russian held a revolver to her head. His meaning was clear.

The woman, for her part, held very, very still.

"Don't do it," Blancanales said. "Just put the gun down and everything will be all right."

The shooter said something in Russian.

"Hermann, I don't think he speaks English," Blancanales ventured. "Do you? Do you speak English?"

The Russian chattered something more, sweat breaking out on his forehead.

"Hermann," Blancanales said in soothing tones, "I want you to get ready to put a bullet in him. Miss, when I say 'now,' I want you to duck your head to your left. Can you do that for me, miss?"

"Yes..." the woman managed to whisper. The Russian looked at her, obviously recognizing the word, but he looked back to Blancanales with only confusion.

"Okay. Now."

The woman ducked her head to the left.

Schwarz fired a single shot.

The Russian went down, falling backward. His revolver hit the carpet unfired. Blancanales moved in, making sure, covering the fallen assassin, but the bullet had taken him in the forehead diagonally. He would not be getting back up, ever again.

The woman screamed.

"It's all right," Blancanales said. "It's all right. Everything's all right."

He did his best to calm her and looked back at Schwarz. "Better check on Ironman," he said. "I'll make sure things are policed up here, check the bodies."

Schwarz nodded and hurried off.

"Miss, it's all right," Blancanales said again. "I'm a representative of the Justice Department. These men were wanted fugitives." It did not hurt to give a simple cover story. "Nobody's going to hurt you." He picked up the hotel phone and called the front desk, identifying himself as a government agent and then making sure medical personnel were on their way. Then he made sure the woman was settled into one of the chairs in the room. Satisfied, he started going through the pockets of the dead men.

He produced several weapons, including a Makarov pistol and another revolver. Two of the dead men carried inexpensive folding knives. One of them had a WTS unit, which would be code-locked and unreadable by anyone other than the owner bearing the code.

One of the dead men had a wallet full of identification.

The driver's license might or might not be real. It listed the bearer's name as Darren Nikitin. There were several credit cards in the wallet. This was the first enemy they'd managed to bring down who had such potentially useful information.

He removed his secure satellite phone and dialed the speed dial for the Farm. The scrambler indicator was green; he could make his call safely. Barbara Price picked up.

"Yes, Pol?" she asked.

"I've got some credit card numbers I'm going to read you," he said. "They belong to a very important fellow, someone the gang and I met on our visit to the city. We'd like to know where he's been."

"Understood," Price said.

Blancanales read off the numbers. "Can you check those for me?" he asked.

"Having Carmen run them now," Price said. "One moment."

He waited patiently. Then she was back.

"All right, we have a possible hit here," Price said. "Most of the charges are for gas or meals in local eateries," she reported. "One of them, however, is for lodging. At a motel in your area. Hunt called the motel and checked, claiming to be a credit card fraud investigator. We have their room numbers."

She read off the numbers and the address. The card had been used to secure half a dozen rooms at the motel.

"Thanks, Barb," Blancanales said. "I'm out."

"Good luck," she said. Blancanales put the phone away. "Ironman, Gadgets, we've got something."

"Good. You'd better get down here." Lyons sounded surly.

"Down where?"

"Out front."

"Why?"

"The cops are here. We need someone who's good at diplomacy."

"On my way," Blancanales said. Somewhere in the room, a voice began speaking in Russian. Blancanales started, bringing his gun up, but there was no one there. The woman in the room gasped in fear, but he ignored her for a moment.

The voice was coming from the WTS unit. He picked it up and listened, briefly. The code had been entered, but never cleared. It was displayed on the unit's digital readout.

Blancanales smiled.

CHAPTER FOURTEEN

Zone of Dispute, Central America

Javier entered the hut, looking over his shoulder before closing the wooden slat door. He carried a duffel bag over his shoulder. At a rickety wooden table in the center of the room, the men of Phoenix Force sat cleaning and reloading the weapons they had appropriated at the Strong Man's base.

"I was able to find a few more magazines and also 7.62 mm cartridges for the rifles," he said. "Nothing for your .45, I am afraid," he told David McCarter.

"That's all right." McCarter shrugged. "The magazines I have so far should do. We have the AKs, and those will get us there."

"I did get this," Javier said. He removed from the duffel an M-79 grenade launcher and several 40 mm grenades.

"There is also food," Javier said, removing candy bars and cans of soup from the bag. The men were already drinking bottles of water that Javier had earlier obtained.

"Well, then," McCarter said. "What did you learn?"

"It is as I feared," Javier said. "El Hombre Fuerte is much hated in the village, but also much feared. There were those willing to tell me what I wished to know, for a price, but there will be no one to help us with what must then be done."

"Not a surprise," McCarter nodded. "What are we up against?"

"A dirt road, created by the Strong Man's men, leads into the jungle to the base," Javier said. "The distance is four, five miles. Not far by the road. The base itself is like a prison. Those inside almost never leave. A supply run, every two weeks, brings food, ammunition and other supplies to the base. There is no wall, but there are machine guns and towers, and some of the villagers claim there are land mines and other traps. The only safe access is by the road."

"This supply run," McCarter said. "Any chance we could sneak aboard?"

"No," Javier shook his head. "The last run was only two days ago."

"So we can't take the direct route," Encizo put in, "and we can't sneak in. What does that leave us?"

"There is a man," Javier said, "a Russian scientist. He is said to be El Hombre Fuerte's missile expert."

"Some sort of former Soviet nuclear technician?" Hawkins asked.

"Yes, he is said to be this." Javier nodded. "What he knows must be very important, for the Strong Man treats him like a king. He is the only man allowed to leave the base regularly. He has a home here in the village, which is kept filled with whores and drink. He travels to and from this home several times a week, spending most nights here in the village."

"What's the catch?" James asked.

"The 'catch'?" Javier looked puzzled for a moment. "Oh, yes. I understand. The Russian, Sukarov, is guarded, never alone. He travels with four bodyguards. They come in a jeep or another of El Hombre Fuerte's trucks. They stay with him, always. When he is here in the village, they guard the house. Never do they spend time with the whores or drink even a single drop. The Strong Man has told them their lives, and the lives of their families, depend on this Sukarov's continued service to the Strong Man. Should he be killed, kidnapped, or even hired away, much death will the Strong Man visit on those who have failed to protect this valued tool."

"Sounds about right." McCarter rubbed his chest. "We've seen what sort of operator this man is. What have you heard about the main camp?"

"It burns." Javier frowned. "Word reached the Strong Man in the second camp that his prisoners had escaped, that the men in his base had been killed. He returned with trucks, the trucks you heard pass by when I was among the villagers. He announced, on his return, that he had defiled the bodies of those who failed to protect his property, and that he burned everything. I am told the trucks contained everything of value that could be salvaged from the base."

"So he sent a message but wasn't willing to really give up anything," McCarter said thoughtfully. "That tells us a little more about him."

"There is not much you need to know," Javier said. "Long did I make a study of this man. He is cruel. He is power-mad. He understands the need to appear brave and strong in front of those loyal to him. He rules through this fear he creates, through the perception of power. But in his heart, this cruel, ugly, large man is also a coward."

McCarter, still rubbing his chest absently, nodded.

"Well, there's only one thing we can do," Hawkins said

casually. "We've got to take the place of those guards, put a gun in Sukarov's ribs, and make him take us inside the base. Once we're in there we can light 'em up."

"This plan, it is dangerous," Javier said, "but I can offer nothing else."

"It's the only option available in the time we have," McCarter said. "If the uranium is to be used to fuel nuclear missiles, every minute those missiles are available to the Strong Man is a tick on the nuclear clock. It's an unacceptable national security risk, one that endangers both the United States and the rest of the world. We can't abide it, mates, and we can't afford it."

The other members of Phoenix Force had no comment. This was a truth they well understood.

"I can lead you to the dwelling," Javier said. "The guards will be there, waiting and alert. The threat of death, and of the deaths of all they love, keeps men very vigilant. It will require caution."

"Right, then," McCarter said. "Let's gear up and get moving."

He looked at Javier. "What sort of resistance are we likely to face once we do hit this place?"

"Very little," Javier said. "Most of El Hombre Fuerte's men never leave the second base unless it is as a large security force. They have been to the first camp and returned, having salvaged what they wished. There are none within the village this night, except for Sukarov and his guards. At least, there should not be. There may be spies."

"We'll have to take that risk," McCarter said.

"I see no other choice," Javier agreed.

Most of the unnamed village was comprised of small huts of local materials, but there was no missing the large, wooden structure guarded by the Strong Man's soldiers. The four bodyguards moved in and around the single-story, square house, the roof of which was made of layers of tarps stretched across wooden slats. A gas generator chugged away at the back of the building, and the interior was lighted. Music was playing inside, loud enough to be audible for some distance.

"Party time," James said.

"What *is* that?" McCarter's brow furrowed.

"Soul Finger, I think."

"What?"

"The Bar-Kays, man."

"Never heard of them, mate."

"You're a musical Philistine, David."

Javier crept up. His machete was on his belt and an AK, captured from the Strong Man's men, was in his hands. "I will clear the way," he said. "Follow as I move."

McCarter nodded.

Javier slipped quietly from hut to hut, visiting those dwellings nearest Sukarov's home. In two of them he apparently found locals, whom he hustled out without much fuss. Long used to living under the Strong Man's thumb, the villagers were more than happy to remove themselves when they learned that conflict was about to break. They had no desire to run afoul of El Hombre Fuerte's temper, nor did they wish to be caught in the cross fire.

Javier returned when he had made a full circuit around the house. "I have made sure no one is near who might be harmed," he said.

"Good man." McCarter nodded. "All right, mates, split up. We need someone on each corner to take the guards. Rafe, take the left rear, by the generator. Cal, take the right.

Gary, you take the front left, and T.J, you take the right out front. Javier and I will try to go straight in the front in the confusion, to capture Sukarov. We need him alive if we're going to pull this off. He's our ticket inside the second base. Move, now."

The members of Phoenix Force fanned out, the huts surrounding Sukarov's dwelling providing concealment but dubious protection. It would have to be enough. Unless the Russian was using flak jackets for wallpaper, the flimsy walls and tarps of his building weren't going to offer him much in the way of stopping bullets, either. McCarter only hoped Sukarov didn't catch a stray round—or get plugged by one of his own bodyguards. There was no telling what sort of orders the guards might have in the event that an attempt was made to kidnap Jiminez's nuclear scientist. McCarter listened as each member of the team reported in using his personal transceiver.

"Calvin, in position."

"Rafael, same."

"T.J., ready."

"Gary, ready."

"On my mark," McCarter said softly. "Three, two, one, *mark*."

Kalashnikov fire rattled through the night. The Briton watched and waited, crouched next to a hut with Javier waiting patiently beside him. He enjoyed watching his teammates operate, even at a distance. Each time he got the rare opportunity to see it from the outside, relatively speaking, he was impressed by the skill and teamwork Phoenix exhibited.

Calvin James put a 7.62 mm round through the head of his target, dropping the guard in his tracks. The fallen soldier didn't make a sound or react in any way. He simply dropped where he stood, dead before he knew the fight was on.

Simultaneously, Encizo fired a short burst from his AK, stitching his own guard through the head and neck quickly and efficiently. The bullets likely penetrated Sukarov's dwelling, but there was no way to prevent that.

Half a heartbeat later, the third guard was brought down, this time by a single shot to the head from Manning's rifle. He fell like a pole-axed steer.

The fourth man, however, didn't die cleanly. Hawkins fired a burst from his captured AK, but the weapon fired terribly low. The bullets caught the guard in the legs, bringing him screaming to his knees. He managed to pull a grenade from his belt before Hawkins got a follow-up shot into him. The bullet took the guard in the throat just as he threw the bomb. It went up in a wide arc and landed near McCarter and Javier.

"Grenade!" McCarter dived for it. Javier turned, saw the fragmentation grenade and snatched it up. He threw it into a nearby hut and then fell flat on the ground near McCarter.

The explosion did enough damage to collapse the hut, but nobody was hit by shrapnel from the grenade or the building it wiped out. Javier got to his knees, looked at McCarter and grinned.

"What was that?" McCarter looked at him, incredulous. "You could have been killed, mate. Might to have blown off your hand, at the very least."

"I did not want this gift," Javier said, "and so I sent it back."

"What do you mean?"

"That empty hut? Well do I know this place. It was used by Hector to commit rape. When he found a girl in the village he wished to have, he would have her brought here, where he was safe near Sukarov's bodyguards. Now Hector is dead, thanks to you, and I have erased his stink from the village." He laughed.

"Well, I can't fault you for the quick thinking—" McCarter shook his head "—but you've got one hell of an odd sense of humor, Jav."

Javier laughed again, the odd sound catching in the back of his throat like the staccato bark of a dog. McCarter just shook his head again. It took all kinds, out there, and everywhere.

"Gary, securing the house," Manning reported.

"Come on," McCarter said to Javier. "Let's get in there."

They found Sukarov and a prostitute huddled on a mattress in one of the building's two rooms. There was a Desert Eagle pistol on the gouged end table next to the mattress, but he made no attempt to pick it up.

"I will not resist," he said. "Do not kill me."

"Well, at least there's that," McCarter said. "Put on some clothes. You're coming with us."

Gary Manning picked up the pistol. "This," he said, "is mine."

"You're welcome to it," McCarter said.

"No," Manning said, shaking his head, "it's *mine*. This is the pistol they took from me when we were captured."

"Oh, really?" McCarter looked at Sukarov with renewed interest. "You and the Strong Man were sharing the spoils of war, eh?" He jerked his chin toward the pistol. Manning was searching through the drawer of the end table and had found his extra magazines, as well as the shoulder holster that had been taken from him. It had been resized to fit the smaller Sukarov and Manning spent a few moments readjusting it.

"He probably got it from the hand of El Hombre Fuerte himself on his return," Manning said.

"Let's scrounge what we can from the guards," McCarter said. "Then we'll need their jackets. In the dark that should be enough to fool anyone before we get close."

"We will need to find their vehicle," Javier said. "There are only so many places it could be. I will check the village and return with it. They do not keep it too near this place, for security reasons."

"Can't have a single grenade taking out both their boy and the only means of getting the hell back to base," McCarter stated.

"Trust the Strong Man's boys to field an AK that shoots two feet low at kissing distance," Hawkins said as he entered the room, disgusted. He unloaded the AK and set it aside. He had taken one of the dead guards' Kalashnikovs to replace it. "I had a busted old hunting rifle that shot better than that, after it broke."

"As long as his jacket is usable, it won't matter," McCarter said.

"Come," Javier said to the prostitute. She couldn't be more than nineteen or twenty, to McCarter's eye. She didn't look badly abused, and his guess was, based on Sukarov's demeanor, that he was more scientist than sadist. But being a working girl among the Strong Man's men couldn't be particularly pleasant.

Phoenix Force policed up the guards' bodies, searched them and removed any items that were useful, including spare magazines and magazine pouches for the Kalashnikovs. Manning, who was quiet and calm under most circumstances, had a little bounce back in his step, McCarter thought. Getting captured had annoyed the burly Canadian, and having his personal handgun back helped alleviate that irritation somewhat. McCarter didn't expect to see his Hi-Power again, though it could be stuck in the belt of El Hombre Fuerte himself, for all he knew. He could get another just like it, as he had so many times before. The Tavors had been nice rifles, and he regretted their loss in a bureaucratic way. Cowboy Kissinger was likely to be a bit miffed about that. But, again, they were replaceable. Weapons, to McCarter, were simply tools to be used and, when necessary, discarded or dismissed.

Still, he was happy for Manning.

The sound of a vehicle outside alerted him to Javier's return. At least, he assumed it was Javier. He snapped off the AK's safety for a moment, just long enough to go outside to check. The grinning operative was behind the wheel of what looked like a brand-new four-wheel-drive Jeep Patriot, and damned if the Briton could see any way the Strong Man or his goons could get their hands on something like that out here.

"She is quite the vehicle, no?" Javier said.

"I'll say." Encizo stepped up, whistling.

"Well, everybody in," McCarter said. "It ought to be a comfortable enough ride."

"You have not seen the state of the road to our destination," Javier told him.

They bundled in, taking their liberated uniform jackets with them. Manning took up position in the back seat of the vehicle with Sukarov and the others piled in around him. McCarter road up front and let Javier drive, as he was more familiar with local conditions. It was a tight fit, the seven of them in the truck, but they managed it. Javier turned on the air conditioner full-blast and breathed a contented, almost obscene sigh of satisfaction when the cold air hit him.

Manning stuck his .357 Magnum Desert Eagle into Sukarov's ribs, to keep the Russian nuclear scientist from getting any ideas. He didn't look the type to put up much fuss, though. He was a little pale and kept glancing around at everyone, wild-eyed, as if he expected to be killed and dumped by the side of the road any minute. McCarter wanted to tell him that their ways were not those of his boss, the murderous dictator Jiminez, but that would have been counterproductive. Better to let Sukarov worry that he could be shot at any moment unless he offered his full cooperation.

"So, mate," McCarter said, turning in the passenger seat to look back at Sukarov as they rode. "I have to know. Just how does a Soviet-era nuclear scientist end up working for a petty warlord in the middle of disputed territory in Central America?"

"How do you know about that?"

"About which, chap?"

"The Soviet Union. I was once highly placed scientist in the CCCP."

"Well, you could hardly be anything else, could you?" McCarter said. "Latter-day Russia isn't exactly winning a any science fairs, is it?"

"You have a point," Sukarov admitted. McCarter almost laughed. For a frightened prisoner, the man at least had a sense of humor.

"So," McCarter prompted, "tell me. Exactly who are you, and what are you doing here?"

"When the Soviet Union fell, I was unemployed," Sukarov admitted. "There was no work for nuclear weapons specialists, only those who were to help with disarmament. I have heard things may be different now, but it is too late. Even if I were willing to go back, there would be no place for me. Glasnost. Perestroika. These words killed us. These words destroyed us. A once proud nation, a powerful nation, a protected nation...I worked to make this so. And then there was no room for me. I was to be reassigned, perhaps to a power plant, to live out my miserable days nurse-maiding. I might as well have been a leper. You have heard Chernyobyl, *da*? Very unpopular, my profession. So I left."

"Left for here?"

"Left for the world market," Sukarov said. "If my nation could not use me, there were others who could."

"They didn't try to stop you?" Manning asked.

"How could they?" Sukarov said. "You forget how it was in those days. The Soviet Union was no more. Crime, the *Mafiya*, were everywhere. It was easy to leave the country. All one needed was money. I had some. I left. I go to South America. I worked for some groups here. Consulted for some, how do you call them, Neo-Nazis? My skills, they are marketable among such people, *da*?"

"Sadly so." McCarter nodded grimly.

"My work, eventually, brings offer from a fellow countryman. Come work for Jiminez, he says. Help bring about glorious Communist revolution across the world, he says. Live like king, he says, with money and liquor and girls." The Russian snorted. "Like king. Pah. Is more like prison."

"So you're not happy in your work, eh?" McCarter asked.

"What is to be happy? All day, I work. At night, they let me come to village. Watched, always watched. Is my home the home of a king? That...hovel? Tarps and wood and a television that cannot get any stations, run by a generator that makes always too much noise? Ugly women, or barely women, all from the village, stinking from servicing the Strong Man's other men? Pah. I have been used. Used for my skill, and forgotten, left to rot here. When I am done, the Strong Man will kill me. This, I have foreseen. I thought you were going to do it for him. I thought you were the ones he had finally sent to see to it I did not live."

"Why did you think that? You're still useful to him, aren't you?"

"Useful how?" Sukarov asked. "I have already armed the missiles."

McCarter looked at Javier sharply and then back to Sukarov. "You've armed what with what?"

"Missiles, missiles," Sukarov said impatiently. "Truck-mounted Soviet missiles."

"With?"

"Nuclear warheads, of course."

"Bloody hell." McCarter sighed.

CHAPTER FIFTEEN

The Chicago Suburbs

Schwarz brought the battered Suburban to a halt in the parking lot of a chain drugstore. From there they could see the motel that was their target. Stony Man Farm had obtained, and uploaded to their individual secure satellite phones, a basic floorplan of the building. Where that had come from, the team members didn't know; they took for granted that Kurtzman and his cybernetics wizards could ferret just about anything out of the ether.

Senator Harrington had been grateful for Able Team's intervention, but she had also insisted that her appearance at the conference go on as scheduled.

"Can't you simply reschedule the conference?" Lyons had asked her as they drove her to the government safehouse to which Stony Man Farm had directed them. "It's not worth dying for."

"A conference on environmentalism, with a bunch of sign-waving greens chanting about Earth Day?" The senator had laughed with surprising cheer. "No, young man, that's not worth dying for. Conservation and environmentalism, global warming and sustainable development...

these are important issues. But they're not worth my life. There is a bigger picture here, however."

"What is that, ma'am?" Lyons had not been sure just how he earned the title of "young man," but he let it slide.

"Call me Marcia, please," Harrington had said. "All this 'ma'am' and 'Senator Harrington' business is making me feel old." She smiled, then her expression grew serious. "Don't you see? If I call this off, they win."

"Who is 'they,' ma'am—I mean, Marcia?" Schwarz had put in. "We're talking about a plot to assassinate you, if those hired assassins are any indication. If they don't get a shot at you, the killers lose."

"But American democracy loses, too," Harrington said. "I know it sounds corny, even overwrought. But don't you see? If we stop participating in our political process every time someone makes a threat, or even pulls a trigger, we're letting them dictate our politics to us. It shouldn't work that way, and it *can't*. I know in these days of cynical and painfully self-aware politicians, the idea that I'm a public servant has kind of gotten lost. My peers in Washington are the worst offenders and the biggest contributors to that evolution. Maybe I'm kidding myself, but I like to think I'm a throwback. I like to think that I can put the people's business ahead of my own gain, and ahead of even my own life. No, gentlemen, I will not back down. I will go to your safehouse until it's time for me to speak at the rally. Then I will make my appearance as scheduled. We cannot afford to let them think they can beat us, even in this small way."

The big former cop had to admit that the woman had a lot of guts and, regardless of whether one agreed with or disagreed with her policies, she was one hell of a woman.

There were a lot of politicians, male and female, on both sides of the aisle, who could learn a thing or two from her.

"GIVE ME THE THINGY," Lyons said, reaching back to Blancanales.

"Stop hitting him with technical lingo," Schwarz said with a chuckle. "Pol, Ironman would like the WTS unit, please, also known in geek jargon as a Seever."

"Whatever." Lyons scowled. He took the device as Blancanales handed it across the seats. Then he looked it over and, finally, found the transmit button.

"Hey," he said into it. "Pick up the dingus, numbnuts." When there was no immediate answer, he transmitted again. "Hey! Pick up the damned space phone, will you?"

"Who is this?" a voice said in Russian-accented English, shaded with anger. "Who is violating the communications orders?"

"Oh, sorry," Lyons said, "I didn't get that order. See, I got this Seever thing off of one of your goons. Well, one of my men did. And he couldn't relay anything because we'd just waxed him. And all the guys with him. And a whole bunch of their friends. And now I'm comin' for you."

"I see," said the voice, strained but now sounding amused. "And where will you do this, my American friend? You are an American, yes? A policeman, or perhaps a government officer?"

"Perhaps," Lyons said. "Why do you ask?"

"Because it will be difficult for you to apprehend me," the Russian's voice was growing more glib, more oily, "if we are thousands of miles away. I could be anywhere in the world, you fool."

"Well, that's true," Lyons said. "You *could* be anywhere

in the world, and these Seever doodads make it possible for you to talk to all of your people. But I've got this theory, see."

"What theory is that?"

"Well, we've been whacking Russian assassins like they're going out of style," Lyons said. "And that's kind of unusual. Some of these guys barely speak English. We've run a few of their IDs and they've come back as only recent visitors to this fine land. The virtual ink on their forged visas is barely dry, if you get me. So I'm thinking, how are these guys possibly going to manage coordinated, goal-directed effort in a foreign land with only a rudimentary grasp of the language and the culture?"

There was no reply.

"What's the matter?" Lyons asked. "Nothing to say? See, we figure, while whoever's directing these clowns *could* be anywhere, thanks to these little gadgets of Butler's, it's much more likely that he's right here, where he can keep an eye on his foreign troops and orchestrate this rodeo. So, yeah, we're comin' for you. Any minute now."

The Russian swore vehemently. The WTS unit's indicators changed color from red to yellow and then to red. The Russian had cut the connection and disrupted the transmission, changing whatever code made it possible for Able Team's leader to use the WTS device.

"Thought so." Lyons grinned. He looked at Schwarz. "I'd call that confirmation, wouldn't you?"

"As close as we're going to get." Gadgets nodded.

"All right. They'll be good and freaked out now. Let's go," Lyons said.

They piled out of the Suburban, then moved on the motel. Lyons and Schwarz took the front, while Blancanales skirted around to cover the rear in case anyone tried to slip out the back.

Before making the WTS transmission, they'd placed a call to the front desk of the motel. It had taken a little convincing to make the clerk understand that they were really calling on behalf of the Justice Department and that this was not a prank call of any kind. He had agreed to quietly move the other guests out of the motel as quickly as possible. Fortunately, there were only a few other guests. The place was too far off the beaten track to be booked full of convention goers or, for that matter, attendees of the environmentalism conference to which Senator Harrington was so set on going.

Calling the Russian like that would alert those inside, of course. In any other circumstances that would have been the last thing Lyons wanted to do. But in this case he wanted the man off balance. There would be no way to break down six sets of doors without alerting the Russian and whoever was with him that an attack was coming anyway. Better that they get the guns out and waving so Able Team could tell friend from foe, heading into it. So they'd cleared out the innocents as best they could and were now rolling on it.

He hadn't been impressed with the Russian mercenaries. Sure, they were men with guns who would kill Lyons, Schwarz and Blancanales if they got the chance, but tactically, this mission had been strictly amateur night from the outset.

They took the first door on the list, purely arbitrarily. Schwarz and Lyons took up positions on either side, weapons at the ready. They had considered involving local law enforcement for backup, but discarded the idea; Lyons had not wanted a bunch of dead cops on his conscience. These Russians might not be up to his professional standards, but one cop was dead already simply for having been in the wrong place at the wrong time when they came calling. Frankly, Lyons was pissed off.

Pressing against the wall on the side of the door, Lyons rapped on the door with the knuckles of his support hand. When there was no answer, he knocked again, harder.

"Who is it?" came a voice from inside in Russian-accented English.

"Candygram," Lyons said.

The shotgun blast tore a hole in the middle of the door. Lyons had been expecting it. He heard the pump shotgun rack back, and as the sound echoed, he shoved the barrel of the Daewoo in through the ragged hole and pulled the trigger. A brief automatic burst of double aught Buck sprayed the interior of the room, shredding the Russian gunner.

"Go," Lyons urged Schwarz.

THERE WAS SHOUTING from within.

Schwarz took the adjacent door, next on the list they'd gotten from Price. He didn't wait; he simply kicked it in, planting one boot against the door next to the jamb and breaking the relatively weak lock. The hollow-core door came apart under the assault.

The Able Team commando threw himself into the doorway and into the room. Two men were inside, each wearing nondescript civilian clothing, each grabbing for a handgun. Schwarz gained his feet and fired a 3-round burst into the chest of the first man, dropping him. He turned to engage the second man, the muzzle of his pistol moving to acquire the second target.

A meaty fist clamped onto the barrel of the 93-R, shoving it up and out of the way. The second man, seeing his partner go down, had forgotten his pistol and gone straight for the intruder. He was big and incredibly strong, reaching out and clamping a hand around Gadgets's neck.

The electronics expert could feel the air being choked off in his throat as the big man's fingers tightened like a vise. "I have killed three men this way," the big man rumbled. "You shall be the fourth."

Schwarz saw no reason to fight the big man for the gun. He let it go. The sudden absence of resistance surprised the big Russian, who found himself in possession of the 93-R, gripped by the slide.

Slapping his pocket, Schwarz drew the Columbia River M-18 folding knife and snapped it open. Without hesitation, Schwarz reached up and carved his way around the Russian's other arm, the one holding his neck.

His adversary emitted a high-pitched scream, then dropped the 93-R and clutched at his maimed arm as he backed up, suddenly pale.

Schwarz dropped to the floor, scooped up the 93-R with his left hand and punched a single round through the Russian's face. Immediately he could hear running feet outside.

Several men dressed in khaki pants and black T-shirts were running out of the adjacent rooms, heading for vehicles in the parking lot. They carried submachine guns in their hands, Uzis from the look of them. Schwarz raced after them, catching Lyons out of the corner of his eye.

Automatic gunfire cut through the air. Schwarz hit the deck, slamming his knees and forearms painfully on the tarmac of the parking lot, as 9 mm gunfire chewed up the front of the motel where he'd been standing. He drew a bead on the nearest gunman with the 93-R, but the man ran behind a parked car. Schwarz waited, dragged in a breath to steady himself and targeted the man's foot beneath the vehicle.

The burst blew the front of the shoe apart. As the gunner went down, screaming curses in what sounded like Russian, Schwarz was up again and circling, using the parked cars for concealment and cover. He almost got tagged by a second submachine gunner, but Lyons tapped the man once with the Daewoo shotgun, taking him out forever.

The third gunman had gotten into a pickup truck parked at the far end of the lot. He gunned the engine and shot straight at Lyons. The Able Team leader held his ground and pulled back the trigger of the Daewoo, emptying the mighty shotgun's 20-round box magazine into the front wheels and engine block of the truck. It came apart nicely, grinding to a halt a few feet from where Lyons stood. As he changed out the magazine, Schwarz flanked the truck and targeted the driver behind the wheel.

"Don't bother," Lyons said, circling around to the driver's side. "He's had it."

Schwarz could see that, too. The gunner was slumped over the wheel, the windshield pocked with pellet holes.

"I have someone out back!" Blancanales said urgently over their earbud transceivers. "I've got him pinned but he's working his way around to a vehicle."

Schwarz and Lyons hurried for the rear of the motel. They took opposite sides in an effort to catch the straggler between them. Schwarz could see, as he cleared the rear of the motel, the back of Blancanales's head as the Able Team operative exchanged gunfire with someone else. Pol was behind the engine block of a Chevy Malibu parked there, which was taking heavy fire. The gunman was crouched behind a concrete abutment that was part of a barrier erected to keep drivers from clipping the motel building itself as they came around the tight corner.

"I'm going to lose him," Blancanales said. "I don't have the position here."

"Don't worry." Lyons's voice was calm and steady. "I've got him."

As Schwarz watched, Lyons unhurriedly stalked up behind the gunner, having come around his side of the motel. The gunman turned at the last moment, perhaps sensing Lyons, perhaps hearing something. The Able Team leader slammed the butt of the Daewoo into his face.

"Think it's him?" Lyons asked.

His teammates joined him, and Schwarz rolled the unconscious man onto his back. He searched through the man's pockets.

"Nothing," he concluded. "No Seever unit, no ID, not much of anything."

"All right," Lyons said. "Let's search the rooms and—"

An engine roared out front.

"Goddamn it. It was a diversion. Go, now!" Lyons ordered. The three Able Team operators ran for it, but as they reached the parking lot, all they caught was the receding tail of a Chrysler minivan. Schwarz, thinking fast, had his minibinoculars up and out.

"Go after him?" Blancanales asked.

Lyons glanced back at the Suburban, which was visible but too far.

"We'll never make it," he said. "By the time we get on him, he'll have lost us."

"But," Schwarz said triumphantly, "I got the plate number."

"Good," Lyons said. "Call the Farm. We're still in this." They began hustling back toward the Suburban, Schwarz holding his secure satellite phone to his ear as they ran.

"Price," the mission controller answered once the scrambled call was routed to her.

"Barbara, this is Gadgets," Schwarz said. "I need a plate trace done." He read off the numbers.

"Switching you to Bear," Price said.

Kurtzman didn't answer right away. Schwarz could hear the big man's fingers flying over the computer keyboard in front of him. He pictured Aaron Kurtzman at his workstation, where he was king of all he virtually surveyed, a master of data and electronic incursion surveying all that came within his ever-extending virtual reach.

He was glad Kurtzman was on their side.

"All right," Kurtzman's gruff voice cut in. "The vehicle is registered to a Norman Hickey. I've got his file up now. He's a traveling salesman with a home address in Illinois. No criminal file. Let me check a few things… No, nothing, unless you count a speeding ticket eighteen months ago. The minivan is probably stolen."

"I don't suppose it has a GPS antitheft system."

"Nothing we have a record of," Kurtzman said after another delay and some more keyboard tapping. "But there is good news. I have Hunt retasking a satellite to give us some real-time imaging."

"Real-time imaging…do you have a bird that good?" The type of imaging Kurtzman would need to spot the minivan by license plate was not unprecedented, but the average orbiting bird didn't have that sort of capability.

"I've got one of NSA's darker black bag fliers," Kurtzman said. "Right in position. Checking traffic in the area of your location..." Schwarz knew that the phone he carried was itself equipped with a GPS tracking device, enabling the Farm to locate the person carrying it anywhere in the world. The feature had come in handy more than once, particularly when Able Team and Phoenix Force members had been captured or, at least once, simply lost in adverse weather conditions. It was giving Kurtzman the reference point he needed.

"All right, now I'm acquiring...well, the bird is. It's processing plates and reading the tags, comparing them to the search field. I should have it in just a moment... Gotcha! Okay, Gadgets, I'm sending streaming data to your phone now. You can use it to follow the car."

"We're on our way," the electronic specialist said. They had climbed into the Suburban. Schwarz looked at the simplified map overlay and compared it to the tracking blip that Stony Man Farm was streaming him.

"Left," he told Lyons. "Then go straight."

Lyons nodded and got the truck moving. He pushed hard, wheeling in and out of busy traffic, the large truck intimidating some vehicles out of the way when Lyons didn't deliberately cut them off.

"If this guy is the one we think it is, the one in charge of the hit teams," Lyons said, "then we're halfway home. We just have to keep the rally from turning ugly."

"Meaning you expect that whatever they've got planned for the rally will still go on?" Blancanales asked.

"It would explain why they were suddenly in such a hurry to mobilize everything." Lyons nodded. "And it fits with the fact that these Russian assassins did their thing today. This is their last chance to take out the senator before she makes the conference. With them out of the picture, it leaves the fringe green whackamoles and maybe a few advisers. We've seen more than a few of these Russian mercenary types sprinkled in among the WWUP and EAF true believers working toward the cause, whatever they think that cause is. No, I think once we nail this guy, we ask him some questions."

"The kinds of questions he can't help but answer?"

"Yeah, those," Lyons said. "And then we'll know what we're up against. And like I said, we'll be halfway there."

"That would be nice," Blancanales said. "I'm starting to get car sick."

Lyons shot a look back at Blancanales and pulled the Suburban through a tight, fishtailing, tire-burning turn.

"Wuss," he said, slamming his foot to the floor.

"So then what?" Schwarz prompted.

"Then what, what?"

"Once we nail down these people targeting the rally, where does that leave us?"

"Well, I have a theory about that, too," Lyons said. "I want to ask our friend with the Seever a few questions, and then we're going to arrange for a fast jet."

"Butler," Blancanales said.

"Butler," Lyons agreed. "If we can get it from the horse's mouth that he's in bed with all this, that's two different sources. I'm going to have the Farm fly us to his front door."

"Won't the Farm already be working that angle?" Schwarz asked.

"Sure," Lyons said. "Maybe if we're lucky they'll even arrange for some Congressional hearings. I was thinking of something a lot faster and a lot more direct. Look, Butler already contracted with those hire-a-thugs to take us out, didn't he?"

"True," Blancanales said. "And Butler and those upstream of him exerted political pressure on the locals. That's how the carport commandoes knew how to find us. Somebody got to the local authorities, who rolled over, before Hal set them right again."

"Well, if he was nervous enough to send hired guns after whoever was monkeying up his plans stateside," Lyons said, "can you imagine the size of the brick that will hit his shorts when we show up on his front door?"

"You've got the soul of a poet, Ironman," Blancanales said.

"Whatever," Lyons nodded. "But my point is that when we show up, he'll probably throw whatever he's got left at us. And that'll pull all of this out of the marble-tiled, two-grand-a-plate-dinner crowd and back into the arena of direct action. Then we can put a stop to this joker's antics once and for all. Murder, political corruption, conspiracy, obstruction of justice…you name it, this character's got a lot to answer for. I plan to show up and ask."

"And then?"

"And then—" Lyons shot another glance at his teammate "—somebody's in big trouble."

CHAPTER SIXTEEN

Atlanta, Georgia

Reginald Butler was in big trouble.

Richard Cross had tipped him off. Word was filtering through the halls of power in Washington that Reginald Butler and, more importantly, campaign contributions from Reginald Butler, were to become a liability. If you had any funds coming in from Butler Telecommunications, word was that you should return them and disavow them. Such a ripple of warning typically made its way through Congress when someone leaked word of an investigation.

Investigation. Butler rolled the word over in his mind a few times. This was bad. Cross had told him that he'd heard Butler was under investigation for, among many other illegal pursuits, campaign finance violations, various and sundry racketeering and corruption offenses, and participation in influence peddling. He hadn't asked Cross if this meant Cross, too, was under investigation, for any influence Butler had tried to buy had come more or less through Cross.

It had all seemed so reasonable a plan. Make Senator Marcia Harrington look bad by making it seem as if the fringe environmentalist groups to whom she'd become a hero were dangerously unstable. A few demonstrations that got out of hand, a few acts of high-profile vandalism, all of this culminating in a big mess at the environmental rally Harrington was headlining. Krylov had made it seem so simple, so bloodless. Once Harrington was damaged political goods in the eyes of the American people, Cross could step in and take her place. He was well-positioned, good-looking, and held moderate ground from which he could lay claim to most of her platform. He'd get the presidency, Butler would get a very powerful ally in Washington, and everybody would be happy.

Except none of it had gone as it was supposed to. It was as if that damned Krylov had been actively working at cross-purposes to what they were trying to do. Why were none of the protest events going off without violence? Why the escalation? And he'd gotten word through Cross that Senator Harrington's office was screaming bloody murder because she'd suffered an assassination attempt.

Butler wasn't stupid. This was too much to be coincidence. He'd tried to contact Krylov on the Seever, but there had been no answer. He had no idea if this meant something bad, or if the Russian coordinator was just asleep or something. What was the time difference between here and Europe? Come to think of it, Krylov never was very specific about where he was hiding. He could be just about anywhere in the world. Butler had always assumed somewhere in Europe or thereabouts, some modern industrial nation from which he could control his troops' movements. But really, Krylov didn't need to be anywhere particularly special, not with the WTS units that Butler had supplied him with so liberally. He could coordinate his people from a snow cave in the Arctic Circle, and it wouldn't matter. That was the beauty of the devices, after all.

Well, whatever. Krylov wasn't answering, and Butler was now dealing with the mess he'd let himself get sucked into.

It was over, of course.

He had millions of dollars in assets on which he could put his hands quickly. He had a net worth that ranked him among the world's billionaires. He was something of a celebrity and regularly appeared in commercials for Butler Telecommunications. He had rubbed shoulders with countless politicians, greasing the wheels of national politics and telecommunications law with money from his coffers.

None of it would save him.

Now that he had the taint of corruption on him, his political allies would run from him as if he had the plague. The great game of Cover Your Ass would begin, and they would fall all over themselves to disavow him.

He had searched around for somebody local who could help him, somebody who could put boots on the ground around the Butler Building. Somebody who wasn't too particular about what he did wrong, or who he did it to. It had taken an awful lot; he'd had to pull out a lot more stops than when he'd found Fleisser. But of course the stakes were considerably higher.

He had considered running sooner rather than later. He could liquidate enough assets and empty his bank accounts quickly enough to be on a plane in hours. The problem was that, if these investigations went as deep or as high as Cross claimed they were rumored to, he'd never make it onto a commercial or even a chartered plane. He could assume his private jet was being watched. The government and its operatives would be looking for just such an admission of guilt as Reginald Butler making a run for it. Even if his lawyers had enough up their sleeves to give the courts grief, he'd never survive with that on the record.

It was to be a package deal, then. It was inevitable that the goons who had been making so much trouble in Chicago, or others just like them, would show up in Atlanta for him. He knew enough about how these things worked to expect it. Therefore, he needed someone to cover his ass long enough so he could get out of the country, and he needed to do it in a way that was not traceable. In other words, he needed to circumvent traditional border authority and air traffic regulations to get out of the country, and he needed men who were willing to kill to get him there.

It was amazing what money could do, he reflected.

He looked around his office. He looked at the trappings of power. None of it would save him now. The best he could hope for would be to set himself up in exile in a country with no extradition treaty. What was left of his fortune, what he could convert to liquid funds, would see to it that he lived relatively comfortably if not fabulously opulently. But he would never again be able to return home. He would have to live looking over his shoulders for maverick bounty hunters and government agents, coming to collect him and take him back. He would live the rest of his life, not as a player on the national scene, but as a fugitive. He would be a comfortable fugitive, yes. But that was all he would ever be again.

It beat prison.

He would not under any circumstances allow himself to be sent to prison. That was not the end Reginald Butler had in mind for his life, no matter how ignominious a come-down he was to experience in making his escape. They could take a lot from him, but he would not let them take his freedom.

The man sitting across from him was here to see to that.

His name was Kurt Hinshaw. He was a huge man, six foot two and three hundred pounds, easily. His dark eyes flashed from within a jowly, bulldog face defined by a mustache and goatee. He had a tuft of hair on top of an otherwise balding scalp. He wore a flight jacket, a black T-shirt, and a pair of cargo pants. Butler had noticed his combat boots when he entered the office, and he was just experienced enough in these matters to recognize the hang of the shoulder holster under Hinshaw's jacket.

"So," Hinshaw said with a grin. There was no mirth whatsoever to that gesture. The smile never reached his eyes, which remained cold and merciless.

"You are here for a reason," Butler said.

"Yeah, I know." Hinshaw smiled that sharklike smile again. "I'm here because you're up to your ass in alligators and you need a paddle."

Butler started to object, but it was as realistic and honest an assessment of the situation as any. He simply nodded. "Yes," he said.

"And you finally got around to hiring the best." Hinshaw postured, though Butler knew there was weight behind his words.

Kurt Hinshaw, in certain less than reputable but nonetheless accurate sources, came highly recommended as a man who was willing to do things, violent things, for money. What was more, he had a reputation for being efficient and, to this point, discreet. He had never done a day of time in his life, said those who recommended him, and it was not for lack of trying. He owned an organization of like-minded individuals, most of them former military, called the Daggers. As lurid as the title was—he could not help but be reminded of Fleisser and Black Bag—few had the temerity to poke fun at it. Kurt Hinshaw had, the rumors went, personally broken the jaws of two men on different occasions, when they had called him an "armchair warrior" based on the name of his group.

Hinshaw was noisily cracking the knuckles of his ham-like hands as he sat in the chair facing Butler's desk. "You realize," he said, "that this is a one-shot deal, and it's going to cost you like it."

"Yes, I know," Butler said. "But at this point I really have no choice."

"That's fine for you," Hinshaw said. He had the broad sketch of Butler's problem and knew the man needed to flee the country, permanently. "But I have a pretty good thing going here, as do the men who work for me. If we help you, if we kill federal agents, we're undertaking about the worst risk it's possible for men to accept. We'll be wanted fugitives, most likely facing life or the death penalty if they ever get to us. That means we've got to disappear with you, and you've got make it worth our whiles to do so."

Butler understood that, but he also knew that a big score like this, and the chance to retire to some tropical country to sit on the beach and be serviced by lithe young local ladies, was the sort of thing of which men like Hinshaw frequently dreamed. Hinshaw was not getting any younger, and the men in his service, while they might not be as old as their employer, would likely be the sorts of rootless hired guns who would likewise welcome the chance to retire in wealth and luxury. Fortunately, Butler had enough money to make it all happen.

"I will see to it that you are compensated fairly," Butler said.

"Fuck fair," Hinshaw said. "I want to be compensated in a fashion that will eliminate any cognitive dissonance I might otherwise feel over my choice." When Butler looked at him blankly, Hinshaw said, "I want you to make me an offer you can't refuse. I have a specific figure in mind."

"How much?"

Hinshaw named an astronomical sum. It was not, however, unreasonable, given the circumstances. It was also lower than Butler had imagined he'd have to accept. He had the money to do it and, more importantly, they had no choice whatsoever.

"That can be arranged," he said.

Hinshaw looked a little disappointed. Clearly he realized that Butler had given in all too readily; that meant he could have gone higher. Still, he was a man of his word. That, too, had been said about him, and it was another reason Butler had chosen to hire him above a couple of other choices that had been presented to him.

"You will make the travel arrangements," Butler stipulated. "I need to get myself and a few pieces of luggage on a plane, after I make some arrangements," he said. "I will be bringing no dependents and very little else. I need a non-extradition-treaty nation as our final destination. And of course we need to be able to get out of the country unmolested by federal or local authorities."

"All of that can be arranged," Hinshaw stated.

"I need men here," Butler said. "Men to guard the building against the agents I mentioned. They'll come looking for a fight, and they'll be well armed. I need you to field as large a force of guards as possible."

"To facilitate your escape should they find you before you leave?" Hinshaw said.

"No," Butler said. "I intend to wait for them."

"Now why—" Hinshaw looked puzzled "—would you want to go and do a crazy thing like that?"

"I don't intend to spend my life running," Butler said. "The men making trouble in Chicago, or men like them, will be sent after me. It's inevitable. Word has gotten out about my involvement in certain matters, certain…extra-legal…matters. That probably happened when another man I hired was made to talk, or it might be I was sold out by people I previously trusted. But regardless, they will send people for me."

"All the better reason not to be here," Hinshaw said.

"I have spent my whole life, and built a billion-dollar empire, by facing my fears," Butler said proudly. "I'm not about to back down now, not about to run with my tail be-tween my legs. That's where you come in. I intend to wait for these men to come here. Then I want you to kill every last one of them."

"That's going to raise the price upward a bit," Hinshaw said. He named another figure. The number was still not at Butler's upper limit.

"Fine," he said. "You will receive it. But I want these men eliminated. Only once they are dead and can't come after me will I even bother trying to leave. Otherwise they would dog my tail to the ends of the Earth, most likely. Better they come to me so we can find them, and then eliminate them. Once they're dead I'll have some breathing room."

"What if they have friends?" Hinshaw said. "Them, or men like them, you said. Well, what happens when one group of these bastards comes looking for payback for what you've done to the other group of them?"

Butler honestly hadn't considered that, but it didn't

change a whole lot. "It doesn't matter," he said. "I've got to draw a line somewhere. With my immediate pursuers gone, we'll have room to work. Then you can get us out of here, and we'll all retire someplace warm and friendly."

"Now you're talking." Hinshaw smiled that humorless smile again.

"The arrangements will have to be made to defend this building, and as quickly as possible," he said.

"Of course," Hinshaw said. "I'll have men and weapons here within the hour."

"What sort of weapons?"

"Why?"

"Well," Butler said, "you'll want heavy weapons. Grenades, that sort of thing."

Hinshaw whistled. "You really have made some powerful enemies, haven't you?" he asked. "Well, you just leave that to me. It wouldn't be the first time we'd had to break out the heavy stuff."

"Just see to it quickly," Butler said. "I have no idea what type of timetable I'm looking at, but I can only assume things are coming to a head."

"Aren't they always." Hinshaw took out a small notebook and consulted some notes. "You hired Fleisser and Black Bag out of Illinois before," he said. "How's that working out for you?"

"If you're asking, you obviously already know," Butler said.

"Yeah," Hinshaw said. "The circles in which I travel, the soldier-of-fortune types who are willing to do what I do, there aren't that many of us. We know each other. We also know the pretenders. I got to tell you, Butler, you picked a real winner there. And by winner, I mean loser."

"I suspected as much when he failed."

"You dealt with him yourself?"

"I did," Butler said. "It was not the wisest course of action."

"Sure wasn't," Hinshaw said. "You can bet he rolled over on you first chance he got."

"He insisted he would only deal with the man in charge," Butler said lamely.

"Yeah, don't they all," Hinshaw laughed. "Word of advice, Butler. Next time, use a cutout. Guys like me, we want your money. We may be doing you a service, but trigger-pullers are cheap. You'll always be able to find a guy willing to kill for you. Hell, throw enough money at the problem, and you'll be able to find a killer who even knows what he's doing."

"I don't imagine it will be an issue," Butler said. He, too, was envisioning the tropical locale in which he would live out his days in exile. He might have to accept a major demotion in his station in life, but that did not mean he could not console himself with a retirement of hedonistic luxury.

"Me," Hinshaw said, unasked, "I've been looking to retire for a while now. You know why?"

"Because men always wish to retire?"

"Hell, no," Hinshaw said. "I'd rather stay working. It's fun. I like being able to do what I want, when I want, to who I want, within reason. It's a lifestyle choice, you might say. You carry a gun and use it in anger, well, for most people, they don't want any part of it unless it's a matter of self-defense. All those good citizens out there, your responsible NRA-course-taking gun owners, your fine upstanding patriotic American citizens, they'll use a gun, sure, but they don't enjoy it none."

"And you?" Butler asked. "Are you saying you enjoy shooting people?"

"What's not to enjoy?" Butler grinned, showing even teeth. "A guy gets in your way, you put bullet in him. Guy smarts off to you, you bust his face or stick a knife in him. It's livin' for yourself, and to hell with anybody else. That's how a man was meant to live, Butler."

"I'll give your…philosophy some thought," Butler said.

"No, you won't," Hinshaw was still grinning as he stood, looming over Butler with his massive hands on the polished surface of Butler's desk. "But that's all right. As many guys as I've talked to, only a few have understood what I'm getting at. Those are the guys I hire." He laughed deeply, the bass of his voice rumbling against Butler's chest.

He reached into his pocket and produced a small automatic pistol. "You got a piece?" he asked.

"No," Butler said.

"Then take this," Hinshaw rumbled. "You know how to use it?"

"I am familiar with its method of operation, yes," Butler said, resigned.

"Good. Use it if you have to. I'd recommend eating a bullet if we get to that point, though, 'cause it's going to mean they've gotten through all my guys before they stand in your office."

Butler paled. It was not a comforting thought.

Hinshaw laughed at him. He turned and lumbered out.

Butler watched him go, wondering how he'd managed to hire such a complete psychopath, and fearing that even this might not be enough.

CHAPTER SEVENTEEN

Suburban Chicago

Carl Lyons thought to himself, with a certain grim detachment, that they were never going to get out of the Chicago suburbs, and if he never saw them again, it would be too soon.

The minivan was parked in front of the house, which looked like all the other houses packed in closely around it. Price had phoned from the Farm, telling him that they'd run the address and come up with a mortgage registered to a holding company. That company was owned by an international interest with ties to a Russian firm. The trail led, ultimately, to a former KGB operative named Fedor Krylov, on whom the Farm had extensive files. He was linked to more than a dozen communist and socialist radical groups, including the Purba Banglars and the WWUP, and the files contained rumor and speculation to the effect that Krylov could have his mitts in a dozen more organizations. It was, in effect, the dossier of a man who could very well coordinate a coalition of communist radicals and violent environmentalist fringe groups toward some common goal.

"So we figure our fugitive for Krylov?" Lyons has asked.

"Unless he's an operative for Krylov," Price had said. "You tell me." She transmitted the file photos just to be certain. None of the Able Team members had gotten a very good look at him, however.

Not like it mattered.

They parked in the driveway fronting the house. Piling out, Lyons had a moment in which to feel vaguely self-conscious. They were standing in a residential, suburban neighborhood with heavy weaponry in full view.

"I guess I'll get over it," he muttered, jacking a 12-gauge double-aught buck shell into the chamber of the Daewoo.

"Get over what?" Schwarz asked, checking his 93-R machine pistol.

"Nothing," Lyons said. "Come on, let's do this."

They approached the front door. Lyons stood to one side and rapped with his knuckles.

"Just don't do the candygram thing again." Schwarz rolled his eyes.

"Pizza," Lyons said loudly.

"Gentlemen," came a calm, Russian-accented voice, sounding fluent and yet clipped at the same time. "Let us not engage in any pretense. We all know what is happening. You have tracked me to my final bolt-hole, and I am attempting to extend my life by whatever means necessary." The voice seemed to be coming from a speaker set above the door.

"Call the locals," Lyons said to Schwarz. "I don't want this guy getting away."

"You sure?" Schwarz asked.

"Absolutely." Lyons put a finger by his nose. "I want you to call in backup."

"And I am not supposed to see that?" the Russian asked. "I have a camera on you, gentlemen."

"It was worth a try," Lyons muttered. He looked around,

but the camera was not visible. He knew enough about the gear from hanging with Schwarz; there were microminiaturized fiber optic cameras and others that could be hidden just about anywhere. There was no point in looking for it.

"I have to admit," the Russian said, sounding almost amused, "that you have outdone yourselves. You tracked me here, where I thought perhaps I might still be safe, *da*? And calling me on Seever unit, that put me off balance, made me think first of running, rather than organizing effective defense. You have done well."

"You're not so bad yourself, Krylov," Lyons ventured.

"So you know," Krylov said. Then he sounded annoyed with himself. "Or you do now. Damn it all, I am still not myself." The man's sigh was carried through the speakers. "I do not think I have quite the courage to shoot myself. And so you will try to get me in here. But I shall not let you in, and it shall not be easy."

"Well, I guess there's only one thing to do," Lyons said.

"What's that?" Schwarz asked.

"Knock on the door." He raised the barrel of the Daewoo. His teammates moved back, around the sides of the recessed doorway, using the house for cover. Lyons pulled the trigger. The door handle and lock exploded under the shotgun pellets. The big former cop kicked the door in— and ducked aside.

The answering shotgun blast was startling in the relative silence that had followed Lyons's first shot. There was nothing more after the first blast.

"Son of a *bitch*," Lyons said, getting up.

"You cannot blame me for trying, *nyet*?" the voice through the speaker mocked.

Schwarz cautiously ducked his head around the corner. "Well," he said. "That's about par for the course."

Lyons nodded. He moved cautiously into the doorway. Just inside, beyond the arc of the door's sweep, was a wooden kitchen chair. A double-barreled shotgun had been affixed to the chair with swath after layer of layer tape. A piece of wire ran from the door handle to the triggers of the shotgun. It was one of the simplest and oldest booby traps in the book. Opening the door triggered the blast that was supposed to kill whoever was at the door.

The problem had been the door swinging inward. Krylov had apparently compensated for that by positing the shotgun beyond the door's arc and making the wire long enough for that distance. The problem, from Krylov's point of view, was that an alert invader—that's what Lyons and company were, in this context, invaders, however righteous—had just enough time between the door swing and eventual pulling of the triggers to recognize the trap for what it was. He could, as Lyons had proved, recognize it and get the hell out of there. The experience had done nothing for his blood pressure, not to mention his mood.

"He's in here somewhere," Lyons said.

"I am in here somewhere," Krylov mocked. There were more speakers; Able Team could see them mounted to the ceiling.

"What in hell sort of *Silence of the Lambs* crap is this?" Lyons asked.

"I have long had this place set up for the, how you say, confrontation, the last stand," Krylov said from the speakers. "You would be amazed what one can buy, when one has billionaire friend. I had thought never to use these things, but you have found me. And if I am to escape I must make you unfind me."

"What is he talking about?" Blancanales asked.

"Uh, guys?" Schwarz pointed.

"Holy shit," Lyons swore and brought up the shotgun.

The mechanical device looked like something out of a movie. It was, in fact, a police robot, of the type used to defuse bombs from a distance. It rode on small crawlers, stood perhaps two feet high at its widest point, and was constructed of white-painted metal.

It also had an Uzi mounted to it.

The machine swiveled in their direction and began to fire. Able Team threw themselves in different directions. Lyons landed behind the couch in the living room, while Schwarz threw himself into the adjacent dining room and Blancanales managed simply to hug the wall. Then Lyons pushed himself to his feet, took aim and blasted the rolling metal menace.

Sparks flew. The smell of a burning electrical motor filled the room. Lyons changed box magazines in the Daewoo and lined up on the robot again, but it was no longer moving. It was likely that the Uzi's magazine had been spent, too, and the rubber-faced grippers attached to the single arm holding the weapon would never be capable of performing a magazine change.

"We were just attacked by a robot," Blancanales said.

"Yeah, it's been a real great day," Lyons said.

"Guys! Guys!" Schwarz called. "More!"

SCHWARZ LANDED in the adjacent dining room, only to find himself face to face with a second rolling robot, which was caught in the corner of the doorway leading to the kitchen.

He had time to assess the situation. His 93-R was great for human targets, but it would never be able to stop the robot. Only Lyons's shotgun had the knockdown power they would need to destroy the robot's electronics.

This one, too, held an Uzi in its single gripper, with a wire leading from the trigger to an actuator motor in the arm. A small camera was also mounted to the arm, which was how Krylov could see to direct the little unit. Schwarz had a random thought flit through his head: the robots had to have cost a small fortune. Nonetheless, his respect for technology did not extend to letting killer robots blow him away.

"Guys! Guys!" he yelled. "More!"

The small robot was just swiveling to target him when Lyons charged forward, blasting it with a triple burst from the Daewoo. Just as the pellets hit it, the robot's actuator motor triggered the Uzi. A stream of 9 mm bullets punched into the wall to the right of Lyons and not far from Schwarz's position. Paint chips flew as the Parabellum bullets ripped up the drywall.

Then the robot was a smoking, sparking hulk, and Lyons was looking around for the next target.

"Gadgets," he said, "come with me. We're going to check out the basement. Blancanales, take the upstairs."

"I can save you the trouble," Krylov said. "I am in the basement, in a saferoom with heavy steel doors. You cannot get in. And I promise you that many more nasty surprises await you."

"A frigging robot," Blancanales said, coming to join them. "I still can't believe it."

"Robots, plural," Lyons said. "Like I said, check the upstairs. And be careful. There's no telling what surprises he's got built into this joint."

"But the nice man said he wasn't up there," Schwarz protested, recovering some of his composure.

"And I trust the nice man about as far as I can throw Jimmy Twelve there," Lyons jerked his chin toward the robot. "Come on, let's get to it."

"'Jimmy Twelve?'" Schwarz asked as they moved cautiously through the kitchen toward the basement door. "I think the robot's name was—"

"Can it, Gadgets," Lyons said.

The door to the basement was a simple wooden affair. Nothing exploded or deployed to attack them when they opened it. Lyons eased the door open, took his tactical flashlight from his pocket and shone it down the steps.

"Oh, I just don't freaking believe this," Lyons said.

Arrayed down the steps, on each one of the wooden slats, was a small circular device with glowing red telltales on its face.

"Tell me, Gadgets," Lyons said wearily, "that those aren't land mines."

"Okay," Schwarz said. "Technically, they're stair mines."

Lyons cursed.

"The upstairs is clean," Blancanales's voice announced in their earbuds. "There's an empty bedroom and one with what seems to be Krylov's stuff in it. A few magazines, a television, a bed that hasn't been made. Smells like feet in here."

"Come on down," Lyons said. "Take up a position at the front door. Mind the store. If you hear any loud bangs, that's just Gadgets and I mingling for all eternity."

"Now *there* is a horrifying vision of the afterlife," Schwarz said. He withdrew his own flashlight, turned it on and attached to it an elastic headband. Then he donned the light.

"That," Lyons said, "is the geekiest looking thing I have ever seen."

"Do you really want those to be your last words to me, Carl?" Schwarz asked, pretending to be hurt. "Seriously. Have some compassion, man."

"Just don't blow us up," Lyons growled.

Schwarz knelt at the first step. From his pocket he took a small kit of electronic tools, something he always carried. Using these, and training the light from his flashlight on the first mine, he pried up the outer casing up.

"Well, now," he said as he lifted away the casing. "These are small, but very unpleasant. It's a miniature Bouncing Betty."

"Seriously?"

"Yep. See this primary charge? It punches this little guy—" he pointed to a small disk the size of a hockey puck "—into the air, where it explodes at crotch level and forever ruins your weekends."

"Nice," Lyons said.

"Isn't it? Our Krylov is not a nice man, not at all." He shook his head. "I can reach these next couple from here, but I'm going to need your help in a minute."

"Do what you do, Gadgets."

Schwarz deactivated the next pair of mines, then he gestured. "Okay, big guy," he said. "This is where you get to put your brawn to work instead of your brains. Wait, that's redundant."

"I could drop you," Lyons said.

"Hold my feet, tough guy," Schwarz said. He got to his stomach and, with Lyons holding his feet to steady him, let the bigger Able Team member dangle him over the steps.

From that precarious position, Schwarz continued to deactivate each of the mines as Lyons lowered him. After several minutes of work, even the Ironman was beginning to show the strain.

"We have sirens approaching," Blancanales said through their earbuds. "Local authorities responding to calls about the gunfire, no doubt."

"Stall them," Lyons said. "I'm not too worried about getting into any jurisdictional pissing matches, not after Hal put out the good word and stomped on a few toes to make his point. But I don't want anyone charging into this little do-it-yourself fun house and getting killed. We've seen enough people go down who didn't need to."

"Understood," Blancanales answered. "I'll hold them off until you say otherwise."

They reached the bottom of the stairs. "That's the last of them," Schwarz said. He slipped down on his belly and then got to his feet, brushing concrete dust from his stomach. The basement was dimly lighted by overhead fluorescents.

"Any killer robots down there?"

"I don't see any," Schwarz answered. "All clear."

Lyons went back up to retrieve his shotgun, then descended again. Schwarz had the Beretta 93-R out of its holster and was still wearing his flashlight on his head.

"I'd say that's the door over there." Schwarz nodded to the large steel bank-vault-style entrance at one end of the basement. "Judging from how much shorter this space is compared to the floor plot above, his saferoom takes up about half the basement."

"Yes, you are correct," Krylov's voice, somewhat shaky now, was coming from still more speakers mounted in the ceiling. A small mobile camera was swiveling back and forth near the door, its red LED blinking. "You have managed to get past the technology that I thought would save me from facing my pursuers. In truth, I thought the mines...I thought you would walk down the steps and be blown up. I see now I was wrong."

"The cops have come," Lyons told him. "Look, Krylov, even if you wait in there for a month, they're going to be out here when you're ready to come out. Unless you're digging an escape tunnel out of there, you've had it. Just come out. I'm a little tired of this James Bond super-villain-lair crap. If you have any poison gas to release, or anything, just do it now."

"Very well," Krylov's voice said. "I am releasing the gas now. As you say, 'so long, suckers.'"

Lyons and Schwarz looked at each other. Schwarz tensed, thinking to make a run for the steps with Lyons.

Krylov's laughter cut through the tension. "Ha ha, I make joke! There is, of course, no poison gas. But I am not coming out. Perhaps I need time to adjust to the notion of taking my own life. I cannot say. But I am not coming out."

"And I'm not waiting one more freaking second," Lyons said. He fished into the cargo pocket of his pants and came up with the small block of Semtex he'd recovered. He held it out to his teammate.

Schwarz nodded, beyond quips and jokes now. He adjusted the size of the block of explosive, removed the rest and handed the modified bomb back to Lyons.

"You just going to walk around with that in your pocket?" Lyons gestured toward the wad of Semtex Schwarz held.

"You did," the electronics expert pointed out.

"Point." Lyons nodded. He placed the Semtex and

pressed the button on the small electronic detonator he'd placed into the bomb.

"Let's go upstairs," he said.

They hustled upstairs and waited a few more seconds. The blast was surprisingly muffled, but the crash of the steel door was not. It hit the concrete floor of the basement like the foot of an angry god stomping flat on an offending bug. The two Able Team commandos hurried back down the steps, jumping over the last two. These were in splinters from the force of the door striking them.

Krylov lay inside his saferoom.

The room had either not been as well constructed as the Russian thought, or he had simply been too close to the door. He was slumped against the far wall of his makeshift vault, a Makarov pistol on the floor next to him, his hand near it but not touching it. Blood flowed from his mouth in a small trickle.

"I…something is…wrong," he said, looking up Lyons and Schwarz. His chest was soaked in blood. Lyons looked around, but couldn't tell what it was that had struck the Russian.

"Gadgets, call 9-1-1," he said. "Get us an ambulance, fast."

"There is…no need." Krylov coughed. "I have seen enough death… Mine is here."

Schwarz took out his secure phone and began calling anyway. When he had done so, he came to stand next to Lyons, who knelt by Krylov. The Able Team leader took the Makarov and placed it beyond the Russian's grasp, but the man's eyes were glazed. It was obvious that fighting back now was the last thing on his mind. Nearby there was a desk, now broken, and the remains of several monitors and electronic remote controls, obviously the devices used to control the antipersonnel robots.

"Krylov," Lyons said quietly. "Spill it. Don't take it to your grave."

"Spill… Oh, yes. This, I have heard." He coughed, but his voice was still quite strong. "There is not much to spill. Long have I wished to see the world remade. Hard have I worked. Always, for me, there was the skill in coordinating, in planning, in organizing. I was KGB and then I was secret police and then I decided that to change the world, I would have to pull together so many, so many groups that were so alike, and so different."

"Butler helped you do that," Lyons prompted. "Reginald Butler."

"Yes." Krylov managed a weak nod. "Yes, he did. Butler was a useful idiot, as you say. He had the communications technology I needed. He thought we worked for the same goals, and we did, but he was, like the WWUP director, simply a sacrificial lamb…I would have used him for something, eventually, some way to take blame from someone else. He would never have lived to see the new socialist worker's paradise we were building…" Krylov began coughing again.

"Tell us who's behind it," Lyons said.

"There is no harm now," Krylov said. "It will never work now…without my coordination, the factions will never work together… Is Harrington dead?"

"No." Lyons shook his head. "We stopped your people. Mercenaries?"

"Some," Krylov nodded again. "Some were former KGB, like me. All, trusted. Butler, he had not the stomach for killing. But I knew we could not merely disgrace her.

We had to kill this Harrington, remove her completely…
Cross, he is like me. He believes in a new Soviet Union.
But unlike me, he is easily led. Easily manipulated. He
would have been my puppet, and I the man behind the
throne."

Krylov stopped talking. His eyes stared at nothing.

"Well," Schwarz said. "That's confirmation for you."

"It sure as hell is." Lyons nodded. "Now we just have
to get to that rally and make sure whomever he's got rolling on it doesn't complete their mission."

As they left, Schwarz took one last look at Krylov's body.

Whatever throne he was standing behind now, it wasn't
going to be the President's.

CHAPTER EIGHTEEN

Base Road, Central America

"All right," David McCarter said as the jeep bounced along the rutted road. "Javier, when we get there, you stay with the truck when we pile out. If you can put the vehicle in a position for a fast escape, do it. Otherwise, wing it. The rest of us will form up on Sukarov and march in with him, just like he's always done it. For his part, Sukarov will march along compliantly and not make trouble. Otherwise Gary here has instructions to put a bullet in his brain. Isn't that right?"

"I told you," Sukarov protested. "I was tricked. Promised much, and left to rot in this place, likely to be killed by Jiminez when he is certain he no longer needs me to maintain the missiles."

"Yeah, well, much as I'd like to have a lot of faith in your sudden conversion to our side, mate," McCarter said, "I'm having trust issues today."

"We will be there soon," Javier said. "I have never been inside, so I can offer no insight to the layout past the gates. They are of wood, as was the first base. There is a guard tower. That is all I know."

"We'll get by," McCarter said. "Sukarov, tell me what you know about these trucks."

"The way for them is difficult," the Russian said. "They were not meant for terrain such as this. We spent some time performing maintenance just on the trucks themselves, for the transportation. If they are to be moved, the way must be cleared ahead of them, and leveled. It takes time and must be done by hand. The jungle, it will rot them, once they move and are parked."

"And the missile systems themselves?" McCarter asked.

"Much better," Sukarov said proudly. "The pride of Soviet Union, in their day. Each missile is capable of carrying its nuclear payload to the United States. Each is mounted on a mobile platform towed by the truck. Is roughly size of tractor trailer."

"That's not small," Enciso said, "but it's not very large, either, by missile launch standards. Are we sure he's not exaggerating the range of the missiles?"

"Doubtful," McCarter said. "They wouldn't be much good to anybody, nor would they justify the expense and effort of getting the uranium out of here, if they couldn't get where the Strong Man or whoever's running him needed them to go."

"I am not exaggerate," Sukarov said, his accenting getting thicker. "Are very good missiles."

"I'm sure they are," McCarter said tolerantly. "Look alive, folks. We won't exactly look the part if anyone gets too close, but in the dark, with luck, we'll be able to get in and get cracking. Make sure your mags are topped off and your AKs are locked and loaded."

They rode mostly in silence for the rest of the bumpy ride, pausing now and then to grunt or groan as Javier took them bouncing and jolting over the ruts. Finally they found themselves in front of the base. A sentry with a searchlight manned the watchtower, but the light was very dim, as if the generator to which it was attached wasn't doing a very good job. The guard took a look at the jeep and waved it inside, looking bored.

"So far, so good," McCarter said softly.

The gate was opened for them. Javier drove inside, moving relatively rapidly to prevent those within from getting too close a look. The trucks El Hombre Fuerte had used to bring salvage back from the first base were parked in a motor pool area not far from the front gate. Here and there a man with a Kalashnikov moved. No one seemed particularly interested in the jeep or in Sukarov. That seemed sloppy to McCarter. The nuclear scientist was vital enough to their plans to be shadowed by four guards at all times. But then, he had to remind himself, would-be dictators of disputed splinters of banana republics weren't known for their slick military discipline.

They climbed out of the vehicle with Sukarov, doing their best to look casual. The Russian had told them that the staging point for the uranium was a low, concrete bunker of a building near the rear of the camp. They started in that general direction, flanking Sukarov, walking at a nonchalant pace.

Somebody started shouting in Spanish.

That was it, McCarter thought. They were blown. And there was only one good reason for it, the reason that had been unavoidable since they hatched this plan. It wasn't practical to leave anybody behind; he was reluctant enough to leave Javier alone with the jeep, where he might well be caught or killed. He needed all of his team members mobile and on the job. Of course, there was one more Phoenix Force member than there had been guards for Sukarov. While the opposition wasn't a bunch of geniuses, they could count to four. Somebody had obviously noticed that Sukarov had come back with one guard more than he'd left.

"Move," he said quietly.

They started running. The shouts in Spanish became more insistent. Finally somebody opened fire. Kalashnikovs chattered from all sides, but the bullets went wide in the dark, hitting nothing.

As they neared the bunker, the bright muzzle-flashes from either side of the doorway told him that there were guards firing at them.

"Calvin!" he yelled.

James nodded and stopped. He took a sidestep to clear his comrades, brought his captured AK to his shoulder and targeted the muzzle-flashes. There was a single shot, hollow and metallic, followed by another. One and then the other muzzle-flash winked out as James's precision fire took the gunner out.

They made the bunker. As they passed through the doorway, McCarter briefly assessed the structure. It could have been a World War II structure, for all he knew; it looked old enough. His knowledge of World War II history did not extend to whether one could rightly expect to find military outposts in Central America, nor did he particularly care. He waited for the other members of Phoenix Force to clear the door, dragging Sukarov behind, and slammed the metal door closed. There was a bar that fit into brackets on the door and the walls next to it, which the Briton set.

They were good for the moment.

He could hear bullets ricocheting off the concrete walls.

of the bunker. Unless the Strong Man's soldiers were willing to bring grenades or other explosives to bear on the structure, they wouldn't be breaking in too soon. McCarter turned and took in what was filling the large space.

No, he didn't figure they'd be too eager to blow up this building.

The room was full of insulated drums. McCarter recognized them from the encapsulated briefing he'd been given by Stony Man. These would be metal double-walled drums, with simple fiberboard and plywood forming outer insulation around another steel and lead core container. The whole thing was airtight, sealed with synthetic O-rings. Here, what was left of it anyway, was the uranium.

"Gents," he said, "I don't mind saying this has been long enough in coming."

Encizo prodded Sukarov over to where McCarter stood.

"Give the man the details," he said.

"Yes, yes, I tell you," Sukarov said testily. "This is the uranium, *da*. What I did not use of it to fuel the warheads."

"Where are the trucks?" McCarter demanded. He could hear soldiers outside banging on the bunker. The metal door began to rattle in its housing, but he thought it solid enough to hold.

"Come," Sukarov said. "I show you."

He went to a topographical map posted on one wall, with red circles outlining three locations.

"Here, this is us, the base," he said. "This one, this is truck one. Not far from here. This one, this is truck two. A little farther, still not far. Both trucks carry one missile, warhead armed and ready. Sukarov is told that should more missiles, more trucks be required, more will be provided. This promise was made by Krylov, Fedor Krylov, the liar."

McCarter nodded. He would have to note that nam and give it to the Farm, once the mission was completed

"How dangerous is this room?" Manning put in.

"Dangerous?"

"Radiation," Manning stated.

"Bah—" Sukarov waved his hand "—uranium, yes, b in insulated drums. Is slightly hot, nothing to worry about.

"Just the same," McCarter said, "let's not spend an more time here than we have to."

"How you plan to go out?" Sukarov said. "Is warm re ception waiting outside." He moved casually to the from door. "Why, I am thinking—"

"T.J.," McCarter said, "stop him!"

It was too late. Sukarov threw back the bolt on the doo The door crashed open and a sudden fusillade of bulle ripped into the Russian scientist. He fell, dead before h reached the concrete floor of the bunker. Phoenix Forc scattered to either side of the space. Bullets hit the floc but stopped short of the uranium canisters. McCarter coul hear shouting outside, close to the doorway. He under stood just enough Spanish to know what was happening Somebody in charge had just reminded the troops that a lo of punctured drums full of enriched uranium fuel were no body's friend.

"Cal," McCarter said, "show them the error of their ways.

James smiled as he loaded a 40 mm round and shoul dered the M-79 "blooper." The weapon chugged as he pu the grenade neatly through the open doorway. The explo sion shook the walls of the bunker and scattered the me outside.

"Once more!" McCarter ordered.

"Firing!" James said. He punched another grenad

through the opening. The explosion was met with more
screams and confusion.

"Up and out, up and out!" McCarter yelled. "Fire as
you go!"

Phoenix Force rushed up the steps and out of the bunker.
McCarter was last out, stepping over Sukarov's body as he
went. For all his protests, for all that he complained he had
been treated unfairly, the Russian nuclear scientist had obviously thought to betray them to stay in El Hombre
Fuerte's good graces. Like so many of those who helped
the strong men of the world, his only reward for his actions
had been a swift death. Well, at least he hadn't endured torture and torment. There was something to be said for that
fast exit, compared to some of the victims of dictators like
Jiminez.

Phoenix Force emerged into a fire-torn hellscape. The
grenades had ignited the two vehicles near the wall, and the
flaming wreckage had rained down doing its deadly work.
The jeep, with Javier behind the wheel, was nowhere to be
seen, and McCarter couldn't worry about it now.

"Gary, you and Cal, head for truck one," he directed.
"T.J., you and Rafe take truck two. Get there and make sure
the launching systems are out of commission. Do whatever
you have to, but don't set off any mushroom clouds."

"And you?" Manning asked.

"I'm going after whatever passes for a radio room in this
base," McCarter said. "We've got to get on the horn to the
Farm and let them know where we are and where to find
this place. They'll need to send in troops, specialists, and
containment equipment for the uranium. The Zone of Dispute will be our friend on this one. None of the neighboring countries want to claim the place, so they can hardly

object to us removing El Hombre Fuerte and his glow-in-
the-dark toys, can they?"

A chorus of affirmatives met him. "Move out, then,"
he said.

The fires in the base continued to rage. McCarter was
surprised at the lack of resistance. Apparently their raid on
the first base had depleted the Strong Man's manpower a
great deal. The Briton put himself in Jiminez's place, pon-
dering what he would do in the Strong Man's situation. The
would-be dictator's most valuable assets, his biggest bar-
gaining chips, were those missile trucks. He would have
most of his reserves deployed around them, McCarter was
willing to bet. And of course communications with the
outside world, that was an issue, too. If it was McCarter,
he would make sure that radio room was well secured.

Lovely.

The Briton kept to the flickering shadows and avoided
the largest of the fires, trusting his teammates to go about
their tasks with their usual efficiency. He spotted a semi-
permanent structure of canvas and sandbags that looked
like a good bet. He slipped up behind it, conscious of the
guard who was standing, nervously, in front of the entrance. The man was obviously quite agitated. He kept
moving back and forth, his Kalashnikov in his hands,
watching the flames. His dilemma was clear: stay or go?
Keep his post manned under the orders of El Hombre
Fuerte, or abandon it and get as far from this destruction
as possible? The fear in which the Strong Man held his
troops and those subjugated by them was obvious in the
man's furtive movements. He would take a few steps away,
then visibly force himself back, all the while hopping from
foot to foot nervously.

McCarter ended his dilemma for him. He slipped up behind the sentry with his combat knife in his fist. Clamping his free hand over the sentry's mouth, he drew the blade of the knife across the man's neck. The Briton managed to avoid the blood spray and left the sentry there, picking up the AK as he went.

It was, as McCarter had correctly guessed, the radio room. There was a table in the middle of the room, a rickety wooden construction missing one leg, propped up with cinder blocks gleaned from the who knew where. The radio equipment was arrayed on it and was, to McCarter's eye, quite sophisticated.

A man sat at the table.

He was wearing, of all things, earbuds, listening to music from an MP-3.

McCarter could not fathom why a man would shove music into his ears in the middle of a firefight. He could only conclude that this poor bastard, like the guard out front, had been told to man the battlements—or in this case, the communications facilities—at all costs and under pain of death. When the world had started exploding outside, the fellow had apparently resigned himself to his fate, and decided he'd rather go out whistling a good tune than watching the rockets' red glare. Well, that was his choice. McCarter, knife in hand, strode up behind him, after first setting down his captured AK and the newly acquired second rifle.

The man surprised him. The fellow was young, but not as young as McCarter had at first thought, and not nearly as helpless. He turned suddenly, an AK-47 bayonet in hand, and lunged in McCarter's direction.

The Briton stepped back and slashed downward, managing a glancing cut on the soldier's knife hand. He grimaced but did not let go; the wound was not deep. Crouching, he kept the knife low and near himself, pointed at McCarter. The Briton was no stranger to the knife game, either, and mirrored the soldier's stance.

"Put it down, mate," McCarter said.

The guard swore at him in Spanish.

"Well," McCarter said, "they say a man who'll willingly engage in a knife fight deserves what he gets."

The soldier looked at him, confused.

McCarter whipped the 1911 from his belt left-handed. There was no point in trying to be quiet now.

The soldier lunged. McCarter shot him, stepping out of the way as the radio operator collapsed on the floor. He aimed the heavy pistol and contemplated a mercy shot, but the man's death rattle was audible enough. McCarter set the pistol's safety and tucked the gun away.

He fired up the radio equipment. Getting the right frequency was not the hard part; knowing he was on a completely open channel was the issue. The radio room doubled as a map room, and the location of the Strong Man's camps was nice and clearly marked on several of these. McCarter rifled through them, memorized the numbers, and gave the room a final once-over before adjusting the radio.

"Phoenix One, Phoenix One," he said. "Code Conflagration, repeat, Code Conflagration. Send support, send containment, coordinates follow." He began reading off the longitude and latitude. While the coordinates would be easily interpreted by anyone listening, and there would be many someone's listening, the Farm would have a containment team standing by somewhere close, staged by Price for this eventuality. That had been the plan as they were dropped over Central America. The close-your-eyes, hope-for-the-best part of the plan had of course been that Phoenix Force would find the uranium and the missiles, if there were in fact missiles, here in Central America where they were supposed to be. Certainly they had expected to be able to contain the threat in India, where all that had happened. Well, that was over for now. They could breathe a little easier. Now he just had to wait for the containment team to show up. And the rest of Phoenix Force would be securing the missile trucks, making sure no one could launch a missile. They just needed time, time to get in place, time to do their work.

"You," came the voice over the radio, "are out of time, my friend."

McCarter glanced at the handset. Jiminez.

"Do you send your men to stop me?" Jiminez asked mockingly. He had to have a portable radio with a scanning feature that picked up the outgoing transmission.

"Well, you are too late," Jiminez said. "I am with one of the trucks. Do you wonder which? And I am pressing certain buttons now. Do you think you can stop the missile before it launches? I do not like your chances. But perhaps, just perhaps, if you guess correctly, you can find me. See if you can. See if you can reach me before the missile takes flight. I suggest you run."

McCarter ran.

CHAPTER NINETEEN

McCormick Place, Chicago

Carl Lyons didn't bother to take in the opulence of McCormick Place. The convention facility, which the Farm had informed him took in more than three million visitors annually, was actually a four-building complex. Their target was the South Building, 840,000 square feet of exhibition space that included the Grand Ballroom. It was there that the main to-do of the convention was scheduled to take place, with various classes and conferences spilling out into the exhibition space above after Harrington's keynote address.

They would be facing amateurs, most likely. Given what they knew of the forces arrayed against them, these attackers would be WWUP and EAF faithful, wide-eyed miscreants with guns and guts but not much else. He figured it likely that they'd capped most, if not all, of Krylov's Russian mercenary help, who had been acting as advisers and, in the case of the arson attack, an external control whose task it was to eliminate pesky witnesses who might be able to talk a little too much, post-capture, about just who it was that had been stirring them up, financing them, and helping them.

Facing amateurs meant that this was largely an exercise in nerve, drive and firepower, but that didn't mean it would be easy. Nonprofessionals were notoriously erratic and unpredictable. They did stupid things that pros didn't do, and as a result they sometimes came out on top simply because the professionals couldn't fathom how anyone could attempt such moves and manage them. Lyons made it his mission never to underestimate the enemy and this was no different.

The men of Able Team had stationed themselves in the grand ballroom, with good fields of fire from raised platforms at the sides and rear of the room. They were dressed as media technicians, in coveralls appropriated from among the media teams covering the event. They had bitched a little, but they'd given in when shown the Justice credentials with which Brognola had equipped Able Team. Lyons's own coveralls were a little snug, but they'd come off the biggest guy they could find. Now he sat next to an actual cameraman from one of the national networks, he forgot which. The man kept glancing at him nervously, as if afraid Lyons would bite.

Schwarz and Blancanales were established in similar positions.

The rally was well under way, and Marcia Harrington had just taken the platform. This was it; this was the critical moment. If the rabble-rousers Krylov had worked up to attack the event were here, they'd choose now, or close to now, to do their thing.

On the stage at the front of the ballroom, several dignitaries were waiting and watching. It amused Lyons that the best seat in the house was actually terrible. If you were one of the bigwigs, you got to sit in full view of everyone else, and when your fellow bigshots were talking, you had great view of their backsides. Well, that's what life was like in the halls of power, he guessed. Probably there was something very appropriate about all that.

Among those sitting on the stage was a very uncomfortable-looking Congressman Richard Cross. His expression was not at all that of a man who was watching his political partner put her best foot forward toward a presidential run, with him on the ticket as vice president. No, Cross looked like he'd just swallowed something foul, and perhaps he had. The assassins had been sent to take out Harrington before she ever took the stage. Now she was there, just as scheduled. Lyons wondered if maybe Cross had prepared a speech, in which he nobly filled in for her and then got to look good when he held his cool as Harrington's supposedly unstable supporters made a mess of the rally. Was that the plan? It did seem likely.

Then he saw the first of the guns come out, and the time for speculating and theorizing was over.

"Gun," he said quietly, pulling the Daewoo from its bag. Given the distance involved and the precision shooting needed, one and only one of Able Team had been tasked with this phase of the rally. That was Blancanales, who even now was leveling his CAR-15 and taking careful aim.

"Got him," Blancanales said quietly.

The CAR-15 cracked. The young man in the hooded sweatshirt, who had pulled a small pistol from underneath it, went down almost without a sound. There was a moment's silence as everyone present tried to figure out what that loud noise had been. Then pandemonium washed across the crowd.

The screaming and running for the exits actually worked to Able Team's advantage. Above it all on their platforms, they had a good view of everyone within that sea of humanity, and Blancanales could pick out those who produced and tried to use weapons. The crowd, meanwhile, was heading toward the exits as fast as a mass of human beings could go. In a post 9/11 world, the threat of terrorist attack was very much on the mind of the public at large. All it took was a few shots to get people moving, to break their paralysis and get them in fight or flight mode.

Blancanales fired again, taking out a man who had raised a revolver.

Per the plan, Harrington's official escorts, who had taken her to the safehouse and guarded her there, were hustling her out of the room via the rear entrance. Blancanales continued to fire away, plucking terrorists deftly from the crowd. Still on stage, frozen in place, was Richard Cross.

Blancanales was taking out one of the last of the gunners, scoring a head shot that separated the woman with the 9 mm pistol from the rest of the receding crowd. It was Schwarz who saw the last of them climbing the stage.

"Pol, we got a climber on the stage!" he reported. The distance was too great for the 93-R, and Lyons had a bad angle for the shot with his Python. Before a bullet could stop him, the young man had put himself in front of Cross, making a shot into him dangerous for the Congressman. Then the terrorist had Cross up and out of his chair and was using him as a shield. He put his gun, a snub-nosed revolver, to the side of Cross's head, making a show of cocking the hammer.

"Damn it," Blancanales said into his transceiver. "I might be able to get a shot, but he's liable to brush against that trigger and blow the man's head off."

"One thing at a time," Lyons said. He looked around; the ballroom had cleared, leaving only the bodies of the terrorists Blancanales had taken down. It was possible there had been a few others among the crowd who thought better of it and left with the rest of the rally-goers, but if that was so they were no longer a threat. The groups involved in this whole mess would be thoroughly investigated, and any individuals with ties to the crimes and conspiracies committed and formulated here in Chicago would be brought to justice. He didn't have any doubt about that. Unfortunately, he did have to save Congressman Cross from getting his head shot off, even if the man might conceivably be dirty, and even—Lyons gritted his teeth—if he was the jerk who had tried to sic everybody from the local cops to the attorney general's office on Able Team.

"He's headed to the stairs," Blancanales reported, "on his way up."

"We can't let him get away." Lyons sighed. "After him."

They climbed down from their perches and pursued. The shooter led them on a merry chase through the exhibit hall area, dragging Cross all the way. When he reached a set of fire doors at the rear of the hall, he was suddenly no longer alone.

They had to have had some kind of plan to provide backup for those in the ballroom, Lyons decided, or else the terrorists targeting the main rally had thought to take everyone hostage and use these men as additional muscle. There were half a dozen of them, mostly young, dressed in the type of paramilitary clothes you could buy in an Army/Navy retail store. The urban camouflage they wore was dyed various colors, ranging from sky-blue to red, and they wore natty little matching bandannas on their heads. Lyons suppressed the urge to retch, reminding himself never to underestimate his foes, even foes with bad fashion sense.

Especially since these foes carried guns.

Each of them had a rifle or a handgun. He spotted a couple of Ruger Mini-14s and what looked like a Beretta and a couple of Glocks, strictly civilian hardware, probably acquired locally, legally or illegally.

Well, might as well start cutting the odds now.

As Cross was pulled past the fire door by his captor, Lyons's field of fire was full of enemies and nothing else. He brought up the massive USAS-12 and pulled the trigger back, riding out the recoil as the shotgun shells pumped dramatically from the weapon. Blancanales and Schwarz did the same, laying down a withering hail of fire.

The camouflaged newcomers were caught completely flatfooted. Expecting helpless victims, unarmed men and women who would cower at the sight of their paramilitary garb and their waving weapons, they could not quite wrap their minds around the wall of death that flew at them. They toppled like dominoes. One man took a bullet to the face, another to the throat; two more men were rocked by the main charge of Lyons's double-aught buck; the last two were gunned down by precision shots from Blancanales's CAR-15. When Lyons moved forward, gliding heel-to-toe on stable firing platforms, one of the grievously wounded men looked up and reached up a hand.

"Why…why…we were just trying to…"

"Trying to terrorize innocent people?" Lyons said. "Maybe commit a little murder in the name of extremism?" He was suddenly disgusted. It didn't matter what cause these people claimed to represent. Really, deep down, they were just thugs and bullies, people who wanted to make the other fellow toe the line by shoving a gun in his face. That sort of thing made him sick. And as long as he was alive and kicking, he would do what was necessary to make sure people like that were brought to justice.

"Come on," he said to the others.

They hurried after Cross. Hitting the stairwell, they saw no sign of him; then the echo of a door slamming filtered up from below.

"Down, down," Lyons instructed. They went, careful to avoid walking into an ambush, but hurrying nonetheless. Lyons didn't think the terrorists they were after would think to lie in wait for him; he was in grab 'em and run mode, probably thinking with an entire congressman in his mitts he could demand a million dollars and a helicopter and a private jet to Barbados, or something. Most of these punks had seen too many movies, and their misconceptions were mistakes they regretted whenever they went up against the commandos of Stony Man Farm.

"He's headed for the parking lot," Schwarz observed.

Indeed he was. That was not good. They really did not want to engage in yet another rolling gun battle. For that matter, the only thing holding that Suburban together was luck and faith. The old girl had been remarkably faithful and sturdy, but you could only punch so many bullet holes in a machine before it stopped working properly.

The terrorist—up close he really was just a kid—had stopped, unsure which direction to take now that he was in the open air. Lyons and the other Able Team members moved in from three sides, Lyons going in forward, the other two flanking the kid at angles so their bullets wouldn't strike each other.

"Don't come any closer!" he shrieked.

"Kid," Lyons said tiredly, "this is not a game we want to play."

"I...I have this guy!" he said. Lyons realized then that they had something working for them; the kid had no idea how important his hostage really was.

"Do you have any idea who I am?" Cross said, visibly upset. "I'm Congressman Richard Cross! I will see to it you never see the light of day again!"

Lyons struggled, very hard, to resist the urge to slap himself in the forehead.

"I want a chopper!" the kid said predictably. "I want safe passage out of here! I'm not going to prison! This is all a mistake...a mistake. I didn't hurt anybody..."

"Kid," Lyons said, "you see those two men to either side of you?"

"Yeah, tell them to back off!" the kid ordered.

"Yes, if you are law-enforcement officers, I invoke my authority," the Congressman blustered. "You will withdraw immediately."

"Congressman," Lyons said, "shut up." He looked the kid in the eyes again. "What's your name?"

"I'm not telling you anything!"

"Your first name, then. So I know what to call you other than 'kid.'"

"Michael."

"Well, Michael, we have a situation. You see, those two men are federal agents. So am I. We are here for one reason, and one reason only. That is to stop those who sought to murder the attendees at this rally in general, and possibly Senator Marcia Harrington specifically. Now, do you know anything about that?"

"I'm not going to admit to anything!"

Lyons sighed. "Fine, Michael," he said. "Let's stipulate that you've taken the Fifth, shall we? Now, you have more important things on your plate. Did you see what happened to your comrades in there just now?"

"You murdered them!"

"Specifically," Lyons said, "the man with the black rifle pointed at your head shot all of your little terrorist buddies. One bullet per, just like in the movies. They died before they knew what hit them. Are you getting what I'm saying?"

"You can't intimidate me, you corporatist thug!"

"Michael," Lyons said, growing tired of the youth's rhetoric, "I'm not here to argue politics, religion or economics with you. I'm telling you that if you don't immediately put that gun down, my friend there will put a single bullet through your brain. I want you to think about that."

Michael looked at the barrel of Blancanales's CAR-15 and did indeed look very much like he was thinking about that.

Movement in the periphery of his vision distracted Lyons. He looked, only to find himself covered by a man with an Uzi, who was inside one of the nearby parked cars. The movement Lyons had seen had been the car window descending. He risked a glance back; Schwarz and Blancanales were similarly covered by men in fatigues who were sitting inside nearby parked vehicles.

"Do not move, any one of you," the man covering Lyons said. He had a distinct accent.

"So Krylov wasn't out of Russian mercs after all," Lyons ventured.

"No," said the first Russian. "I would say he was not."

"Let me guess—" Lyons tried to engage the man, get his brain working on the conversation and not on Able

Team "—you were here to nursemaid these greenie wee-nies, these junior grade Commie Youth. It was your job to see to it they got the job done."

"No, actually," the Russian replied. "It really would not matter what they managed to do in there. Either way, the event would be marred. This does not concern me. My job was to make sure none of them lived. This was to be the escape route."

"So Krylov was covering his tracks, like always," Lyons said. "Eliminating the tools after he was done using them."

"*Da*." The Russian nodded. "I do not know who you are, but I can suspect. You will join them."

"Think so?" Lyons asked.

"I know so," the Russian with the Uzi smiled. "Bring up your weapon and I will kill you."

"That'd be a damned shame," Lyons said. "I guess I'll have to tell my boys to surrender. Guys?" Lyons allowed himself a smile. "Now."

From the hip, Lyons yanked back the trigger of the Dae-woo, one-handed. The weapon bucked terribly as it churned its deadly payload into the car where the Russian hid. The door was blown apart and the man behind it was shredded along with it. The Uzi discharged, but the shots never came near Lyons.

At the same moment, Schwarz and Blancanales dropped to the ground. As they did so, each drew a bead on the Russian mercenary behind the other. Blancanales's 5.56 mm bullet punched through the throat of the man behind Schwarz, who blasted hell out of his own car door with the falling Uzi. Schwarz fired a three-round burst of 9 mm lead that took the gunner behind his teammate in the forehead, snapping him back and ending him.

Richard Cross, exhibiting a fairly keen sense of survival, had also dropped to his knees. The only other participant left standing in this little tableau was the terrorist who called himself Michael. He looked around, confused, as if unsure what to do now that the grown-ups were shooting it out without him. Finally, he started to bring the revolver back on target.

"Don't!" Lyons ordered.

Michael didn't listen.

From the ground, Gadgets fired a single bullet that punched through Michael's jaw, up and out. He folded. The cocked revolver discharged when it hit the pavement, but the bullet hit no one.

"Jesus!" Cross shouted.

"You're welcome," Lyons said.

CHAPTER TWENTY

Central America

Gary Manning and Calvin James made their way on foot along the ruts that had obviously been made by the type of heavy truck Sukarov had described. The jungle had already started to close back in around the great wound caused by the vehicle or vehicles that had made this path. Manning didn't doubt that the trucks would rot; he had seen enough jungle environments to know what they did to both man and machine over extended periods.

"The truck will be guarded," he said. "Stay low."

They took opposite sides of the road. Each had an AK ready, and James carried the M-79. They would use the launcher on the truck if they had to, but Manning hoped that would not be necessary. He did not want to risk any contamination by releasing the nuclear fuel in the warhead. Blowing up the missile wouldn't detonate it; nuclear warheads didn't operate that way. The fuel itself, though, was as deadly a poison as one was likely to encounter. He did not want to set it loose on the landscape.

There was a bend in the trail ahead. The two Phoenix Force commandos paused to look past the cover of the nearby, surrounding trees. In the distance, lighted like a

Christmas tree with gas lanterns, was a large flat-bed truck. The truck had outriggers firmly set in place extending from the bed.

On the bed was a missile, in vertical launch position, though it did not exhibit any other signs of readiness. There were no fumes, no incipient generator noises, nothing to indicate that a launch was imminent. There were, however, several sandbag nests surrounding the truck. At least one of these had a 50-caliber machine gun mounted within it.

"How do you want to play it, Gary?" James asked.

"How accurate can you be with that thing?" he gestured to the M-79.

"How accurate do you need me to be?"

"We need to take out those nests," he said, "without risking breaching the missile."

James judged the range. "I can do that, no sweat."

"All right, then," Manning said. He adjusted the sights on his AK and shouldered the rifle. "I'll pick off any stragglers."

"You got it," James said. He, too, adjusted the sights on the blooper, judging the range. He arrayed the last of his 40 mm grenades in front of him. There were just enough, if he did not miss any. Then, calmly and without rushing, he steadied himself on one knee and braced the M-79 against his shoulder.

The launcher chugged.

The first blast took the machine-gun nest. The weapon blew apart, spraying deadly hot fragments in every direction, shredding the sandbags from within. Men screamed. James, still operating methodically and without apparent urgency, reloaded the M-79 and took aim once more.

The soldiers in the remaining sandbag nests starting firing into the night. Manning waited; he knew that his muzzle-flash would give him away. The M-79 chugged again, just to his left, and a second nest exploded.

Panicking now, the soldiers began emptying their AKs on full-auto, firing in every direction. Still Manning held his fire. James took aim again, let out half a breath, and fired, blowing apart a third nest. He was lining up the fourth and last of these when one of the gunners finally caught a glimpse of him and Manning at the edge of the clearing where the truck sat.

The muzzle-flashes were brighter as the soldiers desperately targeted the source of the inexorable destruction moving their way. Manning cut loose with the AK, sustained bursts taking out first one, then a second gunner. The blooper's launch was almost anticlimactic. Only two men remained in the last nest when the grenade exploded in their midst, silencing them.

"On we go," Manning said.

James slung the now useless M-79, reluctant to leave it behind even though he had no more rounds for it. Shouldering his AK at low ready, he followed Manning as the big Canadian led the way down to the truck.

The control panel set in the side of the flatbed was labeled in Cyrillic. Manning had no idea what to do with it, so he took a photo with his secure satellite phone and uploaded it to the Farm. Moments later, the phone vibrated. He snapped it open.

"Manning," he said.

"Gary, we've got your analysis here," Kurtzman said. "I want you to find the colored buttons on the upper-left corner of that panel. You should see a pattern of green, green, blue, yellow?"

"Got it," Manning said.

"Good," Kurtzman said. "Now, push the blue button."

"Pushed."

"Did the other indicators turn yellow?"

"They did."

"I want you to push the last yellow button on the right, then the others, moving from right to left," Kurtzman said. "Once you've done that, there'll be an audible tone. When you hear that tone, mash the big red circular knob at the bottom of the panel."

Manning did as he was instructed.

"What's it doing?" Kurtzman asked.

"Nothing," Manning said. "All the indicators have gone out."

"Congratulations, Gary," Kurtzman said. "You've just activated the failsafe on a Soviet-era ballistic missile."

"And?"

"And the missile is now effectively zeroized," Kurtzman said. "It can't be launched now. The containment team is mobilizing and should reach you soon."

"Then I guess we'd better hurry up and finish the job here," Manning said.

"Good luck," Kurtzman said. "Base, out."

Manning snapped the phone shut and looked up at the missile. For all intents and purposes, it was now declawed.

"All right, Calvin," Manning said, turning to James. "There's nothing more we can do here."

"Then let's get to the second truck and see if we can help," James suggested.

"Right," Manning agreed. "Double time?"

"Double time."

They ran.

THE WAY TO THE SECOND truck was barred by a series of sandbag emplacements, arranged like walls across the primitive wheel-rut road leading to what Hawkins and Encizo could only presume was the second mobile missile. Soldiers were there, crouched low behind cover, and they were expecting trouble.

"What do you wanna do, Rafe?" Hawkins asked.

"We're going to have to zigzag it," Encizo said. "You with me?"

"With you." Hawkins nodded. "You want left or right?"

"I'll take the left," he said. "You go right. I'll start, and you take the second round, then I'll take the third."

"Gotcha. See you at the end."

They split up, Encizo going left, Hawkins disappearing in the opposite direction. The maneuver they were about to perform was relatively simple—all successful combat tactics were, for in the field unnecessary complexity equaled points of failure equaled death—but risky, as it involved taking each hurdle while switching off as bait and hunter. Being the hunter was fine; being the bait meant drawing fire. Encizo, an expert in guerrilla tactics, had every guerrilla's adverse reaction to taking fire. For that matter, no sane man wanted to be taking lead, or to have it flying even in his general direction.

Encizo waited for Hawkins to get into position. When he judged that enough time had gone by, he pointed his AK in the general direction of the first emplacement and pulled the trigger. He fired a sustained burst, enough to draw the attention of the opposition, but not to waste his ammunition too badly.

The answering muzzle-flashes came right on cue, as the first set of soldiers targeted his burst and began firing into the night. They were firing blindly, from what Encizo could tell. Their shots did not come anywhere near him, despite the fact that he'd given them an obvious target to track. The single shots that cracked out from his right were much more decisive, much more precise. That was Hawkins, punching 7.62 mm rounds into the guards as they gave themselves away.

The guards at the first emplacement stopped shooting. Encizo gave them another burst and waited before emerging from cover. There was no answering fire. He approached the first emplacement, aware of Hawkins moving stealthily parallel to him. The two Phoenix Force warriors reached their destination at roughly the same time. They found two dead men.

"Okay," Encizo said. "Let's take the next set."

They repeated the procedure. Once more, the soldiers targeted the burst of offering sacrifice fire, this time from Hawkins. It was Encizo's turn to target their muzzle-flashes and bring them down with precise, aimed fire. Mission accomplished. When the two men checked the sandbag nest, they again found two corpses.

The third and final emplacement blocking the road turned out to be a more serious obstacle. Encizo got into position, fired his burst and was rewarded with answering fire. This time, the gunshots came closer to his location, but he was still relatively safe. Hawkins targeted them and fired, again silencing the gunshots and ending the muzzle-flashes. They loosened another burst and another wait, then moved in.

"Looks like we got them all," Encizo said as he put one leg over the sandbags.

As he stepped over, one of the supposedly dead soldiers,

who had been playing possum, brought up his AK from where he was lying on his back. Encizo saw it and threw himself back over the sandbags. He felt a tug at the tip of his combat boot as he landed. The supposedly dead soldier was screaming profanities in Spanish as he lighted up the night. Hawkins hugged the dirt and waited for the man to burn through his magazine. When he heard the AK cycle dry, he stood and popped a single round into the man's head. The soldier folded over without another sound.

"You okay?" he asked Encizo.

The little Cuban was still flat on his back. He was looking up at the toe of his boot, visible in the moonlight. It had a neat chip out of it where one of the enemy soldier's bullets had burned past.

"That," he said, "was very close."

Their earbud transceivers began to emit static. Both men paused. The voice on the other end, at first garbled, began to become clearer. They recognized it as McCarter, who was moving into range of the little devices.

"I repeat," the Briton was saying. "The Strong Man has initiated a launching sequence on one of the missiles!"

"It's not truck one," came Manning's voice. "We've taken that out of the equation."

"Then we're on to truck two," McCarter said. "If you're in range, I assume you're all on your way?"

"Gary and Calvin, affirmative," Manning answered.

"Rafael and T.J., waiting in place at the head of the trail leading to the truck," Encizo reported. "What about you, David?"

"I'm on my way," he said. "I sent the radio message, but the Strong Man himself was on the other end of the frequency, just daring us to come stop him. It's looking bad, mates."

The three newcomers reached Hawkins and Encizo at roughly the same time.

"Together again." Hawkins smiled.

"Good work, you two," McCarter said. "All right, let's get as close as we dare and assess the situation."

They stalked through the night, still staying to the edges of the road. When they came to the truck, finally, they were surprised to find no other guards. What they did see, however, was that the truck was in launch mode. The missile was vertical, and the generators connected to the truck were ramping up. Some sort of vapor was spewing from the launch mechanism. The whole truck vibrated as its systems were powered up and the missile was prepared to hurtle into the sky.

"Where is everyone?" James whispered.

"El Hombre Fuerte is around here somewhere," McCarter said. "He's got to be, unless he lighted this candle and made a beeline for the nearest exit."

"What do you want us to do?" Hawkins asked.

"Only thing we can do," McCarter said. "Move in. Spread out. Don't make yourselves tempting targets. I'm getting that feeling again."

As they crept closer to the missile on its flatbed truck, the hair on the back of McCarter's neck stood up.

A voice, speaking in Spanish and amplified by a megaphone, spoke a command, then gunfire erupted.

Methodically targeting the muzzle-flashes, constantly moving in and around the missile truck, Phoenix Force began whittling down the opposition.

One by one, the muzzle-flashes winked out. Phoenix

Force knew well the rules of low light fighting: stay low, move constantly and don't panic. Each time one of the Stony Man commandos triggered his weapon, he immediately moved laterally, making sure that any answering fire would go where he had been. The Strong Man's soldiers simply could not keep up, and none of them thought to leave what he thought of as safety, as cover and concealment, in order to stay mobile enough to avoid becoming a target.

Each was eventually picked off.

When the shooting died down, McCarter took a head count.

"Anybody injured?" he asked.

Only negatives came back.

"Gary," he said, "call the Farm, do your thing."

Manning placed the call and described the control panel.

"Gary," Kurtzman said, sounding worried, "send me a picture."

Manning did so. As soon as the picture uploaded to the Farm, came Kurtzman back on the line. "Do *not* touch the control panel," he said. "What you've got there is a failsafe launch sequence. It's been keyed in to prevent tampering and it's on a timer."

Manning described the situation to the others and handed the phone to McCarter, who was beckoning for it. "David here," McCarter said into the unit. "How much time have we got?"

"There's no way to tell," Kurtzman said, sounding apologetic. "Only the operator who set it would know. There are no external indicators, probably for precisely the reason the failsafe feature was built into it."

"What can we do?"

"Well, you can't do it from the panel," Kurtzman said. "The operator who set it off will have taken the failsafe remote, a means to either trigger the launch immediately or deactivate it. I'm looking at the schematics now, and the damned thing is also a dead man's switch. You'd better be careful you don't shoot whoever is holding it, or that could trigger the launch."

"Bloody hell," McCarter said.

"Who's got the remote?" Kurtzman asked.

"Not sure," McCarter said, "but I've got a sinking feeling. I'll be in touch. David, out." He closed the phone and handed it back to Manning.

"Spread out," he said. "Find a trail. We're looking for a man on foot, let's hope. If he's in a vehicle, we are well and truly screwed."

They searched. A couple of the dead men had flashlights on them, and these helped. It did not take long for Encizo to find them: a pair of fresh vehicle tracks, leading through the brush and back onto the rutted road leading farther into the jungle.

"Shit," McCarter swore. "I don't like our chances of catching up with—"

The sound of an approaching engine cut him off.

The vehicle approaching was none other than the appropriated jeep, with a grinning Javier behind the wheel. He pulled up.

"Jav," McCarter said. "Where have you been?"

"I had to save this pretty jeep," he said. "They wanted to shoot it all up! It took some time to lose them, but I did so, and I returned to find only dead men in the camp. You have done your work well."

"You're just in time." McCarter waved Phoenix Force

over and they again piled into the vehicle. "See that road? We're looking for whoever's taken it, most likely in another four-wheel-drive vehicle. I have a suspicion it's Jiminez, and I think he's got his fingers wrapped around a dead man's switch that could launch that missile there."

"Not good." Javier pressed the accelerator and the jeep rumbled forward, bouncing over the rough terrain. "We will find him, and we will get this detonator, and then maybe you will let me kill him?"

"Get in line, Jav," McCarter said grimly. "Get in line."

They followed the trail in darkness, the black night broken only by the jeep's headlights and auxiliary lights, and the shafts of moonlight that managed to make it through the jungle canopy.

"Where does this road go, Jav?" McCarter asked.

"I was not aware that there was a road even here," he admitted. "The way was guarded always by Jiminez's soldiers, for to take this path one must go through his base, yes? I have no idea. There is nothing out there but jungle for quite some distance, as far as I know."

"If it's Jiminez, maybe he's just running to run," James put in.

"Maybe," McCarter said. "But this once again smells. He's after something."

They came, eventually, to just what it was the Strong Man was after.

The road ended in a clearing and in its center was a small corrugated tin building with a transmitter dish. An old jeep was parked outside.

"Radio Jiminez?" Hawkins asked.

"That is a television transmitter," Javier said. "But here? It makes no sense."

"Possibly it might," McCarter said, "for the young, up-wardly mobile banana republic dictator on the go."

"You're thinking this is Jiminez's bully pulpit?"

"I do," McCarter said. "Think about it. The Zone of Dispute is his. But what good is being king of a disputed area that's not really a country? Sure, you get to lord your power over the locals, but at the end of the day, what does that get you? Not a lot. But if you're planning on declaring your statehood, well, that's another matter entirely. And of course you need a means of getting the word out, preferably in full color, in your nicely pressed paramilitary uniform and all."

"Jiminez plans to use the nuclear weapons for leverage."

"He sure does," McCarter said. "Or at least, he did. Those were going to be the big stick he used to beat his neighbors into acceptance, and to make sure the rest of the world listened. It doesn't matter for what reasons he was provided with the missiles and the nuclear fuel for them. Obviously he had his own agenda all along, as men like him so often do. That you can take to the bank, I think."

"He may be inside," Javier said.

"Oh, I imagine he is," McCarter said. "I think we should give him a few minutes to warm up to the idea of us being out here. I don't particularly want to startle him. Let's assume he's got his hands on that dead man's switch connected to the missile truck. I want to take that very gently from him, to prevent any bangs or booms."

"What can I do to help?" Javier asked.

"You, my friend, wait right here," McCarter said. "You've proved a capable getaway driver, mate, so I imagine you'll shine in that role."

Javier chuckled. "Very well."

"The rest of you, take up positions outside this building. Secure it. I'm going inside, alone, to talk to a certain Strong Man."

"You don't want backup?" Manning asked, sounding concerned.

"No," McCarter said. "If I'm any judge of men like this, he'll want an audience, but he'll also want to feel like we're dealing with him man to man. His honor and his pride will figure heavily into it. If I can get him talking, maybe I can find a way to avert a launch. I'm not one to take guesses where that bloody thing is targeted, are you? I'm assuming it's pointed straight up the nose of the Statue of Liberty until I know otherwise."

"That's vivid, David," James said.

"As you like. All right, I'm on my way."

He jumped out of the truck, followed by his teammates, leaving Javier in the jeep. The four Stony Man commandos took up their stations around the transmitter building, while McCarter opened the front door.

He stepped inside, unsure if he was simply walking into a bullet, but knowing he had no choice but to move forward.

CHAPTER TWENTY-ONE

The anteroom of the transmitter building stank of death. There were bodies here. The men on the floor looked to be wearing the same OD fatigues that many of Jiminez's men wore. Some sported mismatched camouflage, and one even had a full set of tiger stripe. And if they were dead, that meant...

"Yes," Jiminez said, stepping out of the shadows among the transmitter equipment. A camera was pointing toward both of them and its red light was on. "Yes, I killed them."

"Right, mate." McCarter nodded. "May I ask why?" He surveyed Jiminez. He hadn't gotten any prettier. In his right fist was a Makarov pistol. In his left was the dead man's remote, his thumb pressed over the trigger.

"They failed me," Jiminez said, as if it were the most natural thing in the world. "They failed me, and so they had to die. They *all* failed me." He looked at McCarter and then beyond him. "You were wise to come alone," he said. "If I thought you were attempting to rush me, I would release the switch." He gestured with the detonator.

McCarter was unsure what to say to that. There was no point in provoking Jiminez. He tried the sensible approach.

"Look, mate," he said. "Nuclear war? That's not the way to start a new country."

Jiminez's eyes narrowed. "How did you know?" he demanded. "How do you know what I plan here?"

"Well, isn't it obvious?" McCarter said. "You've carved out a power base here, and you've staked out territory that nobody is willing to try to take from you." He did not add that it was territory nobody seemed to want. That was not the way to calm this man, who was teetering on the ragged edge of his power-hungry dreams.

"That is...true," Jiminez said. "I worked hard to get where I am. I was the leader of the revolutionary party—" McCarter gathered he was speaking of one of the neighboring nations "—and I was contacted some time ago by a man who promised many things."

"The fellow who sent you Sukarov?"

"Yes," Jiminez said. "He sent the missile trucks, too. It was very difficult to smuggle them in, to get them here without those in the West learning of them. The fuel was difficult, too, but Krylov said he would solve that problem, and he did. I would be a nuclear power, he said."

"Well, you are that," McCarter said, nodding. "Surely you're not going to throw that all away?"

Jiminez's eyes narrowed. "And why should I not?" he asked. "My men, they have all failed. My forces have been decimated. My hold on the region is weakening. And now I have no choice but to launch the only missile I can. It cannot be known that El Hombre Fuerte was too weak to hold what was his. Those responsible must pay."

"You do that, and this place will be wiped off the map," McCarter said. He had no idea if it was true. Probably it wasn't, because the nuclear powers of the world would never risk angering the neighboring Central American countries. It sounded like a convincing threat, though.

"What will I care?" Jiminez said. "I will be dead. El Hombre Fuerte will be a memory, but at least his will be a memory of power!"

"Power," McCarter said. "Is that what this place was all about?"

"Yes," Jiminez said. "From here I would broadcast my triumph, my declaration. I would tell the nations of the world that El Hombre Fuerte was declaring a new nation, a new people! We would be a proud, strong nation, and all who threatened us would know that we had the nuclear weapons to make them pay!"

Jiminez was starting to rave, and that was not a good path to travel. McCarter pointed to the detonator, trying the direct approach.

"What do you say you give me that remote," he said, "very carefully, so as to avoid any accidental firings. There's no reason to do it, my friend. You will be remembered as strong and powerful. There's no reason to kill innocent people."

"Innocent people?" Jiminez shrieked. "Have you no idea the harm the intervention of the West, of the Americans, has wrought in this part of the world?"

"Hey," McCarter said, spreading his hands. "I'm just a stupid Brit."

"Bah, you are no better!" Jiminez spit. "Lapdogs of the Americans. I will have my revenge on all those in the West!" He gestured with the detonator.

McCarter was losing this war of wills. There was only one path to take. "So," he said. "This is the brave El Hombre Fuerte. Striking at women and children from the safety of a remote launch."

Jiminez stopped waving his arms. "What…what did you say to me?" He looked and sounded outraged.

"I said you're a coward," McCarter said evenly.

"You dare?" he shrieked. "Why, I will release the missile!"

"And in so doing you'll prove what a coward you are," McCarter scoffed. "Any man can lob a missile at somebody else. Takes nothing at all. Pushing a button, that's all."

"I will show you courage!"

"Will you, now?"

"You will face me," Jiminez said. "You will face me like a man!"

"Hey, I'm doing that," McCarter said, gambling with the lives of thousands, if not hundreds of thousands. "It's you who's hiding behind a lousy rocket."

Jiminez growled. He put the Makarov on a nearby workbench. From his belt he pulled a Kalashnikov bayonet. Its honed edge gleamed in the low light from the bare light bulbs in the ceiling of the shack.

"Now we're talking," McCarter said. He holstered his pistol, then reached into his shirt and withdrew the combat knife. "I've got this for you," he said. "Your boy Hector, he got to know it firsthand. I cut his throat and bled him out."

Jiminez snarled. "I will kill you."

"Well, come on, then," McCarter said. "Shut your gob and do it."

With the dead man's switch in one hand and the bayonet in the other, El Hombre Fuerte charged.

SOMETHING ABOUT THE BATTLE going on inside the little shack bothered Javier. He waited for as long as he could, then signaled to one of the Western fighters that he was going to take the jeep.

"I must check something," he said apologetically. He threw the vehicle in gear, turned, and headed back the way he'd come.

He'd spent enough time studying the Strong Man to know that he never had just one plan. Like the two bases, like the two missiles, El Hombre Fuerte always had a second plan in motion. He may well be preoccupied with the confrontation that could very well end his life, and Javier was disappointed he could not be part of that. But he owed these brave men from the American government—he knew they were not all Americans, of course, but he was not stupid and he knew what power would have fielded such men—and he intended to repay what he owed. He had a gut feeling and he simply had no choice but to act on it.

He retraced the route back to the missile truck. There he parked the jeep and explored on foot. Somewhere, there would be something somewhere. Where would El Hombre Fuerte hide it?

He found the tracks. They were faint, but they were there, leading away, into the trees. He followed them quietly and carefully, his borrowed AK-47 in his hands. There was just enough moonlight to work by.

The first of the sentries almost caught him by surprise. The man was suddenly just there, and Javier wondered if perhaps he hadn't been up in the trees before dropping down at the sound of Javier's approach. Javier was quiet, yes, but he was not perfect, and this man was apparently very good to have been left to guard the Strong Man's final plan-within-a-plan.

The guard had a knife. Why he had not simply shot Javier, the Central American agent did not know. Perhaps there had been a shortage of ammunition. Perhaps the man simply fancied himself a knife fighter. There were certainly plenty of those within the ranks of the Strong Man's thugs. Javier simply raised the AK and fired it once. The bullet drilled into the guard's chest punching him to the ground.

Javier knelt, checking, and was satisfied that the man was dead. He waited for the second sentry, flattening his body. The shots he knew would come eventually did. The second guard fired blindly into the night, his shots passing above Javier's head. The shooter had seen the single flash of Javier's bullet and was now hosing the area in an attempt to kill the unseen foe.

Javier smiled. So many of these men were…not smart. Still crawling on his belly, he worked his way around in a wide arc. Periodically the man in the tree would open fire again, firing in all directions, possibly panicking, or possibly just wishing to make sure after falsely believing to have killed his enemy. Certainly the fact that Javier had not fired back might make a difference, might fool the shooter temporarily.

He placed the AK on the ground, regretfully, when he reached the base of the tree. Then he climbed, swiftly, quietly, like a monkey. He had always been a good climber, especially as a child. The sentry was most shocked to see Javier's face loom out of the night. He was even more shocked when Javier grabbed him by shirtfront and threw him out of the tree. He landed on his head, as Javier had meant him to. The sickening crunch could be heard even from where Javier perched.

With two out of the way, he climbed down, recovered his rifle and continued his search in the area around the missile truck. The missile continued to vibrate and churn and

eject gases. That worried him, but he could not let it worry
him too much. He had a small part to play in this drama,
and he intended to play it well. Sometimes on hands and
knees, but always moving, always hurrying, he searched
the ground, looking for clues to what he suspected.

He strayed a little too far into the brush, and he knew
his mistake when he heard the metallic clicking noise. He
had been afraid of that. The Strong Man was known to
place land mines in and around his facilities. Javier was certain he had just stepped on one. That was bad. He could not
complete his mission with a foot blown off. He would bleed
out and, worse, he would not find what he had come to find,
what he suspected was so very important to the mission.

He crouched as gently as he could, trying not to redis-
tribute his weight. What he found made him almost laugh
out loud. It was a crushed metal beer can. He continued his
search.

When Javier found the matted area in the grass, he knew
he had found his spot, and that his hunch was correct.
Holding the AK by the pistol grip one-handed, he reached
out and threw back the camouflage tarp covering the hole
dug into the earth.

El Hombre Fuerte had once before used a similar ruse.
He had been arranging for the sale of drugs and women
with another warlord, when the Zone of Dispute boasted
rivals he had not yet killed. Jiminez had prepared the meeting site ahead of time, digging holes that he camouflaged.
In these holes he had placed soldiers, who emerged at the
appointed time to kill the enemies of Jiminez.

It was this memory that had prompted Javier to act, and
now he had proved himself correct.

The soldier waiting in the pit was young, the sort of man

who would fear El Hombre Fuerte enough to hold his post here, hidden in the dirt, even after the fighting was over. He held, in his hand, a second dead man's switch. Fearful though he may have been, he had not triggered the switch. The youth looked up and his eyes grew very large. His thumb moved toward the button on the detonator....

Javier reversed the AK and slammed the wooden butt into the youth's face with all his might. The soldier toppled. Javier scooped up the detonator and checked it. The thumb trigger remained open. This device had not been activated, and thus it could not be used to launch the nearby missile.

Javier breathed a sigh of relief.

He had done his part. He had listened to his instincts and they had not failed him. The rest was up to the Briton.

"WE ARE ON TELEVISION," Jiminez said, gesturing with the knife toward the camera. "Our fight is being beamed out for all to see!"

"What's that get you?" McCarter asked, crouched low, the Columbia River knife held close to his body.

"It gets me quite an audience to see you die," Jiminez laughed. The detonator in his hand was steady, but its presence worried McCarter. He would have to be very careful.

Jiminez waved the bayonet in front of his body in elaborate flourishes. He circled McCarter in the small space, ringed with dead men and electronic equipment the Strong Man had apparently upended in his rage over his troops' failure.

"Come on," McCarter said, still trying to calm him. "Why check out like this? Give me the detonator and you can walk out of here. You must have money. You could find someplace else to go, someplace to retire." He meant none of it; Jiminez would answer for his crimes. But it never hurt simply to lie to an irrational man. He couldn't reason with such a person.

"You have no understanding of honor," Jiminez said. He lunged, carving the air where McCarter had been standing.

"I understand honor just fine," the Briton said. "It's pointless death I take issue with, friend."

"Pointless?" Jiminez, starting to tire, stepped forward, slashing the air in windmilling arcs. McCarter avoided him, knowing the confrontation could not go on forever. Eventually, Jiminez would get deadly serious and stop screwing around, moving in for the kill, or he would tire himself out with all this showboating. He was obviously playing to the camera, getting in his final speech for the home audience. That was something else all these would-be dictators had in common. They didn't just want to be powerful; they wanted to be *known* for being powerful. Jiminez was making an eleventh hour play for a legacy, for a legend, before he made his final exit.

That would not happen if McCarter could help it.

"Don't you think we've danced around long enough?" he finally asked. "You and me, we both have things to do. You have a being dead to attend to, and I have a rest of my life to get on with."

Jiminez went white. It was the reaction McCarter's flippant comments had been designed to elicit.

He roared and charged. McCarter sidestepped, slashing at Jiminez's knife arm. He scored a deep cut, and as the two faced off again, blood splashed the floor and dripped freely from Jiminez's wounded arm.

"Very good," he said. "Very good, indeed. You are a worthy opponent."

"Could we cut the third-rate movie dialogue?" McCarter asked mockingly. "Next perhaps you'll tell me we're not so very much different, or some other prattle. That we could have been friends if we weren't enemies."

Jiminez shrieked. He rushed in, obviously intending to gut McCarter by slamming the bayonet into his gut. There was no technique behind the charge, just pure animal rage.

McCarter let the bayonet pass him, then slipped to the side again, bringing his knife across Jiminez's neck. The cut would have scored the carotid artery on that side, but Jiminez jerked away from it, and the resulting wound was no more than a light scratch.

"You are not so good as I—" He stopped, confused. The detonator was no longer in his other hand.

"Looking for this?" McCarter asked. He had grabbed the detonator as his adversary charged past, distracting Jiminez with the neck cut, knowing that a man who was wielding a knife and was reacting to a potential slash across the neck wasn't really thinking about what was in his other hand. McCarter held up the detonator in triumph.

Jiminez looked astounded. "You...you tricked me!"

It never failed, McCarter thought to himself. When you tricked them, they always had the balls to tell you the obvious, and they always sounded shocked. He wasn't quite sure why men who were willing to commit violence, to do murder, thought you were going to play fair with them in the end.

Jiminez looked at the camera, then back at McCarter, and then down at the knife in his hand. He marshaled himself for a final charge.

McCarter took a step back, dropped his knife, and

yanked the 1911 one-handed from its holster, snapping the safety off with his thumb. He brought the muzzle up and on target and pulled the trigger.

The shot punched a .45-caliber hole through the center of Jiminez's chest and dumped him on his behind. He looked up, like a child who had just fallen while skating, his expression utterly dumbfounded.

"But…" he began. "We were…fighting…man on man…"

"And I've just beaten you, man on man," McCarter said. "You think this is a fair fight? You think there are rules? This is life or death, mate. You lose."

Whatever objection Jiminez was going to offer died with him. He stared, unseeing, still looking outraged. Gravity caught up with him and he slumped over.

"All's clear," McCarter said. "Get in here and make the call, Gary. I've got my thumb on the dead man's trigger."

Manning called the Farm again. He held the phone to McCarter's ear as the Briton listened to Kurtzman's instructions.

"Now, I want you to press the following combination into the keypad on the side of the trigger housing," Kurtzman told him. "Ready?"

"Just please deactivate this thing, mate," McCarter said.

"Five, five, four, one, one, two."

McCarter entered the combination.

"There should be a button top that's now blinking red, just behind the thumb trigger," Kurtzman said. "Do you see it there?"

"It's blinking," McCarter said.

"Press it," Kurtzman directed.

McCarter complied. The light went out. "Now what?"

"Nothing," Kurtzman said. "You've done it. You can let go."

McCarter squeezed his eyes shut and released his thumb. Nothing happened. No rumbling sound of a missile launch filled the night.

"At least, I think you can let go," Kurtzman said.

"Why…you…" McCarter sputtered.

James, listening in, laughed. "David," he said, "you used to be fun."

"The countdown will have deactivated at the missile platform, too," Kurtzman said, returning to business after that rare moment of levity. "You're good to go."

"All right," McCarter said, putting down the dead man's switch very deliberately. "The team is still on its way?"

"Roger," Kurtzman said. "Containment and recovery. They'll see to it the uranium is accounted for and properly shipped out of there, and that the nuclear warheads are dismantled and the missiles destroyed. Congratulations, Phoenix. You've done it. We'll be arranging to evac you shortly. We'll arrange to debrief you when you get back."

"What about Able?" McCarter asked.

"The guys are pursuing a parallel course," Kurtzman said enigmatically. "We anticipate a full resolution soon. See you back at the Farm."

"Roger." McCarter smiled. "Phoenix, out." When he had put the phone away, he shared the news with the rest of the team. "Job well done, mates," he said. "Let's hope Able is well on the way to doing the same."

"Hey, David," James called from where he bent over the Strong Man, searching him. "Come take a look at this."

A second pistol was tucked in Jiminez belt. It was McCarter's Hi-Power.

"Well, bugger me," he said. "I just won a bet with myself."

Javier rolled up again not long after and told them what had happened.

"I was certain the Strong Man would have a backup plan," he said. "And I was not wrong. You see?" He beamed again, his uneven teeth shining in the moonlight. "I was some help, after all."

"Bloody hell," McCarter said.

CHAPTER TWENTY-TWO

Atlanta, Georgia

Congressman Richard Cross had been, Carl Lyons reflected, one right royal pain in the ass.

Shortly after Able Team had saved his life, he had started in, demanding to know who they worked for, what agency they reported to, just who they thought they were, and so on. It was the same song so many stuffed shirts had sung in the past that Lyons no longer heard it as a distinct melody. They had left the congressman amid a sea of local authorities, sputtering about just who he was and how many powerful friends he had, and why would nobody listen to him? It was quite a spectacle, and Lyons was happy to leave it behind. He imagined that, behind the scenes, Brognola, the Farm and Justice would be all over the Congressman. He had seen the big Fed face down more than his share of bureaucrats. He didn't envy Cross what he was likely to experience in the near future.

It was a bright, clear morning in Atlanta. The jet provided by Stony Man and piloted by a cheerful Jack Grimaldi, who said he'd have plenty of stories to tell about Phoenix Force's mission once they all came in for debriefing, had brought Able Team to Georgia with Grimaldi's customary efficiency. Now they stood looking up at the Butler Building.

"How do you want to play it, Ironman?" Schwarz asked.

"Let's stop dicking around," he said flatly. He reached into the open trunk of their rental car, produced the Daewoo USAS-12, and jacked a shell into the chamber. Blancanales followed suit with his CAR-15.

"I see," Schwarz said. "The subtle approach." He chambered a round in the Beretta 93-R.

"Let's see if Reggie's home," Lyons said.

They entered the lobby of the building. A uniformed security guard walked up to them as if to stop them.

"Do you really," Lyons said through gritted teeth, "want to pit a blue polyester uniform and a tin badge against this?" He hefted the shotgun. The guard shook his head and backed off.

"Way to make friends and influence people, Carl." Schwarz laughed.

"Yeah, yeah," he said. They stopped at the front reception desk. "Reginald Butler," he said.

The receptionist looked up at the men and their weapons.

"Justice Department." Blancanales waved his Farm-issued credentials.

"M-M-Mister Butler is on the top floor, of course," she stammered.

"Oh good," Lyons said. "Yes, of course." They marched to the nearest stairwell. "Anyone want to take bets on just how many floors that is?"

"I saw the directory out front," Gadgets said. "It's exactly—"

"No," Lyons said. "I do not want to know. Don't tell me."

"I expect, at any minute now, if Butler is true to form," Lyons started to say, "that—"

The grenade bouncing down the steps stopped him in midsentence.

They bolted. They threw themselves back out the way they'd come, putting the fire door between them and the grenade. The explosion, contained within the stairwell, did considerable damage but didn't hurt anyone outside.

The receptionist screamed. People milling around in the lobby began to run.

"You!" Lyons yelled at the woman behind the front desk. "Get on the phone and call for help, now! Police, fire, ambulance. Get on it!"

"What about involving local authorities?" Schwarz asked.

"By the time they get here it'll be over," Lyons vowed. "And I want them here to clean up the mess and see to any casualties these fools produce."

"Who do you figure it is?" Blancanales asked.

"Doesn't matter," Lyons said. "Hired guns of some kind. Either that, or Reggie's at the top of the stairs himself with a box of grenades."

They charged back into the stairwell, this time covered by a barrage of buckshot from Lyons's automatic shotgun. The Able Team leader laid down stream after stream, the pellets ricocheting around the stairwell and pocking the walls. When he was satisfied, he motioned for his teammates to move up.

"We keep moving, no matter what," he said. "I want Butler. Without him and his damned Seevers, without his Russian connection, a lot of people would still be alive. The guy is going down."

On the next landing, the fire door swung open and a man in outdated camouflage fatigues wearing a full load-bear-

ing vest opened fire on them with an AR-15. The member
of Able Team took cover on either side of the doorway.
When it swung open again so the gunner could resume firing, Schwarz pushed his 93-R through the opening and put
a 3-round burst in the middle of the man's chest.

"Their employee screening must be all out of whack in
this place," Schwarz commented.

Lyons ignored him.

They reached the next landing, only to find it blocked
by Claymores, which they spotted from the landing below.

"Freaking Claymores?" Lyons asked. "Now that's some
serious hardware."

"Somebody really doesn't like us, Carl," Schwarz said.

"We take this floor, then, cut around," Lyons stated.

"Which is of course a trap," Blancanales said.

"Of course." Lyons nodded. "So we do what we always do."

"Charge forward, through and past the trap, busting everything in our path?" Blancanales asked.

"Yeah," Lyons said.

They stepped out. Lyons almost sighed when he discovered what was waiting for them.

A large, balding man in combat fatigues and load-bear-
ing vest, with an AR-15 in his hands, was standing flanked
by five other men dressed identically. On chairs in front of
the men, duct taped into place with more silvery duct-tape
over their mouths, were several people. They looked like
ordinary office workers, two men, two women, their eyes
wide and pleading in fear.

"For crying out loud," Lyons said.

"Yeah, well," the man told him. "You work with what
you got."

"And who are you?" Lyons asked.

"Hinshaw," Hinshaw said without fear. "I'm the guy who's been hired to kill you all."

"And you're just good enough to do that, are you?" Lyons demanded.

"Oh, no," Hinshaw said. "I know I'm not. Your reputation precedes you, gentlemen. Who do you work for? Some special tactics team of the FBI? Maybe even CIA, working domestically and extralegally? Wet work, that's what you do, isn't it?"

Lyons frowned. "You've seen too many movies."

Hinshaw suddenly laughed. "I have, haven't I?" He almost slapped his knee, he was laughing so hard. "You caught me, boys. I was just messing with you. Frankly, I'm surprised anybody falls for that crap."

"So what is this little scene you've got set up?" Lyons asked.

"Well, see, that's the thing," Hinshaw said. "I've been contracted to kill you. Frankly, I don't much like the idea."

"That's why you dropped a grenade on us and then opened fire in the stairwell?"

"Not me personally."

"Your men, same thing," Lyons shot back.

"Yes, you're right," Hinshaw laughed again. "I really shouldn't even attempt to hide it. Here's the deal, boys."

"I'm listening," Lyons said.

"Well, I don't particularly want to spend the rest of my retirement dead," Hinshaw said. "And I figure duking it out with you boys, the way my employer wants me to, may just bring that about. I don't like that much."

"Your employer...that would be Reginald Butler?"

"Sure is," Hinshaw said. "You'd find out eventually,

and you'd eventually track me down, so what difference does it make? We're just going to disappear anyway. And you, good sirs, are going to let me."

"Why would we do that?"

"Because—" Hinshaw gestured expansively in front of him "—I've got these nice people all lined up in a little row. If you don't let me and Butler and all of my men walk out of here, and leave us unmolested as we take the plane I have arranged, you'll be condemning them to die. Nobody wants that. I have no desire to put multiple murders on my tab, so I'm not going to kill them unless you make me. Sounds reasonable, doesn't it?"

"Oh, very," Lyons said. "But you say Butler wants you to kill us?"

"The nut-job figured that we'd only have a chance for freedom if we waited here and slaughtered you all." Hinshaw chuckled. "Personally I don't quite understand that. Me, I'd have lit out of here before you ever got here, but he told us if we didn't wait he wouldn't pay. Of course I want to get paid."

"Of course." Lyons nodded slowly.

"So you see my dilemma?"

"Perfectly."

"Wonderful! That means you'll cooperate, right?" Hinshaw queried.

"No," Lyons said. "Not at all." He jerked the Daewoo into firing position and pulled the trigger. The blast of buckshot drove Hinshaw back, as Blancanales and Schwarz started shooting. Their rifle and pistol bullets sought out the hired guns mercilessly, punching through heads and chests. As fast as the shooting had begun, it was over. Hinshaw's men were on the ground.

"Get them," Lyons said, pointing to the hostages. Schwarz went to free them while Blancanales covered his teammates. He moved from man to man among the hired shooters, testing each with the toe of his boot to make sure that the men were all really dead. In most cases, their wounds made that obvious, but all the members of Able Team believed in being thorough.

That was why Lyons bent to check Hinshaw. As he rolled the man to his side to check his pulse, Hinshaw's eyes opened and he grabbed the big ex-cop, pulling him to the ground in a tangle of limbs.

The switchblade snicked into place as Hinshaw drew it. Lyons had lost his grip on his Daewoo when the other, equally large man had pulled him off his feet. He grabbed for the knife hand now, clamping his fingers around Hinshaw's wrist. The two man began to roll over each other, fighting for the knife, fighting for an advantage. They struggled, and Lyons was aware of Blancanales standing over him with his CAR-15, unable to take the shot for fear of hitting his teammate.

"I've got this," he growled. "Don't worry."

"Uh, yeah," Blancanales said, watching the knife blade dance among the two men. "You, uh, look like you're all set."

Lyons pushed himself to his feet, dragging Hinshaw with him. The move pulled the mercenary off balance, and the Able Team leader shot a palm heel up under his jaw, rocking him. As he staggered, Lyons brought an edge-of-hand-blow down across the mercenary's clavicle. Something broke. Then Lyons followed up with a tremendous reverse punch that slammed the knuckles of his big fist into Hinshaw's face, breaking his nose and knocking him to the ground. The knife went flying. Lyons reached it and kicked it away.

Hinshaw was still.

"You think," Lyons said, breathing hard, "that he'd try the same trick twice?"

"You could shoot him in the head, just to be sure," Schwarz said.

"You know—" Lyons grinned wolfishly "—that's not a half-bad idea." He drew the Python.

"Carl, no," Schwarz said. "I was just kidding."

"Got you," Lyons deadpanned.

"You bastard."

"Come on," Lyons said. "Cuff that idiot and make sure he's not going anywhere. Are you people all right?" He addressed the former hostages.

"Yes, sir," one of the men said. "We're okay."

"Make sure you get checked for shock when the EMTs make it up here," Lyons said. He turned to his teammates. "Once laughing boy there is secured, we'll take the great glass elevator up to the penthouse suite to see the Wizard."

"I think you're mixing your pop culture references," Schwarz said.

"Which bothers me a great deal," Lyons said. "It really does."

They did not take the elevator. Elevators were a tactical trap, far too easy for the enemy to booby trap. There was no way, in a fight, Lyons wanted to be trapped in a little room suspended off the ground that was entirely dependent on electricity. Plus, there was the all-powerful nature of gravity to consider. It was unwise to tempt fate.

One floor away from the penthouse they encountered a locked door.

"Blast through?" Schwarz asked.

Lyons rapped the door and was impressed by its solidity.

"Not this one," he said. "This is a reinforced security door. Like a bank vault."

"You don't happen to have another Semtex charge available?"

"Sorry, one per customer," Lyons said. "What did you do with yours?"

"Left it in my other pants." Schwarz shrugged.

"Well, we'll take this floor across and see if we can find another way," Lyons said.

"He's just delaying the inevitable," Schwarz commented.

"True," Blancanales put in, "but when did that ever stop anybody?"

They emerged on the floor below the penthouse. "Fan out," Lyons ordered.

As they did so, they came under fire again. Butler's uniformed security guards were at the far end of the spacious floor, which was open except for support pillars beneath the penthouse. It was apparently some sort of lavish party room. Lyons didn't bother to stop to check out the decor, however; he was too busy dodging bullets to care. The members of Able Team each found a pillar to hide behind, as the guards chipped away at the columns with their handguns. At least, Lyons thought, they weren't up against automatic weapons.

"Blancanales, Gadgets," he said quietly, knowing his communication device would transmit his words to the others. "I want you to work your way around the sides. I'll draw their fire and keep their heads down, not necessarily in that order."

"Roger," Schwarz said.

"Got it," Blancanales answered.

"On three," Lyons said. "One, two, *three*!"

Lyons poked the shotgun out from the side of the pillar and, wincing at the pain in his wrist from the strange angle, pulled the trigger back. The Daewoo bucked, emptying its 20-round magazine and splintering the plaster facade of the pillars at the other end of the vast party hall. Lyons was aware of his teammates moving as he fired, keeping the guards stuck behind cover. When the box magazine cycled dry, he yanked his Colt Python from its shoulder holster and unloaded that, too, to give each Able Team member a few extra fractions of a second. When the revolver was empty, he ducked back behind cover.

The return fire splintered and chipped away at the support behind which Lyons took cover. He was grateful that Butler had spared no expense in the construction of this room. The plaster facade was taking a beating, but the support itself was holding. He was in no real danger as long as he didn't move.

He heard the crack of Blancanales's CAR-15. The Able Team commando was now engaging the guards from the flank, his 5.56 mm bullets cutting down first one, then another of Butler's goons from the side. They were unprepared and this sudden onslaught confused them. Blancanales took full advantage of this, firing into them mercilessly and efficiently.

Schwarz cut loose from the other side. He had switched his 93-R to single shot and was methodically picking off targets, one after another after another. Lyons knew that Schwarz, under fire, was a different man than his usual wise-cracking self. He became all cool detachment when battle was on him. He supposed the same was true of all of Able Team; it was part of what made them so good at their jobs.

The last echoes died away. The guards were all down.

"Wow," Schwarz said, stepping over a pile of broken plaster and one of the fallen guards. "This place is a mess."

"Yeah," Lyons said. "Check them. We'll need to find a way up, before Butler can come up with any other tricks."

"On it." Blancanales headed out to scout for exits while Schwarz went through the dead men's pockets and verified that they were, in fact, dead men.

"I got something," the Hispanic commando said moments later. He beckoned to the two men. There was a door in the far wall, which opened to a grand double staircase.

"Well, I do declare," Schwarz said. "That's like something from *Gone With the Wind*."

"I'll say." Lyons nodded. "Come on. Let's not keep Mr. Reginald Butler waiting."

They ascended the steps, their weapons out and ready, expecting anything and everything in the way of lethal surprises. What they weren't expecting, once they made their way past an outer office and a receptionist's desk, was to find Butler seated behind his own desk in his opulent office, holding his head in his hands.

He was sobbing like a baby.

"Reginald Butler?" Lyons said unnecessarily. Butler looked up. Despite the tears and the rather ragged expression, there was no doubt that he was who they thought him to be. Reginald Butler's picture was certainly on enough billboards for Butler Telecommunications nationwide, and the man had done everything from move cameos to political endorsement ads.

"So," Butler said, "this is how it ends."

"You're under arrest," Lyons said.

"And you are?" Butler asked.

"Justice Department," Lyons said.

"I suppose that's as good as anything." Butler nodded. There was a small handgun on the desk in front of him.

"If you're planning on using that," Lyons said, "I need to warn you that we will stop you."

"I was counting on it," Butler replied. "I have no desire to go to prison. I had thought perhaps to shoot my way out, to go out in a manly, adventurous fashion. It's the sort of thing we put on the cable network I run. But I just can't bring myself to pick it up. Isn't that strange?"

"I suggest you step away from the desk then, sir," Blancanales said, trying to be diplomatic. "We'll take you into custody. There doesn't have to be any more violence."

"They're all dead, aren't they?" Butler asked. "All the men I left between you and me. Hinshaw and his thugs. All dead."

"More or less," Lyons stated. "A lot of people have died because of you."

"Don't you understand?" Butler whined. "I did it to accomplish just the opposite. I wanted to help people." He shook his head. "The country is headed terribly wrong, gentlemen. Terribly wrong. Too much individualism. Too much capitalism. Too many people out for themselves, and not enough people helping their fellow man. Can't you see that it has to change?"

"At gunpoint?" Lyons asked.

"That was just a means to an end," Butler said. "I never meant for it to get so out of hand. Krylov said... Well, it doesn't matter what Krylov said. It's fairly obvious he was using me, wasn't he? But I was sure we both wanted Cross in office. A Richard Cross presidency it would have meant so much. We could have changed so much, made the world a better place."

"And all it took to start it off was political manipulation and murder," Lyons said. "Power games fueled by dead bodies."

"You have a point." Butler shook his head. "I started from nothing. I built an empire. I just wanted to give a little back. Is that so wrong?"

"Give back?" Lyons asked. "Give back what, murder? Do you have any idea how many people are dead, not to mention your own goons? How many good men and women, and hell, even some misguided kids led astray by those you worked with to pull off this scheme?"

"I blame Krylov," Butler said. "It would have been okay, if not for him. It's his fault, not mine."

"Tell us about the late Mr. Fedor Krylov," Lyons demanded.

"It was long rumored that there existed a man, a very talented man," Butler said. "Former KGB, but of course that can be forgiven if somebody sees the light and starts working for the right cause. The KGB were never angels, but they were no worse than our own CIA."

"Can the lecture," Lyons said. "Just get to the details."

"I eventually managed to cross paths with Krylov. He was everything they said he was. They called him the Great Coordinator, some people did. He had a gift for organizing, for bringing different groups of people together, people who maybe even didn't have that much in common. Krylov could find that thread, that common tie binding the people he needed to put on the same page. He could beg, he could persuade, he could cajole. The man was just phenomenal. But of course...of course he must have been lying to me all along."

"What do you mean?"

"He told me it would be nonviolent," Butler said. "You must understand, while I wanted to change my country, I don't hate it. I'm not a pathological murderer. I'm not unpatriotic. Just the opposite. Yes, I wanted to shape the country to my own goals, but who doesn't? Krylov used me. He promised he could pull this off with a minimum of violence. But that wasn't true. It just wasn't. I tried to tell myself I didn't know, that I wasn't sure, and if I wasn't sure, it was just coincidence. That things just were coming off badly despite our good intentions. But it wasn't that the groups were hard to control, even when we were setting them to take the fall so they'd make Harrington look bad by association. Krylov was deliberately stirring them up, arming them, advising them, even sending some of his men, Russian mercenaries, along for the ride. He had his finger in all of it. I should have known. But I didn't. I swear I didn't."

"Your buddy Krylov helped you engage in what amounts to mass murder," Lyons said, "by putting into motion a chain of events that got both the innocent and the guilty dropped into boxes."

"Oh, I never meant for that," Butler said. He started to sob again, collapsing on his desk.

"Stay away from that." Lyons started forward.

"Oh no," Butler said. He had straightened with the handgun in his fist. "I don't think so. I think I'm going to walk out of here."

"But you're not," Blancanales said. "There are three of us and one of you. You can't survive. You can't walk away. You'll be a hunted man even if you get out of this building. You don't want that. I don't for a second think someone like you can live like that."

"You're right," Butler said. "And I must admit that at one time I had much higher hopes for myself." He was holding the gun to his temple. He sat at his desk and pulled out he middle drawer.

"Don't," Lyons warned.

"I'm afraid that's all it took," Butler said. "You see, I had Hinshaw bring in one of his experts. It was one of those little touches. I figured I was going away forever anyway. Why not pull out all the stops, just in case? I think I always knew that it would come down to this."

"What are you talking about?" Lyons asked.

"Pulling out the middle drawer," Butler said. "There's a bomb under the desk, large enough to wipe out this entire penthouse and probably start the building on its way down. I don't know. I didn't pay much attention to the specifics, I'm afraid. I just know the bomb is very, very large. Per my specifications."

"Don't do this!" Blancanales said. "Tell us how to disarm it."

"I can't," Butler replied. He pulled the trigger.

The blast was not terribly loud, but it was more than enough. Reginald Butler, billionaire political player and star in his own way, was dead.

"Oh, crap," Lyons said.

"You're not kidding," Schwarz said.

"Get under there, Gadgets," Lyons ordered. "If the bomb is as big as he said it is, we can't risk letting it go off. We might not even get out of the building in time. There's no way to evacuate everyone, necessarily, if it's going to happen soon. And if the building comes down, countless others will be hurt."

"You don't have to convince me." Schwarz crawled

under the desk. A few minutes went by. "Can I get one of you to shine a flashlight under here? I could use a little more light on the situation."

"Sure thing," Blancanales said, apparently feigning nonchalance. Lyons figured he had to be faking it; otherwise the politician surely did have ice water running through his veins. Lyons himself was sweating pretty badly.

"This is not good, guys," Schwarz announced. "I have several blocks of plastic explosives down here, wired to a funky combination lock that looks like it needs computer assistance to open."

"Can you do it?"

"I can try," Schwarz said. "I'm going to dial the Farm."

"Well, get on it," Lyons said. "I don't want to explode."

"You and me both, Ironman."

There was a knock at the door.

"Oh, you have to be kidding me," Lyons said wearily. He had placed the shotgun on the floor to get a closer look at the bomb under the desk. Now it was too far away. He drew the Python as the door was kicked inward.

More of Butler's uniformed guards were hurrying in. Whether they'd heard the shot and come running from whatever concealed room they had occupied, or they had been alerted by some alarm connected to the desk drawer, or if it was just sheer coincidence, there was no way to know. But now, with Schwarz under the desk trying to disarm a bomb, was the absolute worst time for more of these clowns to intrude, Lyons thought.

He double-actioned the first shot, punching a .357 Magnum round through the head of the lead guard. The others scattered, and Blancanales and Lyons went to either side. They were trying to draw fire away from Schwarz, who at least had some cover beneath the desk, but there was no telling what a stray bullet might do to the whole package.

Blancanales pumped away with his CAR-15. Guards fell one after the next. Lyons stayed clear of Blancanales's field of fire, supplementing the withering 5.56 mm hail with bullets of his own. Finally, they had cleared the field of opposition once again, and Butler's armed guards were lying on the carpeted floor.

"Do you think they even knew that he was dead?" Blancanales asked when the last of the gunshots faded.

"Does it even matter?" Lyons asked. He crouched, alarmed when he saw a bullet hole in the face of Butler's desk.

"Gadgets!" he said. "Are you okay in there?"

"Missed it by *that* much," Schwarz said. He was working steadily away with his secure satellite phone propped against his ear. "Uh-huh," he said. "Yes, okay. Now, I have several numbered circuits. Can you make them out in the photo I uploaded to you, Aaron?"

"Wow," Blancanales said. He was looking through the bullet hole, following the path past Schwarz's shoulder. Two inches lower and to the left, and the bullet would have tagged the electronics wizard.

"That is one cool customer in there," Blancanales said.

"And that cool customer is in the process of defusing a bomb that's big enough to kill all of us and then some," Lyons said. "Let's give the man some room."

"Oh no, you don't," Schwarz said from beneath the desk. "You're not getting out of this that easily. You come right back here this instant."

"We didn't actually go anywhere," Blancanales said.

"Then you keep it that way!" Schwarz said. "What's

that, Aaron? No, not you. Uh-huh. Yes, number 16. It's blue. What do you mean it looks brown in the picture you have?"

"I hope to hell he's just making jokes." Lyons shook his head. He was starting to sweat.

"Uh, guys," Schwarz said, his voice muffled by the wood surrounding him. "I think I'm running out of time here."

"What good does it do to tell *us* that?" Lyons demanded.

"Well, misery loves company," Schwarz shot back.

A high-pitched tone sounded from beneath the desk. It began low in volume, but was gradually increasing. Lyons flinched, wondering if putting his fingers in his ears would do a damned bit of good when they all blew up. The tone gradually increased to almost intolerable levels.

"That," Blancanales yelled, "is one really annoying bomb!"

"What?" Lyons shot back.

"I said," Blancanales tried, almost screaming himself horse, "that is an annoying bomb!"

"Yeah!" Lyons said. "You'd think that they'd have the courtesy to make the bomb a little more considerate before it kills us all!"

"Carl," Schwarz said.

"What!" Lyons yelled.

"Carl," Schwarz said insistently. It was then that Lyons realized the tone had stopped.

"What?" he asked, more calmly this time.

"Why are you yelling?"

Lyons rolled his eyes and sank into one of the nearby office chairs. "This," he said, "has been a really long mission."

"Don't worry," Blancanales said, "you have a nice, long series of debriefing waiting for you back at the Farm."

"I can't wait."

CHAPTER TWENTY-THREE

Washington, D.C.

Congressman Richard Cross sat across from Hal Brognola in the big Fed's office. Cross started to speak, but Brognola cut him off. He was chewing on an unlighted cigar and worked up quite a head of steam that morning. He did not want to be interrupted.

"Cross," Brognola said, "you're in a delicate situation."

Cross stiffened. "That's Congressman Cross, if you please."

"Not for long," Brognola informed him.

"What?"

"I've summoned you here today, to tell you that your political career is over." Brognola stood, looking out the window for a moment, before turning to regard the increasingly anxious Cross. "We know all about what you've been doing. We know you leaked what little you could determine about certain sensitive government operations to your allies. Allies like Fedor Krylov, formerly of the KGB. We also know that you've used your political influence to benefit other individuals like Reginald Butler, not to mention interfering, using Illinois law enforcement, with an ongoing investigation."

"You can't prove—"

"Do I need to?" Brognola said. "By itself, there isn't much fire to go with that smoke. We've got a few law-enforcement officials, an attorney general, and a state legislator who were more than happy to say the calls for action came from your office. They rolled over pretty quickly when they were informed that this went higher than their pay grades, all the way up to, well, here." Brognola spread his hands. "All the way to the Justice Department."

"But that's not proof," Cross insisted. "Just who do you think you are?"

"I think," Brognola said, "that I'm the man now in possession of certain financial records. It's amazing what you can find through the computer these days. Transfers of money to offshore accounts that, when you follow the trail back, can be positively linked to you. Transfers from Fedor Krylov, a known terrorist who was actively working to co-opt and corrupt the United States' political system."

Cross grew suddenly very pale.

"Yes," Brognola said. "I know all about it. You were Krylov's boy, weren't you? All that time you were running hand in political hand with Marcia Harrington, being groomed for the vice presidency slot. But that wasn't the ultimate goal, was it? No, Krylov was playing the long game. And your supposedly moderate stance on progressive issues like the environment, well, that was all a sham, wasn't it? We've found evidence of illegal contributions to your campaign. They were well concealed and took some time to ferret out. But they came, ultimately, from radical Communist and environmentalist groups, all of whom were part of the loose coalition Krylov formed as part of his network."

"I…" Cross said.

"This is all off the record," Brognola said. "You're caught and we both know it. I'd like to know why."

Cross looked down. "The planet—the entire political system—has to change. Krylov had the right idea, and the network to make it happen. It was for the good of the Earth and for the United States that I did what I did."

"So you were going to be President?"

"That was the idea," Cross admitted. "Krylov hatched the whole thing, once we got in touch with each other. Running in the same political circles, however covertly I was forced to do it, it was inevitable that we'd meet eventually. Harrington was the poster child for the progressive movement, yes," he said, "but she wasn't radical enough. She had a really good shot at taking the presidency, and that wouldn't work. Because she wasn't in Krylov's corner and that's what he needed, what he wanted."

"So you decided to maneuver her out of the way first, then kill her to keep her there."

"I never had any part in the assassination plans," Cross said.

"But you knew about them."

"I did," Cross said. "It was the most effective way. The rally was the key, and the terrorist incidents leading up to it. Krylov was working up the WWUP and EAF goons, using some of his own Russian operatives, mercenaries and other former KGB people loyal to him, all people he was able to pull together through his government and military contacts in Russia. The idea was to get the EAF and the WWUP looking dirty, as dirty as possible. We were going to conduct a covert political campaign, setting up some 501(c) organizations not traceable to us, making it clear that she was in bed with these dangerous radicals these terrorists."

"So you were using your fellow travelers for your own political gains. You also used what information you were able to glean to help Krylov put his Russian mercenaries on the trail of Justice Department agents investigating the matter. Didn't you?"

"I did," Cross said. "It wasn't easy. I didn't have a lot to go on. But once I knew what to look for and who to ask I had enough connections and enough callbacks to help Krylov find the men."

"You realize that several people died? Innocent people Cross. One of them was a cop on the doorstep of his own stationhouse!"

"The ends justifies the means," Cross said. He looked Brognola in the eye. "Certain sacrifices had to be made."

"Sacrifices like Marcia Harrington?"

"Yes," Cross said. "Once we made it clear that Harrington was in bed with the radical socialist and environmentalist fringe groups, groups tied to recent acts of terroris violence, Krylov was going to make sure the big environmental rally turned into a bloodbath. Then he was going to get those same groups on the airwaves after the fact through the news media and the Internet, taking credit and praising Harrington's sacrifice."

"Explain."

"She was never supposed to make it to the rally," Harrington admitted. "Krylov was going to have his Russian mercs kill her before she could get there. We were going to blame it on a shadowy government conspiracy, CIA assassins, that kind of thing. The fringe elements of the movement will believe the government is capable of anything. They'd have bought the whole thing."

"So you set her up," Brognola said.

"Of course. We were the best of friends, the strongest of allies. I always knew where she was, what her itinerary was to be. She hid nothing from me."

"And once she was dead, you'd be there to step in for the brave, late and martyred Senator Harrington."

"Yes. Things didn't quite work out the way they were supposed to. She made it to the rally. But even that I could have compensated for. Krylov could have had his terrorist groups take credit for the event in Harrington's name even if she were there; they'd just have spewed different justifications for it. Instead of attacking the rally in her memory, they'd have done so on her behalf, telling the world that the cause wasn't moving forward fast enough and that those who weren't extreme enough in their views were as much the enemy as anyone on the opposite side of the issue."

"Have you always known you would step over her body into the presidency?"

"Not always," Cross said, ignoring the jab. "When I first hitched my star to hers, it was because I saw that she was going to do well. She was charismatic, she had good balance. She was a natural-born politician, competent and savvy. I'm only sorry that, deep down, she was too dedicated to the way things have always been done. She wasn't willing to change. I didn't really want to sacrifice her. Had she been willing to work with Krylov and I, we all could have done it together."

"But you didn't think she'd go for it."

"I knew she wouldn't," Cross said. "She was progres-

sive in her politics. For some reason people seem to think,
wrongly, that being progressive meant she was willing to
change anything and everything. She wasn't. She had a
firm belief in American tradition, in the United States' su-
periority. She wanted it to stay that way. She was really
very old-fashioned in that way, despite her support for
other progressive causes."

"So you used her," Brognola said. "You were going to
manipulate her politically and, in so doing, manipulate
those supporting and opposing her."

Cross nodded. "It was brilliant, a twofold plan," he said
admiringly. "Krylov has a very keen mind for politics. He
was going to make the radicals think that Harrington,
though she was never extreme enough for them, had given
her life for their cause, making them sympathetic to the person they saw as her political heir, namely me. Meanwhile,
thanks to my carefully cultivated voting record, to the
mainstream voters I'd look like the more moderate alternative, the safe choice to continue on for her in the cause
of progressive politics. I'd have secured the nomination and
likely the presidency easily. That's the trick to winning
any election, you know. It's not enough to secure the end
of the spectrum. You've got to appeal, simultaneously, to
the middle."

"And all of it was cover," Brognola said. "In reality
you're every bit as radical as the people you're using and
throwing away."

"'Radical' is an ugly word," Cross said, "used by people who don't understand the necessity for direct action.
As President, I'd have been in a position to affect national
policy and world politics. The most powerful man in the
world would finally have the Earth's best interests at heart."

"In other words, you were Krylov's puppet," Brognola said, holding up his hand when Cross tried to interrupt. "He maneuvered you into the political catbird seat in order to have a handpicked ally in the White House. Where does Reginald Butler fit in?"

"He was useful to an end, like the EAF and WWUP members." Cross shrugged. "He had the technology we needed to keep the various groups connected, keeping them feeling like one network instead of disparate cells. That was very necessary to the model Krylov was following. He also provided a great deal of funding we'd never have been able to provide otherwise."

"And in so doing, dug himself a hole he couldn't get out of," Brognola said. "Desperation makes men do stupid things."

"I don't intend to make the same mistake," Cross said.

Brognola let that go for a moment. "And the uranium? You knew all about that, didn't you?"

"Of course," Cross said. "It was key to Krylov's plan. It was through his contacts in the intelligence community that he learned of the expanded Indian nuclear program. He rightly determined that security was relatively light for the amount of material available. He used his network to hit them and then protect and transport the enriched uranium to his ally in Central America."

"Meaning the Purba Banglars stole the nuclear fuel and saw to it that it reached Jiminez, the man formerly known as El Hombre Fuerte. The man Krylov supplied with Soviet surplus mobile missiles capable of hitting the United States."

"I believe he did arrange for the missiles, yes," Cross said. "And of course the fuel to make the nuclear warheads viable."

"Why would you be party to that?" Brognola asked.

"You don't honestly think he was going use them, do you?" Cross shot back. "The Strong Man was a tool of Krylov's, nothing more. He wouldn't fire those missiles without Krylov's say-so, for that would mean the Russian, probably the most skilled terrorist coordinator in the world, would withdraw his financing, his influence, and his aid. And Krylov didn't want the United States nuked, no matter how bitter he might have been about the USSR going belly up. He wanted the very real and very credible *threat* of nuclear attack, so I could use it."

"Scare mongering in order to wield a big stick at home?"

"Exactly," Cross said.

"You couldn't manufacture the intelligence data required to fake such a threat?"

"Ten years ago, maybe," Cross said. "But today? There are certain retired generals who are only too familiar with what it does to your future political aspirations when you stand in front of Congress or the United Nations, pointing to satellite photos of weapons of mass destruction that nobody ever actually manages to find. No, we couldn't afford to fake something, to manufacture something. The threat had to be real and verifiable." He spread his hands wide. "With the specter of nuclear terrorism galvanizing public opinion in favor of the government, I'd have been free to use my executive powers much more liberally than in the past. There's precedent. Look at the sweeping powers the President was able to adopt after terrorism struck the heart of the United States, in recent years. I would have used that to do a lot of good."

"I'm sure you think so," Brognola said, sounding weary. "I actually believe that you believe it. I won't bother cau-

tioning you about the power-mad decisions dictators and
warlords like El Hombre Fuerte are likely to make, regardless of who thinks they're pulling the strings of such
leaders and power brokers."

"I stand by my actions," Cross said. "It was necessary.
For the good of the planet. For the good of the country."

"Please," Brognola said, rubbing his temples, "just
shut up."

Cross stared at him. Then he said, "So now what?"

"Now," Brognola said evenly, "you're going to resign.
Quietly."

"What?"

"You're in a difficult position, as is the government,"
Brognola said. "Your crimes are treasonous, Cross. You
could conceivably be tried and put to death. It's been a
very long time since anyone was executed for treason in
the United States. And let's be honest, we don't need the
media circus or the months of hand-wringing and political recriminations that's likely to produce. You are an em-
barrassment, Cross, and a huge liability to everyone
connected to you politically. Your actions, if they become
public, could undermine the citizenry's faith in the political process in general and in their government specifically. It would be best for all concerned if you
just…disappeared."

Cross grew pale again. "You can't mean…."

"No," Brognola said, after letting the man's sentence
hang in the air for a few moments. "You won't be meeting
with any convenient accidents, much as I might like you
to. Justice doesn't operate that way, Cross. You're free to
go, provided you announce your retirement from public life
within the next forty-eight hours. Come up with some-

thing convincing, please. Perhaps you should say you wish to spend more time with your family."

Cross looked stricken. "But—"

Brognola held up a hand for silence. "This is not a negotiation. Make no mistake, Cross. If you *don't* do it, if you don't quietly go away, you very well might find yourself accident prone. These things have been known to happen, if the political cost of exposure is high enough. That's out of my hands. If you prove a liability to the security of the United States, and that includes continuity of government and public faith in the government's ability to protect the people, you will be a national security risk. Such risks are eliminated. I have that from the President himself."

"All...all right." Cross was shaken now. He stood to go.

"One more thing," Brognola said. He stood, looking out the window with his hands behind his back. He did not turn to look at Cross as he spoke. "We'll be watching you, Cross."

"Watching me?"

"Listen very carefully," Brognola warned, still looking out the window. "If you continue cooperating with, financing, agitating, or otherwise working with or for radical, extremist political causes, all bets are off. What I'm saying, sir, is that you had better disappear off the political radar completely."

Cross nodded, swallowing hard. Brognola saw him do it in the reflection in the window. The soon-to-be-former Congressman left, closing the door quietly behind him.

Brognola let out a sigh of disgust.

He chewed on his cigar, looking out at Wonderland. It was a strange world in which to operate, this white marble Gomorrah on the Potomac. It was, in its way, much more complicated and much more deadly than the world of violence and subterfuge in which the men of Able Team and Phoenix Force operated.

He would, he knew, sleep well this night. He would sleep well knowing that they had done what was necessary to secure the safety of the American people for yet another day. He would sleep well knowing that Cross had been neutralized and, while not dealt with as harshly as the big Fed might have liked, he would be forever a nonentity in the political game. It would tear his guts out, emasculate him. It would, for all intents and purposes, end him. Brognola smiled at that.

And Brognola would, he knew, sleep well for one more reason. He would so do because he knew that Able Team and Phoenix Force were out there, ready and willing to do violence to fight evil. They did so on behalf of the President, on behalf of Brognola, and, most of all, on behalf of all the American people.

That, he thought, was all that truly mattered, in the end—that good men were willing to *do* something in a world fraught with evil.

It was enough.

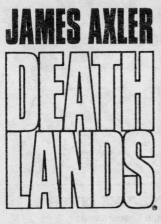

TAKE 'EM FREE

2 action-packed novels plus a mystery bonus

NO RISK

NO OBLIGATION TO BUY

AleX Archer
SEEKER'S CURSE

**In Nepal, many things are sacred.
And worth killing for.**

Enlisted by the Japan Buddhist Federation to catalog
a number of ancient shrines across Nepal, Annja
is their last hope to properly conserve these sites.
As vandalism and plundering
occur, police become
suspicious of Annja—but
she's more concerned with
the smugglers and guerrillas
trying to kill her. As she treks
high into the Himalayas to
protect a sacred statue, she's
told the place is cursed. But
Annja has no choice but to
face the demons....

Available July
wherever books are sold.

www.readgoldeagle.blogspot.com

GRA19